Body and Soul

George Wilkins

Contents

BODY AND SOUL

BY

George Wilkins

FILIAL AFFECTION.

IN the parish of which Dr. Freeman was Rector, one of the principal inhabitants was Mr. Montagu, who, from a diseased constitution, a taste for literature and the elegant arts, and the constant society of two interesting daughters, led a life approaching almost to seclusion. Possessed of considerable property, and inhabiting a mansion, which, from the spacious grounds surrounding it, had all the advantages of the country, he seldom quitted it for more than a few weeks in the spring of the year, when he visited the metropolis. With the exception of the interchange of a few occasional visits with some of the families of the county, his daughters rarely left their home; and unless for the purpose of attending the service of the church, they as unfrequently entered the Town. Indeed, though partially acquainted with the chief residents, they were upon terms of intimate acquaintance with none but the Rector. This sprung from no false motive of pride, for they were accessible to all. In the company of those who were upon an equality, or superior to them in rank, they were animated in conversation, and fascinating in manners; whilst with those who were their inferiors, their affability and openness were such as to remove all distance between them. With minds highly cultivated, and graced by every accomplishment that can adorn the female character, their attention was uniformly directed to the care of their father's declining health, which was such as to make it apparent that his ' days were numbered;' while he, impressed with the assurance that the sand of life was nearly run out, seemed alone anxious to apply the energies of his once powerful mind, to render his existence serviceable, and his memory endeared, to those in whom all his earthly joys were centred. The fresh bloom and beauty of youth, the uniform mildness and suavity of temper, indications of ' souls attuned to Heaven,' and an elegance of personal deportment, alike characterised the sisters; and as the clustering branches of the mantling ivy, clinging to the fostering tree beneath whose shade they grow, at last give support to the trunk in its decay, their accomplishments matured under his guidance were directed to whatever could invigorate the mind, or contribute to the bodily comfort of their father. The Elder possessed the power of throwing a charm into all her conversation; while the Younger, by the same kind of enchantment, infused a spell into all her actions; and thus, both wove a magic wreath, which, when bound about the brow, dispelled, by its inherent power, mental uneasiness, and bodily anguish. Their father, with a mind stored with the elegancies of literature, with a taste refined by the advantages of foreign travel, and an early introduction into polished life, joined to a fine and tempered sense of religion, shone with equal lustre in retirement as in society: and these amiable endowments were transmitted unimpaired to the minds and manners of his children. This was exemplified in the air and character of every thing around them: the pleasure-grounds and gardens, the walks and greenhouse, the mansion and its establishment, all manifested the same unison of taste and feeling. Beauty, produced by elegance, without splendour; liberality without extravagance; and arrangement concealing its mechanism, were the impressions which obtruded themselves upon all who visited this seat: and that ail this sprang from the same refinement which showed itself in the pursuits that engaged the uniform attention of its possessors, was equally conspicuous to the few that visited the family as friends. Indeed, so ac-cordant were their sentiments, that they seemed to emanate only from one mind; an equal interest was excited in all, for the excellencies of each. In the choice of books, in the course of reading, in the selection of subjects for her pencil, Matilda was governed by the taste of her father. In her music, in the arrangement of the flowers, plants and shrubs, and the management of domestic concerns, Ellen was influenced by the desire to please the same director; whilst he, in displaying the natural beauties of the grounds, or in laying out the gardens, submitted his plans to the determination of those for whom he was dedicating his taste.

It was on a bright winter's evening, when the moon was rising in all her pensive beauty in the heavens, through the clear frosty atmosphere, that Dr. Freeman walked out towards the mansion : he had stopped more than once in his way, to gaze upon the beauties which the elevated and massive fabric of his church presented to his view, at a time, and under a sky peculiarly suited to the contemplation of the magnificence of Gothic structures. The shadows of the re-tiring parts of the building are then broad and deep, the soft tinge which the moon-beams cast upon the projections are so exquisitely and delicately silvered, and the whole so mellowed and subdued,

> When buttress and buttress alternately
> Seem framed of ebon and of ivory,

that the mind is awed by the sombre majesty of the scene: and this, associated with the reflection that there stands before the eye the venerable pile, in and around which there sleep in calm repose those who from successive generations have frequented the House of Prayer, and have offered up the pure incense of devout praise and adoration;—these thoughts take possession of the heart, and lay it open to the reception of the best feelings of our nature. On the good Rector's mind, familiarized as he daily and hourly was to the sight of this object, it did not fell to excite a glow of satisfaction in his heart that he possessed the guardianship of a temple, which, in its antiquity, purity of style, and dignified majesty of architecture, assimilated so well with the character of that religion which it was his duty and high gratification to advocate within its walls. But when he reflected upon the momentous charge which that guardianship devolved upon him, and contrasted the extent of the sacred pile with his own frail tenement of clay, he found himself shrink into insignificance, from which, however, he was elevated by a sense of that immortal essence which dwelt within him, and which assured him that he should live, when

> " The cloud-capp'd towers, the gorgeous palaces,
> The solemn temples, and the great globe itself, were dissolved,
> And like the baseless fabric of a vision,
> Left not a track behind."——

From this object of admiration, and these interesting thoughts, he was driven by the keenness of the air; he, therefore, proceeded onward to the mansion, and was soon ushered into the drawing-room, where Mr. Montagu, reclining upon a sofa near the fire, had vainly been wooing sleep.

" My good friend," said the kind host, as the Doctor entered, though in an un-usually subdued tone, " why did you not come and take your dinner with us to-day, if you had no better claim upon your time? I began to think the greenhouse had lost its charms, and my girls their attractions in your eyes, since we have seen so little of you lately: what has been the cause of your long absence ?"

" The cause," replied the Doctor, " is one which has already excited the commiser-ation of this house. There has arisen, from the ex-tireme dampness of the atmo-sphere, an epidemic disorder which daily carries off such numbers, both of children and up-grown persons, that my time has been incessantly occupied in attending the chambers of sickness and death. I have, however, seized the first opportunity which the interval from such employment has offered, to get the exercise of a walk hither, and to enjoy a little of your society; but I have also an additional motive for my visit this evening, in the desire to thank your young ladies for the benefaction which they sent me this morning, for the relief of those many distressing objects which this visitation of Providence has created; already it has been gratefully appreciated by the most necessitous."

" Doctor," said Mr. Montagu, "let me again particularly request that you will increase your own gratuities by adding those of my daughters to them, and never hesitate to call upon them for any thing for which you will condescend to be their almoner."

" My good friend," replied the Doctor, " I have reason to thank you all for your repeated acts of substantial kindness in this respect, which have been faithfully dedicated to such objects as I am sure deserve your charity. In these times of gen-eral and fetal sickness, it is a bestowing of alms on such as will never again claim or require them; and if ever we do the work of heaven on earth, it is by such deeds as these. But tell me, are you not much better ? for I am persuaded you must feel so, or I should never have seen you at church last night; so unexpected a pleasure has made me the more anxious to congratulate you upon your amendment. And my young friends, — how are they?' "

With respect to my dear girls," said Mr. Montagu, in a voice betokening contrary feelings. to those attributed to him by his friend, "thank Heaven they are in perfect health; their cheerfulness and assiduous attentions, as you well know, contribute powerfully to soften all my painful sufferings; but after all, Doctor, I feel the force of your remark, ' our time is short, and our expectations should not lead us to calculate upon any thing beyond the present moment.' The impression these words have made upon my mind, corresponding with my bodily feelings, assures me that I must soon, very soon, ' go hence, and be no more seen.'"

Here the Doctor, about to express his un-feigned sympathy with his friend's feelings, was interrupted by the entrance of the servant with tea, followed by the ladies, who welcomed the good Rector with all the warmth of heart-felt friendship, and both of them drew a chair neat him.

" My dear Sir," said Matilda, with an air of great earnestness, while her sister's countenance betrayed equal concern, " My dear Sir, I Cannot express how glad I am that you are come out to us this evening. We had heard how fully occupied you were with visiting the sick and afflicted at this unhealthy season, of we should have sent for you before. Our patient here," turning to her father, " in vain struggles to conceal his sufferings from us; we too clearly see that he is alarmingly weak, and his physician holds out no hopes upon which we can rest with any satisfaction. We urged every thing in our power to prevent his going out in such inclement and unwholesome weather as this; but we could not prevail upon him to listen to our solicitations, and he would go yesterday to church. He, who at all other times is so perfectly disposed to put himself under our management, threw off all submission, and contrary to our wishes and advice, persisted in doing much more than we think he ought to have done; for you must have been as much surprised at the sight of him as we were at his determination to attend at the late hour of evening service."

" Aye," said the father, erecting himself from the reclining posture in which he sat, " I rejoice, greatly rejoice, that I had sufficient strength to accomplish it. To me it was the most goodly scene I ever beheld; and the words of your admirable discourse, my dear friend, upon the awful subject of death, so suitable to this time of sickness, and so peculiarly applicable to my own case, have left an impression on my mind that, were I destined to reach the utmost limit of existence, never would leave me. On this occasion outward objects also contributed their most powerful aid to heighten my feelings; for as I approached the church, under a thick dark-clouded sky, and caught the first view of that venerable and stupendous pile, with the light issuing from its windows of rich-wrought fairy work of stone, the effect was striking; but when for the first time I had ever entered it at the hour of darkness, and found it illuminated with a brilliant blaze of light, which lost itself in the mazes of the spell-bound vaulted roof—when there opened upon my sight thousands of my fellow creatures, thronged together for the solemn purpose of offering the accumulated incense of the most fervent devotion to that God who knows every aspiration of the heart, I felt as if enveloped in the effulgence of the divine Shechinah; —and when the slow solemn peal of the organ swelled upon the ear, and the choir sang the songs of praise with the mellowed sweetness, the captivating soft-was and solemnity which the stillness of night conspired to render more enchanting, the effect was most imposing. It was only then that 1 felt the full force and value of these outward associations, as calculated to inspire awe, and perceived how powerfully they tended to chain down the wandering senses to the exclusive act of profound devotion. As I walked down the aisle, supported by these earthly blessings, these ministering angels,"—and here he threw a glance of such soft affection on his daughters as drew forth crystal streams of tears,—"methought I was already entering a Paradise of joy: sickness forsook me — respiration became easy — the film was removed from my sight, I breathed nothing earthly, and Heaven seemed opened to my view. Never did I feel so conscious of the excellency and spirituality of our prayers. The sober feeling of pure devotion that pervades them harmonized so well with my own thoughts, and with the hour of worship, that every word of them seemed the word of a seraph communing with heaven, I felt, indeed, that peace which we pray for, ' which the world cannot give,' and I was therefore the better prepared to listen with devout attention and rapture, when you so feelingly aroused the reflection of those around you to the momentous consideration of death and eternity. The words which I heard scarcely seemed the address of uninspired man; I was struck as with the voice and language of an apostle — of a special messenger from on high, who conveyed the solemn admonitions to my heart. Yes; I felt it to have been the une-quivocal summons, the last warning that will ever here be vouchsafed to me; and I left the holy temple with the strong conviction, un-accompanied by any sort of fear, that my next entrance into its sacred walls would be when I should be carried thither for my burial." — He paused; then looking on his daughters, whose deep sobs and afflicted looks wrung the heart of his friend, while the placid countenance of the sick man betrayed no earthly-allied emotions, he continued: —

" Sweet devoted daughters of my fond affection, weep not for me; and oh! weep not far yourselves. — Cheer the last moments of my existence by your wonted se-renity. Though I have had no earthly wish, no other sublunary enjoyment but what has centred in you, yet remember, your angelic mother is in Heaven, and there, ' where my treasure is, there would my heart be also.' My friend,"— extending his hand to the Doctor, whom he saw unable to control his feelings, while his voice, though enfeebled, became not less emphatic — "My friend, my last hour is come! — Oh, stir not! it is in vain to call for any further earthly assistance; the common foe is no longer to be resisted,— No more is left me than to express the desire of my heart, that these objects of my fondest love may derive from your friendship that protection and aid which I know you will ever feel disposed to afford them. Accept then the charge which I now solemnly commit to you, with the prayer that the love and mercy of Heaven may ever continue with you." — Here the Doctor clasped his hand, and pressing it to his bosom, expressed by his manner and countenance what his tongue in vain essayed to utter. Disengaging himself from this last act of friendly regard, the sinking parent again turned to his drooping daughters, whose faces were bowed down by fearful anticipations and deep emotion. —" My devoted, my be-loved children," said he, " come hither, and take from the lips of your dying father, his best and last blessing." .Instantly they were in his arms; when, after a long and almost convulsive em-brace, he raised his hands above them in the attitude of the most fervent supplication, and as he uttered, with a calm and dignified pathos, — " God ever, ever bless you I" death sealed his lips for ever ! I

A scene like this who shall describe ? — for who can adequately represent to the mind the poignancy of that grief which "clouded the souls and overshadowed the countenances of these interesting females, so fair, so lovely, so inexpressibly afflicted, as they hung over the lifeless body of the fondest parent that ever blessed his offspring with his love ? Over them stood the mute, but impassioned mourner — the friend of sympathy — embalming with a flood of silent tears, the sanctity of those feelings to which nothing human can administer relief. No; these are scenes which imagination may body forth, but to which description will in vain attempt to impart an adequate colouring; and though they paralyze the hand that would paint them, yet, when conceived, they tend to soften and refine the. heart---to cut the silver cord which binds us to the world, and to lead our minds and wishes forward to the blissful state of those ' who die in the Lord.'

When the sisters had poured forth the first burst of anguish, and nature had found relief in the transports of grief, the Doctor summoned assistants to attend them to their chamber, while he superintended the removal of the body to another apartment

The Doctor soon afterwards returned to the Rectory, and having made some necessary arrangements, repaired again to the mansion, where he determined to take up his abode for the present. On the following day he visited his young friends in their dressing-room ; and after the burst of renewed anguish had gone by, and he had suffered them to dwell upon the awfulness of the event, and upon a thousand other circumstances, as they were presented to their minds, knowing that in the time of acute sorrow no alleviation is so great as that which arises from the development of every thought connected with the object which has occasioned it, — " My dear friends," said he, " you do not require me to suggest in what way, and for what purpose you are to regard this severe dispensation of Providence. The event has been long foreseen, and might have been expected, though not so suddenly as it has happened; and though this circumstance does not render the loss less afflicting, yet it serves to display the mercy of Heaven in permitting your beloved father to draw gradually to the close of his existence. Engage your minds, by dwelling fully on his acts of Christian love, his humble piety, and tranquil end; and from such a pure source of consolation draw motives to follow his example, and to make your lives as useful as his was to others, that the memory of yon all may be equally blessed.

I have hardly left the house since the event occurred, nor shall I quit it until we have deposited his remains within the walla of that holy temple, which he seems so lately to have visited with a sort of inspiration on his mind. Think now only of yourselves, and whatever I conceive you would yourselves do, I shall studiously perform; and that you may be perfectly relieved on my account, I have the satisfaction to tell you that I have made every arrangement for the discharge of my own duties. I am to be found below, whenever you may wish to see me; and as my desire is to be ser viceable, let me be summoned upon every occasion on which it may be thought that I can be in the least degree useful." The warmest pressure of both his hands to their hearts was their only reply.

On the evening succeeding the day on which the remains of Mr. Montagu had been consigned to the tomb, the two sisters were calmly conversing with the Doctor on the only subject that engrossed their attention, and were deriving all that spiritual consolation which this Minister of God was so capable of pouring into the wounded mind.

" Tell me, my dear Sir," said Matilda, " what are your sentiments upon a subject which has now become so deeply interesting to Ellen and myself, and upon which we have reflected so much; I mean the state and condition of the soul after its release from the body* We have read that there are some who conceive the whole man to be destroyed by death. Others, thence called soul-sleepers, that the soul exists in a state of profound insensibility or torpor. Others, again, that a common receptacle is prepared for the souls of all, whether good or bad; but what do you say ?"

" My opinion," replied the Doctor, " is founded alone upon the Scriptures — that the souls of the righteous, immediately upon their departure from the body, are translated to places of felicity, and the souls of the wicked into those of torment till the great day of the Lord."

" Do you consider," asked Ellen, " that the Scriptures explicitly declare this doctrine ?"

" I do," he replied ; " for though they speak not so much or so clearly as our cu-riosity de-sires, yet enough is revealed to satisfy our minds. To enter fully into the subject, you will readily grant that we are composed of two parts—the body and the soul—and that the qualities of the one essentially differ from those of the other. The body ' was formed out of the dust of the earth,' but the soul 'was breathed into it by the Creator:' now, these, however closely they are combined in the con-stitution of our existence, are still separate and distinct. The body is assàilable by every outward accident, the soul is accessible to no tangible object. You may destroy the one, but you cannot touch the other; for the one is mortal, the other immortal: that is, the spirit exists, whether united or liberated from its conjunction with humanity. This is evident from our Saviour's commending the care of his soul to the holy keeping of God, when expiring on the Cross: — ' Father,' said he, ' into thy hands I commend my spirit;' and you may re-member that the first martyr, St. Stephen, at his death, did the same. There are, indeed, abundant proofs of the perpetual existence of the soul after death. We find the prophet praying to God that the soul of the child of the widow of Zarepta, may be restored to its mortal frame again; ' and the Lord heard the voice of Elijah, and the soul of the child came unto him again, and he revived;' so that it is quite certain, as the preacher says, that ' the dust shall return to the earth as it was, and the spirit shall return unto God that gave it.' "

" This point," said Matilda, " you have clearly established; and we are quite certain that the soul survives the body, but not equally sure that, when separated, it is sensible."

" And this," continued the Doctor, " I can as easily prove. Conceive, only for a minute, that if the soul, that æthereal essence of the divinity within us, exists when clogged with the incumbrance of the body, how much more exquisitely refined and tenuated must it be, when liberated from the trammels of flesh and blood. But what was the argument which our Saviour teed to demonstrate to the sect of the Sadducees the truth of the resurrection? ' Did not Moses,' said he, on that occasion, ' did he not call the Lord, the God of Abraham, the God of Isaac, and the God of Ja-cob ? God is not God of the dead, but of the living, for all live unto him.' Now, how could the dead be said to be living, and to live unto God, if the soul be not sensible?

Did not also Christ upon the Cross promise the penitent criminal, that on the very day on which he died he should be with him in Paradise? And what was the difference, or where the advantage, whether be were or were not with Christ, whether in Paradise or in any other place, if the soul were then insensible to the delights of Paradise, or to the joy of such a meeting?"

" Alt this, too, is quite clear," rejoined Ellen; " but yet there are several allusions to death, as represented by sleep, which I have met with in die Bible."

" I allow this," continued the Doctor; " but such expressions bear an uniform reference to a state of perfect exemption from strife, labour and thought, and all other corporeal human qualities; in the same manner as sleep is a suspension from activity, but not altogether from motion or sensibility. If you shut up, into a state of inactivity, the essence of the spirit, at the moment that it quits the body, you will be compelled to believe, that the body must first be resuscitated, and the spirit again revived; a supposition perfectly irreconcileable to all our notions of the refinement and immateriality of the ' heavenly essence.' And now, if you will allow me to have established my position, that the soul exists in a separate state, and that when disunited from the body it is also sensible, I will endeavour to show you, that it is capable of happiness or misery. In confirmation of this we read that Christ, after his crucifixion and death, descended into Hell, or Hades, the place of departed spirits; where, says the Psalmist, God ' left not his soul to see corrup-tion.' It is in the same place Hades, separated. by a great and impassable gulf, that the parable represents Dives and Lazarus as placed; the one suffering torture, the other enjoying rest Again, we read that Judas, when he put an end to his existence, went ' ***to his own place?*** ' and Peter, upon his death, to ***his***. Now, this is a refutation of that opinion which you mentioned as entertained by some, of a common receptacle provided alike for the souls of the just and unjust ; for if this were the case, both Peter and Judas would have been consigned to the same, and not to different abodes."

" Surely," interrupted Matilda, "this, though evidently established by Scripture, carries a sort of inconsistency with it; for if we are to suppose that the good spirits enjoy felicity and the bad misery, upon their removal from the body, where is the need, or where the justice, of a final day of retribution? You have repeatedly told us that God does not always punish the guilty in this world, but permits evil to exist until the time of restitution, when all inequalities are to be adjusted; and why may not this argument be applied to the soul in its intermediate state between death and judgment?"

" That question," said the Doctor, " is shrewdly put I do not presume to unravel the secret counsels of God; for who can enter into his thoughts ?— ' High as heaven, what canst thou do ? deeper than hell, what canst thou know? Such knowledge is too wonderful; you cannot attain unto it.' I dare not, therefore, charge any of his purposes with folly. I speak only of that which I find clearly revealed. I have already stated the grounds for the belief of the intermediate state being a state of felicity or woe in the cases of the penitent Thief, Dives and Lazarus, Peter and Judas; and I know that the Fathers of the Church not only believed, but maintained the same doctrine, that the souls of the wicked are tormented with forebodings of the just judgment of God, and with the fear that a more dreadful sentence awaits them; while those of the righteous, ad-mitted to the participation of joy, live in expectation of more perfect happiness: for the misery of the one and the happiness of the other are augmented by the reflection which the effects of their wicked or good example have left behind; and beyond the grave we are assured ' our works shall follow us.' And on this supposition we may perhaps, not inconsistently, conjecture that the last great day of account will be one, also, of declaration; that is, the sentences that have already judicially been effected, will, on that day, be publicly pronounced, and the Lord will gather all his people to himself, and be 'glorified in them;' whilst the Devil, his angels, and followers will be cast into the place ' where there is weeping and gnashing of teeth.' You may then safely derive consolation, my dear friends, from the assurance that in the interval between death and the resurrection, they who have died in the? fear and love of God live in holy communion with ' the Saints and Spirits of just men made perfect;9 and consequently that he who has now been removed from us, we may confidently hope, is now in the number of this blessed society. Who, then, would be unwilling to exchange the sure possession of unsul-lied happiness for the participation of uncertain and imperfect joy ? "

" It is this reflection," said Ellen, " which supports us under our present loss; but there is one other question, Doctor, I would fain ask you on this interesting topic — whether there are grounds for believing that the departed spirits have any knowledge of each other in a separate state."

" This is a point," he replied, " which it is impossible for me satisfactorily to determine. I can produce nothing upon which to require your belief, though I may offer something to show it to be more than probable. Knowing that the souls of faithful believers are at peace, and those of the wicked in misery, we have no reason for enquiring further to what degree of happiness or woe they can progressively or ultimately attain beyond what mortals can estimate ; yet it is a pleasing recreation of the mind to draw natural inferences from the developement of revelation, particularly when they have the direct tendency to make us aspire after that blessed state to which we are invited by the promises of the Gospel. We find in the early part of the Bible, that a phrase generally prevails expressive of a notion, that departed spirits of the righteous go to the society of those objects of affection whom they loved and venerated. The phrase of being ' gathered unto their fathers,' signifying death, conveys something beyond the wish for the body to be consigned to the sepulchre of their forefathers. When Jacob lamented the loss of Joseph, who he was told had died in the wilderness, he said, ' I will go down to the grave of my son mourning;' — he could not mean that his body should be deposited in the same tomb with his son, whom he thought the beasts of the field had devoured, but that he should go down through the grave, the gate of death, to the place where there should be this communion between them. Is there any one who, upon the loss of a relative, or one whom he regarded as his friend, has not engrafted on the feelings of his heart a hope that he himself shall one day be re-united to those who have engaged his love? It is a feeling inseparable from genuine affection; it is one inspired by Nature, one that seems implanted by God himself; for ' God is love.' If, then, an impression on the mind, made by Nature herself, be taken as a ground for believing a state of immortality as being an echo of that voice which the Almighty whispers to man; may not a similar impression from the same source be looked upon as affording reasonable grounds for believing, that the feeling for a re-union with those dear objects of our hearts, who have quitted our mortal society, is implanted in the breast by Him who has inspired such affection —by Him who has constituted the ties of tenderness, and the bonds of love? Reason, or perhaps something of a higher nature, suggested this hope to David on the loss of his child, when he consoled himself with the assurance, ' I shall go to him, but he cannot return to me.' That favourite expression, too, among the Jews, of being ' in Abraham's bosom,' in which Christ represented Lazarus to be, carries the supposition that the souls of the righteous are admitted at their departure into the congregation of patriarchs, ' the society of just men made perfect.' And what could have been the meaning of Christ's promise to the repentant criminal, of being **with him** in Paradise, if it did not imply that they should be in the society of each other? Does not, moreover, the request of Dives for the aid and comfort of Lazarus intimate, that in Hades they had knowledge one of another? Whatever might have been the source from which the Heathen Philosophers derived their opinions, it is quite evident they believed, that the souls in Elysium were not only sensible and conscious of each other, but that their happiness consisted in a great measure in a social intercourse. And is it not natural, is it not rational, to conceive that if we are endowed with organs of communication here—if our greatest mental gratification consists in imparting our thoughts to each other, entertaining, improving, and exalting our nature by such means, — there; must be something infinitely more sublime, more refined and heavenly, in a conversation of souls ?"

" And now, my dear consoling friend," said Ellen, " there remains but one point more to render the solace of these considerations altogether perfect Could you but show us any rear sons for conceiving that they who have been taken from us on earth have knowledge of what is here done by us---I mean so as to have a sense of what constitutes our happiness here below, — our satisfaction would be complete. Matilda and I should derive redoubled delight from all our pursuits, could we thus persuade ourselves that the dear objects of our affection still know that we are good and happy."

" Your sister's question," replied the Doctor, " regarded the happiness of our souls at their departure hence; yours refers to the enjoyment which we may derive while we exist in these earthly tabernacles. Neither of them is a point necessary to believe as a part of Christian faith on which our salvation is to depend, and can only be inferred from such deductions of reason as it is optional to receive or reject. To me it appears most probable that the happiness of good spirits is enhanced by the contemplation of those virtuous and holy effects which their example and precepts have had upon their posterity, and of the prospect of greater happiness which shall afterwards be conferred upon them on this very account; while, on the contrary, the wicked will derive misery proportionate to the pernicious effects which their execrable conduct and example have had upon the world, and the expectation of more which all this will bring upon them in the dreadful day of judgment Such a consideration has the tendency, when other motives fail, to arouse the wicked mind by the contemplation of such woe, and excite the virtuous by these pleasing reflections; the one to abhor and flee from sin, the other ' to seek peace and ensue it.'"

" But," said Matilda, " on this supposition, if the happy spirits were to be sensible of the deviations of their survivors from the paths of virtue, and their falling into vice, their happiness would be interrupted."

" Not exactly so," said the Doctor; " because in Hades it may be supposed that they have the enjoyment of a prescribed, invariable portion of happiness; which happiness, while it may be augmented by such causes as we mention, may not be lessened by them below the original standard of it I say, then, that the faculty of departed spirits to take cognizance of our earthly concerns, as they contribute to our virtue, or , draw us from sin, is probable; and the probability rests upon the reflection, that when Dives was in Hades, he, in consideration of his great solicitude for the happiness of those relatives whom he left on earth, prayed that some commissioned spirit from the mansions of the dead might be sent unto them, by whose awful visitation they might be brought to timely reflection, and to that amendment of life which would ensure them a doom different from that to which he was then consigned: and thus, though separate from the body, it is plain, from his reflecting upon the past occurrences of life, he was interested in the fete of his survivors."

" Yes," interrupted Ellen: " but this does not go sufficiently far to show that he was acquainted with any transaction which had happened since his own dissolution; but if it did, you must remember that it was altogether a *parable*, and might be meant only to illustrate some essential points, without being a representation of any thing that really existed."

" I grant it may be so," replied the Doctor; " yet I think even if it were a parable, it was founded, like many others of the Gospel, on actually existing circumstances. Christ, as he delivered his discourses, took the things within his view to illustrate and enforce his doctrines. The foolish man, building his house upon the sand, was a parable grounded upon circumstances which it is well known were common in Judea, where imperfectly-founded houses were not unfrequently washed down by sudden torrents and inundations of rain. The parable of the Sower was grounded also upon real life; that of the wise and foolish Virgins upon what often occurred at marriage festivals; the lost Sheep, the Publican and Sinner, the Marriage Feast, and many others, were built upon the most natural and frequent occurrences."

" I think," observed Matilda, " that we are carrying our enquiries beyond all prescribed limits, when we estimate the sources from which the happiness or misery of immortal departed spirits spring; and though I confess the satisfaction I should derive from this belief would be great indeed, yet it appears to me that the happiness of a pure æthereal essence emanates from something so infinitely refined, as can never enter into the conception of mortality : for ' eye hath not seen, nor hath it entered into the heart of man to conceive the good things which God hath prepared for them that love him.' "

" I admit this, also," said the Doctor, " and entirely concur in the general sentiment which you have expressed; but the happiness of which. the souls in Hades are partakers we are not perhaps to consider so exquisitely refined and æthereal, as that which they are hereafter to enjoy at the consummation of all things. Do not, however, misunderstand me; I open no ground for the belief here of any thing approximating to the doctrine of Purgatory. In the intermediate state there is no putting *off* the corruptive stain of sin: no virtue is there to be acquired, no vice to be washed away; for ' there is no repentance in the grave, whither ye must all go;' and ' where the tree fells, there it lies.' What I would infer is, that we may conceive the soul in Hades to be allied more nearly to what is earthly then, than when it is admitted to its final state of refinement; and yet we have the testimony of Christ for knowing that the Angels in heaven, who have attained the highest and most exalted perfection, look down from above with the eye of watchful solicitude on the frail children of mortality, and exult when they perceive them turning from the evil of their ways unto him who created them; for ' there is joy in heaven over one sinner that repented!.'"

"This," said Matilda, "in a great degree removes my objection; and whether it be the case or not, I shall in future consider every action of my life as known by the blessed spirits of our dear departed parents, and from such a consideration I shall ever derive a stimulus to be good, virtuous, and religious, as I shall conceive it to enhance their spiritual peace and joy; and this I know has long since been your determination too, Ellen."

" At all events," said the Doctor, "you have enough that is clearly and explicitly revealed on this subject to afford you the greatest consolation, and to make it evident that such is the nature of our beautiful system of religion, that while it has an invariable influence to make mankind pious, it has equally the uniform tendency to make them happy."

THE SUICIDE.

WHAT complication of severe distress,
What inward terrors words can ill express,
What starts convulsive, and what inward, throes,
That mark the absence of the soul's repose,
Does conscience kindle in his troubled heart
Who, feels, deep-rankling, Sin's remorseless; smart!
That still small voice more dreadful sounds conveys
Than e'er the syren Vice could pleasure raise ;
Speaks with a tone that all the man confounds,
And probes,with goadingstings,Guilt's lurid wounds.
And thus, all impotent of peace or rest,

The soul's awaken'd feelings are confest: —
" At length 'tis done! The useless strife is o'er;
Vain is resistance, contest is no more.
Long have I braved the still recurring tide
  Of deathless Conscience with a Sceptic's pride;
Long have I held the veil before my eyes,
To perpetrate Religion's sacrifice,
And with a magic web around me flung,
Allured the weak, the credulous, the young:
But now the vision, bubble-like, recedes,
And leaves me prey to hell and hellish deeds.
I, who so long conspired the world to cheat,
Fall, baffled victim! by my own deceit.
In this dread hour, when life itself decays,
And the slow tide in sluggish currents strays,
When strength grows weak, and all the outward man
Enfeebled, gains its constituted span —
I feel—I feel a something living still,
Superior to the body's grosser will—
A something, which, as fades my trembling breath,
Whispers defiance to thy triumphs, Death!
A something, not unknown, that oft has striven
Against my crimes, and beacon'd me to heaven.
To HEAVEN! dread name! oh, how my spirits sink!
'Tis not for me! I stand on Ruin's brink —
Beneath me yawns a precipice—and see!
The grinning fiends their firebrands point to me.
Oh save me! save me! Hold, my bursting heart!
Avaunt, ye demon crew! my inward smart
Needs not your fires! Oh, whither shall I turn?
Burn, burn, ye flames, with quenchless blazing burn!
Alas! I sink. Oh! could I breathe *that name*
Which can alone these raging furies tame—

That name which saves the just,—they would retire:
That name would quench their never-dying fire.

" Were mine the treasures of exhaustless wealth,
And they could purchase shortest space of health,
How eager would I buy a day, an hour!
But, no; 'tis just! a retributive power
Vengeance demands. I feel the flame within ---
Hell gapes; its blazings must atone my sin.
I sink! I sink beneath the Eternal's rod,
And own, in death, thy justice, RIGHTEOUS GOD!"

" These lines," said Mr. Deacon to his venerable Rector, as they drew round the fire after a social dinner, distinguished rather by simplicity than sumptuousness, " These lines were an early production: they are somewhat rough, but I well remember that I felt myself much interested in the composition of them. I was on a visit to a highly-respected dignitary of the Church, when an event occurred which gave rise to them."

" Deacon," said the Rector, " yours is a happy disposition. You seem to have employed your early years well, and spent in observation that time which is too frequently given up to idle and unprofitable pleasures."

" That I have in some measure been enabled to do so, I thank God. The satisfaction to be derived from a retrospect of a youth well spent, must, I am sure, be great indeed; for to me, who can but very imperfectly apply to myself your observation, there is a perpetual source of thankfulness: what, then, must it be to those who have measured their time by an improvement much superior to mine! But there are others, for whom one cannot but feel very deeply, who enter upon the first scene of active life with all the eagerness natural to their years, and, at the same time, with all the vice which is generally acquired by a longer collision with the world, and too frequently with that part of it which is the hot-bed of folly and depravity."

" I cannot but regret," said the Doctor, " that things are in this respect changed since ' first life's journey I began.' Young persons are now men and women before they cease to be children; and too often become old, not only in vice, but by vice old in constitution, before their years attain to maturity."

" I know one young man," said the Curate, " who is, alas! too strong a proof of your observation. He was not only a schoolfellow of mine, but a townsman. Our years are equal. When children, our pursuits and studies were the same. Where one was to be seen, the other was not far distant And though I cannot say with the poet, that we had ' one house, one bed,' yet we had one school, one teacher. As years advanced so did our communion grow stronger. There was sometimes a tartness about him that threw an occasional gloom over our bright hours of friendship, which, however, was always transitory; like an April day, the cloud that awhile dims the æther, when past, leaves it more bright and pleasant. It was his misfortune to have parents too indulgent; parents whose affections were stronger than their reason, and whose kindness was manifested rather by acts of inconsistent fondness and overstrained indulgence, than the love which chasteneth and the affection which wins, whilst it corrects. The consequence was, that though they were much averse from having their son what is commonly termed a spoiled child, their treatment of him was the most direct way to entail that curse both upon him and themselves: and unhappily it came upon them very severely. Their son, their darling Henry, the hope of their lives, and the anticipated comfort of their declining years; so far from realizing their fond expectations, brought their prematurely-grey hairs with sorrow to the grave. Every year seemed to add to his waywardness; and though towards the com-mencement of each vacation he was much im-proved, from the discipline of our dear and excellent teacher, whose memory I highly venerate, yet the time he spent at home not only undid the good that had previously been done, but * materially added to the corruption of his once amiable disposition. At the age of fifteen, he left that respectable school, in which for six years we had been drawing in the nurture of a sound and classical education, and was transplanted, unfortunately for him, to an overgrown establishment; in which, in his case at least, whilst talents expanded, virtue died. I now only saw him once a year; and though he expressed for me unalterable friendship, yet I could easily perceive he felt neither the easiness nor happiness in my society which had marked his early years. There was an unbridled wildness in his conversation that sometimes sparkled with wit; but it was the wit of libertinism. The sacred name. of God was never uttered but in an oath or idle exclamation; and religion was sometimes a jest, sometimes a form. To me, who had from my cradle been taught to utter the name of God with reverence, and to entertain a kind of holy respect for religion, there was something in such conversation very shocking; and when I remonstrated with him on the levity of his conduct, and the profaneness of his speech, he laughed at my simplicity, as he called it, and asked, ' Who made me a judge in Israel ?' — said that I was inexperienced, knew nothing of life, had no spirit, and that a few gay scenes in the world would make me think differently. ' Fashion, all-powerful fashion,' said he, ' requires that we should free ourselves from such antiquated forms as you talk of; for what says the epilogue ---' Fashion in every thing bears monstrous sway.' ***Thus*** would he run on. In vain I endeavoured to recall the remembrance of the days of childhood, when innocence gave pleasure, and ignorance of vice conferred contentment. The pure delights of life's opening spring he termed insipid : well enough, indeed, for that, early age, but not worthy to be remembered, when the busy scene of maturity, with all its pleasures, fascinations, and bewildering enchantments, invited his. acceptance."

" How frequently," said Dr. Freeman, " do young persons argue thus, and alas! how fallaciously ! I can easily divine that your friend became a complete worldling: but proceed, for 1 am anxious to hear the rest of your story."

" Your surmise is true. Finding that he could not bring his conversation to the standard of decency which I always wished to be observed in my own, and that of my associates, he became less desirous of my society, and sought out others of a disposition more congenial with his own. His visit into the country was only for a few weeks: his other vacations were spent in places better fitted to his taste and affording a wider sphere for his dissipations."

" But how, with respect to his parents ?" interrupted the Doctor. " Did they use no endeavours to stem the current of his career; or were they blind to his faults; or did they consider them only youthful indiscretions ?"

" His parents, though he contrived to hide from them the blacker shades of his character, began now to see, too late, the error they had committed in his education, and would gladly have done any thing to cancel the past. They entreated, they wept, — in vain; they threatened, they promised, — but it was to no purpose. At the age of twenty-one, so rapid is the progress of guilt, he was an adept in every debauchery, and practised in every kind of li-bertinism. At the university, where he had now been two years, he was any thing but what he ought to have been; till at length he was expelled. This circumstance greatly added to the weight of sorrow that already pressed heavy upon the drooping spirits of his afflicted parents. His mother, in particular, with all the softness of. her sex, and tenderness of maternal solicitude, felt most poignantly this new but merited disgrace of her only child. ' Alas ! ' she would say, ' I go sorrowing to the grave; no child of mine shall close my eyes: I have no daughter, and would to God, I never had had a son: but his will be done !' The deep and mournful traces of affliction were lessened by the placidity of her heart, which, while it knew its own bitterness, felt the consolation which Religion ever bestows upon those, who, brokenhearted and humbled in spirit, seek to him who came to heal every wound, and raise the fallen; but though the influence of our blessed Religion materially checked the violence of her inward grief, yet nature fell beneath the struggle, and her changed looks gave evident marks that her days were numbered. Like a tranquil evening which has succeeded the bursting of the storm, whose depth is mellowed by the still lingering rays of the setting sun. In a little time she sank, and her ' place knew her no more.' Never shall I forget the day of her death. Though I had left my home, and was entered upon the theatre of busy life, yet I was at that time op a short visit to my parents. As usual in the days of my infancy, I was a constant guest at Mr. Farnworth's, to whom my presence now gave a sensation of pleasure. mingled with a secret pain, because it seemed to remind him and his aged consort, of one who ought to have been there: but where was he? His mother one day sent for me, and addressed me in nearly the following words : —

" ' My dear young friend, companion of the early days of my beloved but prodigal Henry, hear the words of one of whose spirit is about to leave its earthly tabernacle. Should you ever see my boy,' — and here the tears followed one another in rapid succession down her blanched cheeks, and her feelings choked her utterance, — Should you ever see my boy, tell him not that I died broken-hearted; reproach him not on my account, for his conscience will one day need no other censure or punishment than its own sting,* Tell him my prayers, my thoughts, my hopes, and my wishes were ever for him; tell him I forgive him, as I hope to be forgiven; and that my last breath shall whisper his beloved name. Dear young man, you are no stranger to the troubles of my heart; but may my child never know, and never feel what I have suffered; — though I fear---But,' she continued, ' there is a God, and there is a Heaven,' raising her heavy eyes, whilst a feint flush of rapture gleamed over her care-worn visage, —' a God who is abundant in mercy,' and a Heaven ' where every tear is wiped off every eye.' — Oh Henry, Henry! shall we meet there ? — Shall we, my Henry ?'

" Here, overcome by the exertion, her tongue faltered, her head sank, and she lay as one devoid of sense. Presently she recovered; I took my departure; and in one hour ' the silver cord was loosed, and golden bowl was broken.' The tidings of this event were conveyed to his son by the afflicted father, in a letter scarcely legible through grief. The day appointed for the funeral arrived, but no Henry came. On the morning of the day which was to see the mortal remains of his parent consigned to their kindred dust, and whilst every heart that had known her, beat in sorrow, and every eye that had once blessed her presence wept sincere tears, — her son, on whom she had doated, was far from his country, a voluntary exile, a supposed murderer; Of this, the public prints gave an account, which of course could not escape the notice of all his friends, who took every precaution to prevent the dismal tidings from reaching the ears of his only surviving parent, already so deeply stricken. His mother was buried in the grave of her fathers; and his father breathed among men, scarcely conscious that he was reckoned among the living."

" Righteous, indeed, is the retribution of Heaven !" said the Doctor: " how ' wonderful are his counsels, and his ways past finding out!' You said, that on the day of his mother's funeral, the son was an exile and a murderer.— Dreadful! Tell me how this happened."

" Expelled from the university, the prodigal immediately went up to London, and ran the career of profligacy with augmented eagerness. The whirl of dissipation excluded thought; the bewildering of gaming stirred up in him so insatiable a desire for play, that it absorbed every other consideration. Success followed him, otherwise his pecuniary means must have failed. Short, however, was his career: one evening he grossly insulted a young officer, added a challenge to the insult, and, though a bully and a coward, escaped unhurt, whilst his victim fell, to all appearance never to rise again. Delirious with fright, and filled with the imagination of the consequence of his baseness, and the danger he incurred from the violated laws of his country, he fled. This was on the very day his mother died. Paris received the exile, not changed in his habits, or disposed to amend the evil of his ways. On the same day tidings reached him there, of his mother's death, and of the recovery of his opponent: the former information slightly overshadowed his soul, and inflicted a pang, which however was soon healed by the rapture with which the latter intelligence inspired him. The father soon became acquainted with his son's complicated viciousness. He saw him no more: — in six months from the death of his partner, ' one grave contained the hapless pair.'"

" And did not this rouse the young man from his dream of madness, for such it must have been ?"

" For some little time after this event there was no account of him, during which period it was charitably hoped that he had withdrawn from his former habits, and was devoting his hours to grief, repentance, and contemplation: but alas! he soon reappeared on the stage of dissipation: his short seclusion had only increased his appetite for vicious pleasures. The last account I heard of him was, that he had left Paris, and was following nature in the society of some of our countrymen and countrywomen who look upon religion as a jest or trick, and marriage as a civil dealing quite inconsistent with the freedom of human beings."

" It is lamentable," observed the Doctor, " to hear that such things are; and that men of rank, talents, and literary fame, are the persons who thus scandalize society and mock the ordinances of Heaven. How strangely must their understandings be perverted, and their hearts vitiated by their passions and prejudices ! How debased is sunk their reason, who can love to live as beasts! Is it possible that there can be affection among such people? They must be strangers to all those pure delights which religious virtue gives, and all those nameless sensations of refined happiness which wedded love bestows. Theirs may be the halo of enjoyment and sensual gratification; but the sun of contentment, the full orb of the unclouded pleasure of ' the happiest of their kind,' animated by the noblest feelings, and best aspirations of our nature, has never, and can never shine on them with its almost divine radiance."

" And yet," replied Mr. Deacon, " this perversion of reason, and open defiance of the laws both of God and man, may be less wondered at, when we see Senators, and those of the highest rank in the legislature, gravely advancing the bold hypothesis, that marriage is only a civil contract."

" I am willing to believe," replied the Doctor, " that such assertions were the unguarded ebullitions of warmth rather than of reason; for, I cannot suppose that a Christian who reads the word of God with any attention, can so far allow his understanding to be darkened, as temperately to conclude that marriage is only a civil contract. The lives of those who practise these principles will always be a standing proof and antidote against this unscriptural doctrine. Is there one among that society who has not been deeply sunk in the mire of guilt, before he leagued himself with it ? The career of your friend is but a transcript, perhaps of the darker kind, of what is too frequently taking place: dissipation, gaming, debauchery, irreligion, duelling, and infidelity, make up the black account; and though all these may not unite in one person, or come in all at once, yet these are so closely allied, and so consecutive to one another, that where one is found, the other is not far off. As for duelling, to which there lately have fallen two *victims*, it is a practice in direct opposition to the spirit of the Gospel, and inimical to the interests of the' Christian world. It is unquestionably murder, and murder preconcerted under the aggravated circumstance of a pretended merit; and, however human laws may acquit the duellist, there is registered in Heaven a solemn charge for him to answer."

" And yet," observed the Curate, " Dr. Johnson advocates this practice."

" I know he does," was the reply; " but. on a false principle. It is curious to see
that Leviathan of learning floundering in the shallows of sophistry. But in spite of
all his reasoning, he has failed to make good his argument. And, indeed, no wonder;
for all the reasoning in the world can never subvert a plain precept of holy writ. '
Thou shalt commit no murder,' is at once so expressive and. full, that no ingenuity
. can elude its authority. And is not duelling to all intents and purposes murder?—
foul, aggravated, hypocritical murder? And why? What is the object it has in view
? To satisfy a real or imaginary insult. As if the taking away of life, or even the attempt, could be any satisfaction to a mind regulated by the principles of Christianity, the purest spirit of which breathes only ' peace and good-will to man.' It ought
to be discarded, abhorred, detested. It is the worst of vices, without one redeeming
quality. It possesses all the basest features of cowardice, for it fears the censure of
worldly men — it carries with it all the hardihood of the most abandoned sinner,
for it fears not the wrath of (rod. Obnoxious as it is to all that is good and moral,
how infinitely more so is it to Christianity! For if that heavenly quality which '
never fails,' because it comprehends all our duty both to God and man, were to be
exercised between two angry opponents, who are ready each to send the other

> ' to his great account
> With all his imperfections on his head,'

the hand directing the murderous engine would unconsciously be extended in
token of fellow-ship, whilst the heart that is palpitating in doubt between honour
and nature, would beat with kindness; and the eye that flashes with rage, beam with
gentleness, and smile where late it frowned. As when the raging element heard
the voice of I AM, as he walked upon the waters, and simultaneously were hushed
to silence at his command, so would the raging passions of discordant hatred, and
fictitious honour, settle to instant calm, and be soothed to. fellowship, to amity and
love, would men once listen to the heavenly dictates of Christian charity."

The Doctor was proceeding in a strain of unusual animation, when a servant
entered the room, and announced that there was a person in the hall who wished

to speak either with the Rector or the Curate.

" Show him in," said the Doctor. The waiter of one of the principal inns now made his appearance.

" Gentlemen," said he, " there is a stranger at our house who came by coach this morning: he is dreadfully ill; and my master begs as a favour that one of you would visit him, for he suspects that the gentleman stands in need of religious consolation."

" As it is a wet evening, sir," said Mr. Deacon, "and I know you are not particularly well, you must permit me to go to this sick man."

He accompanied the waiter to the inn, where he found the medical gentleman who was in attendance on the patient

" Sir," said the surgeon, " I fear my skill is unavailing: I cannot 'administer to a mind diseased.' There is more need of your assistance than mine; but I fear that both will be to little purpose." So saying, he led the way. - The room was imperfectly lighted; and the curtains of the bed were drawn, so that the invalid was in a great measure hidden from view. A deep groan announced intense suffering; and a convulsive start which caused the bed to shake, indicated to Mr. Deacon that some one was there who was no ordinary sufferer: this impression was confirmed when a hollow frantic voice wildly broke forth in these incoherent words:

" Off! off! I' cannot bear to look upon you: father ! mother! Whip me not, ye furies ! See, see, there they sit! — Don't you see them grinning, and shaking their hellish goads ? Oh, this is, indeed, agony! The furies are tormenting me! Oh, hide me! hide me !"

Here he covered himself with the bed-clothes, and for a few minutes remained quiet, as if afraid to move: then suddenly throwing his covering aside, and starting upright on the bed, with eyes distended and wildly rolling, and with a velocity that marked the madman, he continued :

" Ha; they are gone. — No, I did not murder them: tax me not with that:—they died at home, and I — where was I ? Is that Captain Martin?— Ha! ha! ha! I shot him! — Seven's the main — a thousand pounds — lost, undone: — fool! madman! — Ruin ! ruin ! — Father, mother ! —hush ! they are asleep;— tread lightly on the grass — I will not awake them

" Alas ! I cannot; — they are dead! dead ! dead! I am following them — following? — Yes, to the grave, but not—no, no ! Oh, I feel! I feel!" straining his clenched hand with convulsive vehemence to his heart; " I feel it here, — it is too much— I cannot bear it —"

Nature again sank beneath the struggle, and the patient lay a lump of repulsive humanity. By this time Mr. Deacon had recognized his former friend Henry Farnworth; — but, oh ! how changed! there was no longer visible in his features the playfulness of youth, that indescribable appearance which marks immunity from care. In its place were depicted the haggardness of remorse, the indented marks of dissipation, and the crooked lines of guilt

Alas! thought he, what a havock is here! How is he who was formed to be the delight of society, and the comfort of a domestic circle, "rendered obnoxious to strangers, and an alien from his friends! Talents abused, blessings prostituted, and advantages misapplied, have brought on a dreadful consequence. Instead of the comfort of virtue, behold the poignancy of vice. Instead of the corrupted nature of man ennobled by. the atoning grace of Heaven, behold that nature more corrupted by the impurity of wicked deeds and voluntary debasement! The wretched man at length revived, and in a lucid interval of comparative composure said:

" Is there any one who will do a friendly deed to a stranger to happiness, and an outcast from society ?"

Mr. Deacon here came close to his bedside, and sitting down by him, took one of his hands, and in accents of mildness softened by compassion, said:

" Farnworth, in the name of Heaven, what is the matter? Why are you here?"

Startled to hear himself accosted by a name he had so debased, and in a place where he believed himself totally unknown, he looked intently on the Curate, and enquired:

" Who's that says Farnworth? — Surely I once knew you. That voice sounds like memory of former days. I have some faint recollection, too, of that face (scrutinizing him with an ar-dent glance). Are you — (and he passed the back of his hands across his eyes and forehead, as if to remove the film that prevented recognition) — are you Deacon ?" Here the Curate motioned assent, and Henry Farnworth thus continued: " I sicken at the name, for it brings before me the memory of things I dare not dwell on. It reminds me of those happy days, the happiest I ever knew, when we were lads together— Oh, how have I sinned and suffered since.—I have scoffed at God, and now I feel his power, and it is just that I should. I have done every thing to abet vice and to offend Heaven. Religion I have scorned, and hence have I in-dulged in blasphemy. I joyed in infidelity, and hence have I lost all principles of virtue. I am a murderer! the worst of murderers, a parricide. My victims were my parents, (and here he shuddered,) a young officer, and my own reputation and peace of mind. And, now, to complete the enormity of my guilt, I am a SUICIDE." Then rising in height and vehemency of voice—" Oh ! look not so mildly and compassionately upon me! I am a wretch of the basest, blackest, worst description. There is no sin that can disgrace a man, which I have not been guilty of. I can bear reproaches, for I deserve them, — but those pitying looks, so unmerited and unexpected, — oh ! they kill me. Tell me — for you cannot harrow up my soul with more terrifying feelings than I have long experienced—tell me, did you see the authors of my wretched being before they died?"

" I saw them," said the Curate, and the emotions of his heart flooded his eyes; " I saw them but a very short time before." " Did they curse me ?"

" Oh, no! they were Christians in life and death. They forgave you, they blessed you, they prayed for you."

" Did they, indeed? Then — (and a ray of hope shot transiently across his countenance) No: that is impossible! (and his countenance was again dusked with gloom.) Deacon, I am a Suicide; this morning I swallowed poison: my limbs are chilly and benumbed, but my brain is on fire." His looks were those of madness, scowling, dark, and repulsive: his pallid cheeks were flushed with mounting and contending feelings — his lips quivered, whilst a livid blue o'ermantled them — and his tongue in vain strove for utterance.

" Unhappy, guilty mortal!" said Deacon, '.' what can be done ? I pray you, Sir, (turning to the surgeon) use all your art, and, if possible, protract his life; for though he is not fit to live, yet it is dreadful to think, that he is less fit to die. Add, if you can, under Providence, but a few short hours to his life, that he may think upon his God."

The last word acted like a talisman upon Farnworth, and he uttered: " Who talks of God ? Oh! —name him not. There is terror!— there is destruction in the sound ! Talk not to me of his mercy, — mock me not by mention of his pardon. There is no atonement for me. My sins are beyond all reckoning. Once, indeed, I thought that I never could feel afraid of Him, because I credited the opinion, that Religion, with all that belongs to it, was a mere cheat. But now — oh terrible ! terrible! I tremble, I shudder — I sink in despair. Despair, despair is my portion; and if there be a hell, it lights for me its hottest fires. I cannot, I dare not think, Deacon, the world says you are a good man; it will never say so of me."

" Think not of what I am," was the reply, " but think of yourself: think of repenting; think of praying to that God whom you have so in suited, and looking up to that Saviour who died for all."

" Repenting, praying: — and can you talk to me of repentance and prayer? I cannot, cannot It is too late —the cup of wrath o'er-flows, and I must drink it to the dregs — and it is just — dreadful as it is, I have deserved it all. Oh! that I was again a boy, that I might lead a better life. That may not be — I dare not ask you to pray. Oh ! that those whom I have undone, and who helped to undo me, were here now; they would learn a lesson of bitterness and remorse. Deacon, tell than, tell the world, that the career of guilt is full of stings, and its end is — hell. — Passion, ungoverned feelings, lewdness, gaming, and blasphemy, these, these have been my ruin. I will not tax God for this. It was my own stubbornness and wilfulness, and I must now pay the dreadful, but just penalty. Oh vice! thou has no satisfaction in life, and in death, thou causest bitterness and despair —"

" Think, I exhort you," said the Curate, " think more rationally; and, as you feel the sting of vice, let the wound incline you to turn yourself to that great Physician, in whose hands are the issues of life and death."

" Death! horrible thought! He is here — he is here! hide me from him.—Deacon, stand between him and me; for oh! he is dreadful; I dare not look upon him, for he is the messenger of wrath. Life and death, said you? One I have abused, and it is passing from me, and the other — oh ! my brain is maddened. Death! what art thou? Canst thou quench this agitation which I feel throbbing, beating, fluttering here? Thou canst not. Thy look is full of horror. Thy bony, quivering hand is full of flaming darts, that flash with sulphureous blazings, and raise up before me terrific phantoms. —Keep off, and come not near me. Yet I would hail thee, if thou art the end of all worldly care — if thou canst take away all memory of the past—if thou canst blunt those sharp torments which rack me with remorse, and fill my soul — My soul! oh, no ! It may not be. — Too true for me it is, there is a God, and there is an hereafter, in which — (raising his agitated voice) — in which, where shall I appear? — where, where ?" and he continued repeating the last word, till his former friend broke in upon his reverie, by asking him if he would hear a prayer.

" No 5 I cannot bear it. How can you prayexcept to that God, whose goodness I have outraged, whose blessings I have converted into curses, whose mercies I have rejected, and whom I dare no longer call my father. Oh ! Deacon — (and he raised one hand of the minister to his burning forehead, and the other he strained to his heart, which beat in sad uncertainty, as if suspended between life and death) Oh!— Deacon, vain are your prayers—lose not, waste not a thought, a word on me — drop not a tear— (here nature for a moment triumphed, and the big drop stole down his sunken cheek, which had long been a stranger to such moisture)—drop not a tear over the memory of one, for whom it would have been better that he had never been. My senses waver; and yet I know and feel that I am an outcast — that 1 have sinned beyond redemption. Warn others of my misery when I am gone — and may my example deter them from—but I am faint — I go — but, oh! whither?"—

After a short, but violent struggle, all that remained of the once handsome, graceful, and accomplished Henry Farnworth was livid, cold, and revolting.

Who, on contrasting the events of such a scene with the innocent days of infancy, and the simple, but pure pleasures of early youth, could have Med to indulge, like Mr. Deacon, in serious contemplation. The review of the hours of friendship, which they had passed together, was a striking reverse to the period which had elapsed up to this awful time, and the prospect beyond was painful and sickening. To a sensitive mind like his, the death of his former friend, under such a horror of circumstances, suggested various feelings. He saw, lifeless before him, one who had possessed every advantage, and had been endowed with every faculty, the use of which ennobles, and the abuse . degrades humanity. He contemplated also the secret, the inscrutable workings of Providence, which is extended over the evil and the good, the just and the unjust. And from comparing these together, he felt more than ever assured of the truth, that human nature is corrupt, weak, and sinful,: unable to save itself, and consequently dependent on the gracious assistance of some higher power; which assistance, he felt equally assured, is always extended to all who seek, or strive to obtain it. From these considerations, also, he derived additional reasons to believe in that great work of heaven, which, without diminishing its fulness, prepared a way to purify, enlighten, and confirm mortality, by the sacrifice of one who, uniting both natures, exacted, and paid the penalty for all, which man could never have paid; and who conferred the means of redemption, from which his still imperfect ability may obtain continual supplies of assistance to enable him to " fight the good fight of faith," and come " to honour, and glory, and im-mortality." How sickening, therefore, was the sight before him—" The noblest work of God," so " infinite in faculties," and embellished with all that is " express and admirable," is now un-occupied and laid in ruins, whilst the tenant, whom God himself housed there, is driven away by a rash act, the fatal consequence of a complexity of vicious practices, to appear before his Creator, unsummoned, unprepared. This was an awful thought, and though as a man he might not pronounce eternal death upon a fellow mortal, yet the page of Revelation too clearly denounces ' tribulation and anguish,' and everlasting punishment on all those, who wilfully rush from a life they received for gracious purposes into an eternity of endless woe and never-dying misery. He could not fail, also, to feel what he had often preached, and thought, that whilst the Christian unfearingly meets his end, and relying upon the merits of the Saviour to be imputed to him, with the eye of hope anticipates the pure delights of heaven, the hardened sinner, however vice may have bewildered his sense, and blunted his feelings, finds his pilgrimage of life full of suffering, and, filled with dreadful doubts and gloomy fears, shrinks in the hour of death from that futurity which it is not permitted man to fathom.

PHILOSOPHY AND RELIGION.

ARTHUR Oswald had been left an orphan in early life, when his guardians sent him to a large school, through which he rapidly passed by the force of a natural and powerful genius, which like a strong current, carried him impetuously forward, despite the various obstacles which presented themselves to check him in his career. As a very moderate exertion was sufficient to buoy him on the surface of that scholastic distinction which his companions by more laborious efforts attempted to gain, no studies were to him difficult; and as there was nothing to excite application, he was altogether a stranger to it. This was a circumstance to be regretted, for they only can truly appreciate fame who acquire it after much toil and difficulty. Diligence in itself constitutes one of the most refreshing and invigorating exercises of the mind, by which, alone, the intellectual soil is loosened and turned over, and adapted to the reception of the seed to be implanted in it. The facility with which his exercises were accomplished, while it gave him greater leisure than was profitable, had the effect to restrain the powers of his mind, as it was expedient to retard his progress to admit of the advancement of those with whom he was classed. His lessons were prepared in half the time which they commonly engaged others, and thus while his companions were busied in making their way up to him, he was left to the indulgence of exclusive amusement, to the idle thoughts of a fanciful imagination, or to the perusal of trifling works of wit and genius, which, while they contributed to make him a more agreeable companion, had the tendency to fill bis mind with unsubstantial acquirements.

As a young man, he was prepossessing in his appearance, and not less so in his address. Tall and well made, his manly countenance and decisive gait commanded attention, while a brilliancy of intellect, a vivid fancy, and an uniform flow of language, gave him a marked superiority in every circle in which he moved; and though neither retiring in his manners, nor reserved in his opinions, he never obtruded his sentiments, nor manifested any thing in his conduct which could either be construed into arrogance or self-conceit. In the possession of what *are* called " easy circumstances," he mixed in the society of polished life, of which he was the admiration and delight His. taste and feelings were such, that though he neither unwillingly nor unfrequently mixed with the gay and fashionable world, he imbibed no effe-minate or immoral habits. The love of virtue was in him so strong, that his conduct exhibited a practical proof, that wealth and pleasure might contribute to the enjoyment of life without vitiating the heart; and that a strictly moral course might be maintained by a prudent mind amidst the manifold temptations to which such a public life was exposed: in the same manner that a ship may be safely directed by a skilful pilotage through shoals and hidden reefs, though to ignorance and mismanagement such dangers are attended with inevitable ruin. But the society in which Oswald commonly lived was that of educated men, such as blended taste with genius, and science with fortune; and with these he passed both an agreeable and an useful existence. Yet among all his acquisitions, in the midst of all these brilliant assemblies of wit and talent, and a dedication of his time to the refined pursuits of literature, Religion seldom obtruded either herself or her doctrines upon his reflections. Lost in the contemplation of the beauties of classic lore, the maxims and morals of heathen authors were those on which his creed was founded; beyond these and the works of nature, he looked not far to satisfy the temporary doubts which occa-sionally presented themselves to his mind; not that he did not venerate the Book of Life; to him it offered beauties which he considered unrivalled; but they were the extrinsic ornaments of composition; height of language, sublimity of thought, artless simplicity, perfect harmony, and deep pathos; these were the just objects of his admiration, which, in comparison with the writings of antiquity, were as the blaze of the sun to the light of the moon. All this was allied to taste, but it was removed from higher feelings: his was the eye of the lover of sculpture gazing upon the attitude, the execution, and the garb of a statue of Religion, and not upon Religion herself; upon the resemblance, and not the reality; on the shadow, and not the substance.

It was from ambition, inspired by a constant appeal to his judgment, and a desire to obtain his sanction in all matters of literature and arts, that he was brought gradually to vanquish that negligent supineness which, though induced by circumstances, and confirmed by habit, was not inherent in his nature. His application now became intense, and produced with it all those fruits which a mind endowed with such a taste and genius was calculated to bring forth. Well digested reading and a comprehensive mind, when united to the graces of elocution and elegance of manners, elevate the possessor of them above the ordinary level of his species, and are sure to be regarded by the liberal among mankind with a veneration due to superior qualifications. Though young, Oswald took the lead in the literary world, and was regarded as 'possessing a considerable knowledge of arts and sciences. As a natural philosopher, experimentalists pressed upon him their discoveries; as a chymist, he was besieged by all the blue-stocking conoscente from the Institution; as a lover of vertu, he had access not only to all the academies of science, but to all the galleries of painting and sculpture in the metropolis; and as a scholar, his aid was solicited by the conductors of all the Journals of eminence. Thus constituted a chief in the kingdom of the Belles Lettres, he received the homage of its subjects with a pride that was tempered by suavity of manner, and openness of communication, which showed itself allied to no narrow conceits of superiority; a pride it was that sprung from the purest principles, from the desire of being useful to others, and not the object of admiration or envy.

It happened as he commenced a tour into the interior of the country, for the purpose of viewing the distinguished residences of the Nobility, inspecting the

manufactories, and visiting those places remarkable either for the beauties of nature, or the discoveries of subterranean productions, that he came to Burleigh, the
seat of the Marquis of Exeter. The fineness of the morning had invited him to walk
from the Inn at Stamford, through the magnificent park, to the house, which he
reached at the moment when a carriage was setting down a gentleman and lady,
who had evidently arrived with the same intention. Attended by the housekeep-
er, they commenced the inspection of the place together, and were immediately
launched into the great conservatory of paintings. Here the taste of the strangers
seemed so perfectly to accord with each other, that their attention was continually fixed upon the same object in every room which they entered; passing as if by
common agreement over many intervening pictures to rest upon some one, the
perfections of which simulta-neously caught their eyes. The expression of their
sentiments — the effect which the object before them had upon their minds — the
colouring of this — the relief of another — the grouping of a third — the keeping
and exquisite " colouring of a fourth, obtained the tribute of admiration from the
spectators with hardly any difference of language; but this sympathy of taste was
more strongly called forth when they reached the little closet, where, in dignified
retirement, hangs suspended that masterpiece of the art, the Saviour of Carlo Dolce!
Here the three stood rivetted to the spot for a length of time gazing in silent devotion upon an object which excited unutterable feelings, and longer would they have
remained had not their conductor, betraying symptoms of restlessness, roused them
from that fit of abstraction into which this exquisite performance had thrown them.
They now proceeded slowly onwards through the remaining apartments, though
the sensation which the closet picture had produced, induced a fastidiousness of
taste which suffered their attention to dwell only on the choicest objects of the
remaining part of the collection. They arrived at the state-bedchamber, where the
little regard they paid to the objects pointed out to them by their guide, began to
excite in her sentiments bordering upon contempt; for in the eyes of the visitors the
curtains and drapery which she displayed, the luxurious crimson chairs which she
set forth in all their regal pomp, the steel-cut grate which she partially uncovered,
and the glittering andirons which she dexterously, but vainly, brandished in the
rays of that sun which had only just before been permitted to enter —these, with
many other little arts to attract attention, were all disregarded; at length finding her

labour fruitless, she only thought of pushing on her strangers with all imaginable speed. It was in one of the last of the suite of rooms leading to the grand staircase, while looking upon some of the many pictures with which it was stored, that Oswald perceived the eye of his fair companion fixed upon the face of a youth in a group of figures which had captivated her complete attention, and as she viewed it, a silent tear gently stole down her face; but finding it perceived, she complacently turned aside. Oswald now directed his eye particularly to the object that had elicited this proof of sensibility, and continued gazing upon it for some minutes after he had been left by his companions.

Such an accidental collision as this meeting occasioned stands in the place of the best intro-duction between strangers. In this case it was evident that the one was ranked highly in the esteem of the others, from the observations thrown out, by their manners, and by the similarity of their sentiments. As therefore Oswald, when the carriage drew up, was about to take leave of his fellow visitors, he was politely asked whether he were going to Stamford, and upon his answering that he was, he was as kindly prevailed upon to occupy the vacant seat. It was soon afterwards discovered that all were sojourners in the same house, when Oswald was further solicited, rather than break up the party which he had joined, to accept an invitation of dining at the same table, a request which he felt in no way inclined to refuse. Be-fore, however, they assembled, the stranger had enquired of the waiter the name of the person who had returned with them from Burleigh; and Oswald from the same fruitful source of intelligence had instituted a similar enquiry; so that upon the announcement of dinner, when he again made up the trio —

" Give. me leave, Mr. Oswald," said the stranger, advancing to him as he entered the room, " now to introduce my daughter and myself to your acquaintance. My name is Lorraine, one which I think can hardly be known to you: I was not aware until now that we had had the gratification of enjoying the society of one whose talents and character are so generally known, and so deservedly appreciated. I think myself happy in having thus casually fallen upon your acquaintance; and shall, with no less pleasure, be desirous of improving it."

" Pray," replied Oswald, " may I be permitted to ask, whether you were related in any Way to a young man of your name, whose friendship I had begun to cultivate when he suddenly died at the University ?'

" Alas!" replied Mr. Lorraine, looking at his daughter's sudden change of countenance, " I had both the happiness and misery of call-ing him my son!"

" I ask pardon," said Oswald, " for having thus unwittingly alluded to a circumstance which must give you pain; but suffer me to add, that with his remembrance are associated reflections more than commonly interesting; for in a short, but intimate acquaintance with him, I witnessed that which will ever endear him to my memory, and it is gratifying to be able to give additional testimony to his merit and worth as a scholar and a man, to those who must naturally feel a lively, though now a melancholy, interest in whatever related to him. I think too," continued he, addressing himself to Miss Lorraine, " now I have touched upon the subject, I can discover that this amiable person was presented to your mind by the picture which I saw you observe with marked concern just before we left Burleigh; I assure you so great was the re-semblance, that it powerfully recalled his image to my remembrance." If the similarity of taste and feeling excited by the exhibition in the morning had opened an acquaintance between the strangers, the discovery of one who had entertained a regard for the worth of a departed son and brother forced that acquaintance into a rapid maturity; and while the philosophical painter found an enlightened companion, whose taste, in the science he had once professed, was pure and correct, and whose open communication evinced a mind amply stored with the valuable treasures of literature, Maria discovered in the same, one whose manners and conversation displayed the most refined feelings, — feelings fully appreciated and welcomed as emanating from a heart that had united in its sympathy the friendship of a beloved brother.

This day was certainly one of great enjoyment to the travellers; their conversation, impeded by no interruptions, flowed calmly on like a river in its course, rolling smoothly onwards, enriched by a continued variation of scenery; nor did the party separate at night until Oswald had accepted the offer of accompanying them on a tour through some parts of Yorkshire, Cheshire, and the picturesque scenery of Derbyshire. In this journey some weeks passed agreeably and rapidly away, during which their acquaintance had gained an accession of strength which had ripened it into friendship, and that friendship seemed, with regard to Maria and Oswald, to be bordering upon a feeling which, if it were not a-kin, was not very distantly allied to a tie of a closer nature. It was impossible that two such minds should come into contact without making such an impression as that, which though not very evidently, was very certainly effected. Maria, as we have before mentioned, was not more distinguished by the graces of her manner and person, than by the cultivation of a mind quick and penetrating, a temper gentle and open, and a heart alive to every finer feeling of her nature. Educated under the direction of the most experienced teachers, and ambitious of exerting the full energies of a vigorous intellect, she. possessed a refinement which blended in true harmony with the softness of her sex, and the purest touches of religion; her mind occasionally displaying deep and broad shades, and exhibiting a strength of thought and conception beyond the ordinary range of feminine acquisitions. Ever backward in acknowledging, and averse from displaying her powers, it required the efforts of time and intimacy to lead to their developement. She was ever more ready to listen to the discussion of topics in which the generality of her sex forbore to enter, than to take any part in them; yet none could be more ready to return a judicious reply to any thing casually submitted to her opinion. No wonder then, that to a mind like Oswald's, she appeared engaging and worthy of something more than common admiration, or, however dear and sacred, more than even com-mon esteem. A feeling which received an additional impulse and strength by an event which happened in the latter part of their journey, and which powerfully excited in their breasts an ad-miration of each other, founded upon the sen-sibilities of their nature.

When pursuing their route through Derbyshire, as often as they arrived at the foot of those lofty hills with which the romantic parts of this county abound, Oswald alighted, that he might walk by the side of the carriage, not only to lessen the draught of it, but that he might get exercise and a view of the country on his ascent. As he was climbing one of these eminences, he perceived a country-lad riding upon an ass with frightful precipitation down the hill: the animal, with short, quick, bat unerring footsteps, speedily brought the Mercury on his back to the spot where Oswald stood gazing upon his progress, and the boy would have passed with the same rapidity, had he not previously made signs for him to stop. The lad, in suddenly pulling up the animal, threw him on his haunches, and with alarm in his countenance, and tears in his eyes, asked him what was his pleasure.

" Pleasure!" said Oswald; " there's no pleasure at all, my lad, in seeing you risk your own neck and that of your Rosinante, by riding at this unmerciful rate down this very steep hill; what makes you in such an unaccountable hurry ?"

" Oh, sir," said the boy, " poor sister Mary is dying; and as mother is in yonder fields near the farm-house below, I am going to call her."

This circumstance, and the pitiful manner of the boy's relation, had arrested the attention of Maria and her father, who, as they caught the latter part of it, alighted, while the carriage proceeded slowly onwards.

" Where, my good fellow," said Oswald, " is your home where your sister lies ?"

" Our house," replied the boy, " is on the side of the road when you get down into the next hollow."
" And what," said Maria, " has happened to your sister?"
"Oh, madam," replied the tender-hearted youth, as distinctly as his sobs would allow him, " she is almost crushed to death: but indeed I can't stay longer."

" Stop another moment," said Oswald: "do you conduct this lady and gentleman to where your sister is, and I will return presently with your mother. What is your name ?"

" Aspendale," replied the boy; and Oswald ran quickly down the hill.

The boy walked by the side of Maria and her father, until they came to what was called the hollow, where, among the trees, a few paces from the road, was situated a picturesque cottage. Here on a bench before the door were seated two labouring men in evident perplexity, whilst another, holding the bridle of a horse, stood before the little railing in front, and a single female seemed hurrying round and about the house with noiseless steps. The strangers were at once conducted to the room in which the sufferer lay. It was a large back-ward apartment, the casement of which, shaded by the shrubs which grew before it, denied entrance to the glaring rays of the sun. The clean brick floor — an old shining bureau, supported on either side by a polished oaken chest — a three-legged table—two or three chairs with high perpendicular backs, grotesquely carved, were the articles of furniture which accompanied a bed that had no curtains, but whose patchwork coverlet and coarse clean linen designated the comfort and respectability of its inhabitants. The patient, whose groans were deep and piercing, showed symptoms of excruciating agony, but the expression of her countenance indicated that more was suppressed than she betrayed, for there was evidently a struggle to resist all she felt. At the side of her bed was seated a youth, whose head almost resting upon his knees, was buried in a handkerchief, while on the other sat the medical attendant in silent abstraction, watching the countenance of his patient.

" What," said Lorraine, addressing them, " what has happened to this poor creature; for the little boy who conducted us hither can give us no account beyond her having met with an accident ?"

" Sir," said the surgeon, " she has had the misfortune to be dreadfully crushed by the blast-ing of a piece of rock, and is terribly mangled."

Here the youth on the side of the bed waved his head and body in bitterness of sorrow, and wept aloud; upon which the sufferer, in all her agony, laid her hand upon his arm, and looked at him with a fondness that drew tears from those who witnessed the expression of so much tenderness. After a little while the mother, accompanied by Oswald, entered the apartment, and, throwing herself by the side of her daughter, evinced the deepest sympathy and grief as she gazed upon the tortured countenance of her child.

" What, what, my dear Mary," she exclaimed, "has happened to thee? I left thee so well and so cheerful but a few hours since, and to return so quickly and with such alarm is almost too much for me. Edward !" said she, turning to the distracted young man, " do tell me what it is that ails ye both ?"

" My good friend," said the surgeon, " let me tell you in a few words that your daughter, passing down below the hollows of the quarry, was unexpectedly struck by a mass of blasted rock, and is severely bruised ;" and he betrayed the extent of his fears by the touching manner in which he spoke.

" How," said she, " struck by the stone ? What were there none to warn stragglers of their danger ?"

" Alas, alas!" sobbed the distressed Edward, " the fault, the fault is all mine ! I thought nobody could be near — I gave no signal — I set no warners, — and I, yes I have killed her. Oh Mary, Mary ! how I wish I could suffer all this instead of you !"

" Tell me," said the mother, addressing the surgeon, "tell me, is she in danger?"

" That question," said the afflicted girl, making a painful effort to speak, " my dear mother, I can best answer. I feel, aye, I am sure, quite sure, that it is all over with me!" Here Edward on the one side, and the mother on the other, caught each hold of the sufferer's hands, which they pressed with the greatest fervour, and bathed with floods of tears. " I wanted," she continued, " to take Edward by surprise at his work — I went to carry something to refresh him, and something, too; I had to say to him; but it is all over! Mother, thank, thank you for the care you have always taken of me,—you have always been kind, very kind, and I hope you have never thought me ungrateful ?"

" Never," would the agonized parent have uttered, could her tongue have spoken what her countenance expressed.

The sufferer, now turning her head, added— " Good bye, Edward; don't take on so hardly; don't I know that you would rather die before I should suffer?—When I am gone, comfort my poor mother, (here her fortitude forsook her,) and take care of James," turning her moistened eyes to the corner of the room, where the poor little fellow had squeezed himself with his face turned to the wall to hide his woful countenance.—" Let me be laid in that corner of the church-yard where we have so often walked together, waiting for the Sabbath service. — God bless you all, and you, kind strangers, who show such pity for us—bless, bless you all, and oh! may my heavenly Saviour have mercy upon me!"—Here her voice failed her, and after one or two slight distortions, the tender-hearted Mary breathed no more!

The travellers, with deep affliction, shortly took leave of the inmates of the cottage, and proceeded, without exchanging more than a few words, to the Inn at Matlock, where, as soon as they were shown into their apartments, they separated. Mr. Lorraine, from the window of the sitting-room, gazed upon the romantic scenery before him, and he looked upon it with feelings of interest heightened by the impressions of melancholy, which his mind had received from the wretchedness he had witnessed. Maria in her chamber sought composure, from meditating upon that volume which can bind up the broken-hearted, and pour balm into every wound Oswald, with the view to soften that despondency and gloom which these circumstances had oc-casioned, by diverting his mind with different reflections, climbed the hills above the village, and dived into the dark recesses of the caverns, where, instead of shaking off the depression which hung upon his spirits, he only increased it by the silent and dismal scenes around him, scenes that were assimilated to nothing but the grave. Never till that day had he witnessed a real scene of death; he knew of calamities and human sufferings only by description; he had never been thrown into the way of those who laboured under bodily afflictions; what he had seen at the cottage, therefore, had quite unnerved him. He began to reflect, and to feel that he himself was of the same nature, and liable to the same calamities with those whom he had so lately beheld distressed, and with her whom he had seen suddenly removed in the very morn of life and vigour, from this transitory state. She who had risen that day full of expectation, and with the prospect of long-continued happiness before her, was now, ere the setting of the same sun, inanimate,—the residue of dust and ashes! She who had built upon the hope of repairing to a home of her own, in the company of one she loved dearly as her life, was now to be consigned to the dread regions of darkness, and to be laid in the cold grave, a prey to the reptiles of the earth! And yet he reflected,— " she betrayed- no fear of dissolution; she lamented, indeed, being suddenly cut off from the bosom of her family and her friends; but no expression, no symptom of apprehension, escaped her; and when I remarked this striking circumstance to my fair companion, she made no other reply than that such was to be attributed to. the power of religion on the heart If this be so, religion has more in it than I have ever conceived. I am resolved to make it more my study, that I may derive a fortitude from future hope, which nothing I have met with yet can give me. How often have I heard Maria, with all her wonted sensibility, declare that true and deep feelings of religion were frequently impressed upon the heart by the sight of human woe and misery—often by becoming the spectator of calamity and suffering, and then by fleeing to Christianity for the knowledge of the end and purport of them, has the mind by these means been led eventually to the best knowledge of our God!"

In such a train of musing, Oswald indulged for some time, when, at length, he returned with a mind more troubled, but with a heart more softened, than when he first set out.

The party was soon afterwards summoned to partake of a cheerless dinner, when, upon the removal of the cloth, the conversation still turned upon the melancholy occurrences of the day, and thence to reflections upon the accidents and distresses to which life is perpetually exposed. Their attention was suddenly arrested by Maria holding up her finger to invoke silence, while she listened to the conversation of a person speaking to the waiter in the passage.

" I am persuaded," she exclaimed, " that I hear the voice of our friend Dr. Freeman," and she hastened to the door, at no great distance from which she saw the good Doctor, who expressed both his surprise and delight at the meeting. Her father rose eagerly to receive him, and in a moment they conducted him into their apartment

" To what good fortune, my dear friend, are we to attribute this unexpected pleasure?' said Mr. Lorraine, " for though you were not the last person in my thoughts, I had not the most distant expectation of your being within the circuit of many miles of us."

" Why," replied the Doctor, " I am as fond, though I have not the same taste for picturesque scenery as yourself, and as I have been recommended by my physician to change the air, and to try the effect of relaxation from professional studies and duties, I determined to seek both here, calculating at the same time on a distant chance of falling in with you at the close of your journey, and I am not a little gratified by my early success."

" My dear Sir," said Maria, " you give and you take away pleasure at the same moment; how happens it that you, who generally possess health, should have been induced to take the advice of a physician ? but, indeed, upon looking more attentively, I do not think you appear to be so well as we have been accustomed to see you."

" My dear Maria," said he, " I fear my ap-pearance betrays me, and that it speaks truly when it manifests that a change has taken place in my general health since we last parted; but as I am marvellously recovered, and am come in search of pleasing and agreeable objects, let me sit down and talk with you, and hear the detail of your wanderings, since you took your leave of us."

" Then, as one of the most agreeable circum-stances that has since befallen us," said' Mr. Lorraine, " has been owing to our acquaintance with our kind friend here," pointing to Arthur; " let me introduce you, Doctor, to Mr. Oswald, a name, I am sure, familiar to you, as it is con-. nected with every thing allied to taste and talent. -—Mr. Oswald, this is the venerable and good friend,' Dr. Freeman, of whom you have heard Maria and myself so often speak.— Well (he continued) I am happy indeed, that you have come at this particular juncture, for we stand in need of all your aid to raise us from a state of pensiveness, into which a scene of sudden death we witnessed this morning has thrown us."

" What, then," said the Doctor, " it was you who were at the cottage of the poor Aspen-dales ! Ah! ah ! I now perceive (looking at Maria) who it was that so strongly sympathized with, and so bountifully administered to the temporal wants of the distracted and forlorn mother, and who, also, it was (now looking at Oswald) that so liberally paid the surgeon for his attendance upon that, and for some future occasions; and I know that both of you have made separate appointments to meet at the cottage to-morrow, but as I cannot allow you to go thither without me, I beg you not to forget that I am to be one of the party."

" Pray," said Maria, manifesting the greatest astonishment, " by what power of divination have you arrived at the knowledge of these particulars?'

" By means," replied the Doctor, " altogether simple and natural, for on my way hither I was overtaken by Mr. Williamson, who, on a former occasion, attended upon my wife in a sickness which seized her here; and from him I learnt all the particulars of the scene, in which it seems you were actors, for the good man's mind was labouring under the same depression which has laid hold on yours; little did he or I suspect how much1 was interested in the strangers of whom he spoke, for I am, indeed, greatly pleased, though not at all surprised, to find the good Samaritans were those of my own fold. Now, my good friends, if you desire such occurrences as these to have a wholesome effect, suffer them to take possession of your minds while impressions are the strongest—reason and argue upon them.— reflect upon their tendency, and then turning the mirror of Religion towards your own breasts, learn not only to know yourselves better, but to see how utterly incapable you are to proceed without the guidance of that Spirit which can alone reconcile you to things here, and prepare you for existence hereafter — it is by such spectacles as these that you perceive the instability of human nature, and know how that instability is connected with higher and more permanent objects."

" In other words," said Oswald, taking up the subject, " we must exercise our philosophy to bear up against the untoward accidents and miseries to which human life is subject, knowing that they are inevitable, and that our state of suffering cannot be of any very great duration."

" If," said the Doctor, " from the shortness of life, you derive the hope of pressing onwards, through a Redeemer's love, to a future and a better state, your philosophy is supported by Scripture; but if the passive endurance of afflictions be merely the result of considering them unavoidable, and not from the desire of showing resignation to the will of heaven, Philosophy and Religion are at direct variance."

u I look upon it, Doctor," said Oswald, " that the difference arises from our entertaining different notions of the same thing. Philosophy, I consider to be the Religion of Nature, and distinct from any consideration of Revelation; now what is your opinion ?"

" Sir," replied the Doctor, " my opinion is, that true Philosophy is ever the companion of genuine Religion, whether that Religion be called natural or revealed; for truth, whether it be philosophical or religious, must always be consistent with itself. It has been the habit of writers to speak of philosophers in opposition to men of religion, conceiving the one who derives his wisdom from the observance of the operations of Nature, to be contrary to the other deriving it from Revelation. And because the wisest of the heathen world, who have attained to wisdom almost beyond the reach of man, by their own natural and intuitive powers, have, in some few instances, arrived at the same conclusions with those who have been aided by Revelation, some have drawn the false conclusion, either that the study of nature is sufficient without the aid of Religion, or that Revelation super-sedes the necessity of having recourse to the works of nature; whereas both ought to be employed."

" Doctor," said Oswald, " I must confess that I have hitherto considered philosophical, so far removed from religious truth, as, in many instances, to amount to an essential difference: indeed, I think I am not going too far when I say, that the philosophy of Scripture varies in several particulars from that of Nature."

u This," said Maria, " appears to me quite unaccountable; I have, indeed, known those whose philosophy has led them to deny the truth of Scripture; but my imperfect knowledge of Religion, and great tenderness for its concerns, would rather incline me to reject all philosophy, than forego the consolatory assurances of Revelation."

" There are," said the Doctor, " two descriptions of persons who, on these grounds, have taken their stand. They of the former class scorning to know the Almighty Author by any other means than the book of Creation, deny the necessity of Revelation, and not unfrequently show their contempt of it by turning all that is sacred into ridicule, and thus professing themselves wise, they become fools. Such I call *Philosophical Infidels*. On the other hand, in these days there are others who, taking up the volume of the sacred Scriptures as their Encyclopedia, will connect no other study with it indeed, some in their over-zeal to become serious Christians, regard the prosecution of any other pursuit, though not directly an act of profaneness, yet as bordering upon it, — though not as a positive evil, yet a negative good: these may be termed *Anti-philosophical Religionists*"

" Of the latter," said Oswald, " I know nothing; but of the former, if you will extract the discordant feature of attempting to convert what is held as sacred into jest, you draw, I believe, pretty accurately the character of my belief."

" How!" exclaimed Maria; " is it possible that you, with your highly gifted powers of mind and talent can be a disbeliever of Revelation? Can you dispute the truths of the Gospel, or deny its manifold evidences? Oh, pray recall your words, for you cannot possibly conceive the distress which such opinions have already occasioned me, although it has been relieved by a thorough change of sentiments in him to whom I allude."

" Mr. Oswald," said her father, " I do not hesitate to acknowledge that my daughter alludes to me; and I am proud to bear testimony to the uncommon proofs of her affection to me in this respect, and to the zeal manifested by my excellent friend the Doctor here, which have jointly had the effect to bring me to the renunciation of my errors; and I am now, by the permission of a kind Providence, as desirous of advocating the cause of Christianity as I was once adverse to it.". " Do not mistake me," replied Oswald; " I have read and considered the evidences of Religion with some attention, and I have brought such conviction of the truth of Christianity to my mind, that could I get over the obstacles which stand in the way of philosophy, I would cheerfully subscribe to the same articles with yourself Mr. Lorraine. . I confess, indeed, upon every return to this subject, I have found the difficulties to lessen; and I could now almost declare myself a firm believer. cm the same grounds that Mahomet demanded assent to his creed."

" How was that.?". asked Maria.

" Why, that impostor demanded belief of the Koran Upon (the simple grounds of the sublimity of its language, affirming, that as it was superior to. ail human compositions, it was necessarily of a divine origin ; now, all the beauties of this description which it possesses have actually been taken from our Scriptures; and certainly the sacred volume affords such uniform simplicity, such consistency of precept, and such exquisite examples of rhetorical figure and ornament, as can be found in none of the works of the most celebrated writers of antiquity: still, as I before said, the philosophy of it is at variance with that which is confirmed by science."

" For my part," said Mr. Lorraine, " I declare, as this is a subject on which I may venture to give an impartial opinion, for I have formerly held much greater objections to Scripture than such as you have made, —that after the most scrupulous examination of it, the impression on my mind is now, that the truth of all its parts, whether taken separately or together, is founded upon a rock, — an immoveable rock ! My good friend here has told me a thousand times that our Religion invites en-quiry, and that the deeper we go, the stronger is the proof of its reality; and I think myself now qualified to maintain, that no where does the Bible inculcate erroneous notions of science; and that the apparent contradictions between the philosophy of Scripture and that of nature are all of them reconcileable."

" You are to consider," resumed the Doctor, that the object of the Bible is to teach men Religion, and not Philosophy; to instruct men in moral, not in physical knowledge; to make men Christians, and not Naturalists. At the same time philosophy serves to expand the mind, and to open it for the reception of religious truth, and to make it more susceptible of religious impressions, and thus invisibly to lead us from * Nature's works up to Nature's God.' It is true there is no developement of philosophical principles to be found in Scripture, not because it is derogatory to blend the one with the other; not because the study of the Bible supersedes the necessity of investigating the works of nature, but because it is supposed these principles are already known and understood, and that men are conversant with them: but point out to me any passage in which there appears any such variation, and I will undertake fairly and reasonably to show that Scripture and Nature, Revelation and Reason, Divinity and Philosophy, harmonize with each other."

" I cannot say," replied Oswald, " that I am so well versed in these matters, or have considered them with so much attention as to be able to bring the particular instances which · I have mentioned immediately to my Blind; still there are some more prominent than others which readily force themselves upon my notice. For instance, with respect to the formation of the World — Many are the conjectures of the heathens; some of which bear a resemblance to that of Moses, whose description, after all, barring his account of the firmament and the lights of heaven, is more rational, I admit, than all the others : for that the globe was originally formed of a *fluid* matter, is confirmed by the discoveries of science, from the circumstance of the equatorial, being greater than the polar diameter, which is the natural result of any tenacious fluid whirled around an axis; but as to the situation and description of a. firmament which, at one and the same time, is said to be both ' in the midst of the waters,' and yet ' dividing the waters from the waters;' and ' of there being two great lights, the greater ruling the day, and the lesser the night;' when there is properly but *one* source or fountain of light, these are positions manifestly unphilosophical."

" So I once thought," continued Mr. Lorraine; " but if the Doctor will tell you, as he has already informed me, that this word *firma-ment* signifies the atmosphere, which is supported by the waters of the earth, and bears above it the waters of clouds and vapours, the difficulty vanishes; and with respect to the two great lights, without considering whether they are both actually bodies of fire, whether they are either primary or secondary orbs, all the philosophy in the world can never disprove that one of them rules or governs the day, and the other the night"

" Well," continued Oswald, " but how shall we get over the difficulty in the article of time assigned by Moses for the creation of the World? If it were altogether a miraculous operation, six days are an unnecessarily long period for Omnipotence to have done it; if, on the other hand, matter were possessed of an inherent directing quality to form itself into the globe we now inhabit, the term of six days was much too limited for physical causes to produce this effect."

" My dear sir," said the Doctor, " this is the common error into which we are all so liable to run. We cannot refrain from attempting to explain divine things by a reference to natural causes, and when man puts his limited faculties in the scale against the infinite wisdom of God, it is no wonder that he loses himself in the mazes of perplexity: but why the Almighty was pleased to select this stated portion of time for the performance of this great object is explained by himself, when he says, that in six days he ' made heaven and earth and all that therein is, and rested upon the seventh day, and hallowed it.' Thus establishing the observation of a Sabbath, so necessary and so important to man, and which, in after times, served to overthrow the worship of the heathens, who paid adoration to creatures instead of the Creator."

" This explanation, also, I admit to be satis-factory," said Oswald; let me then take you at once to the great stumbling-stone in the way of philosophy, which I should rejoice to see satisfactorily removed; I mean, how it came to pass that *the Sun* was commanded by Joshua to remain stationary for a whole day over the valley of Ajalon, instead of the Earth being made to stop in her course; surely the prophet, speaking by the inspiration of God, should have used language more consistent with true philosophy."

" And had he done so," interrupted the Doctor, " who was there then that could have understood him ? Addressing himself to those who had no other belief than of the globe's being a stationary object, would he not have exposed himself to something more than ridicule, had he not adapted his language to the comprehension of those whom he aimed to instruct? We know that in more recent and more enlightened times, an attempt to correct the error into which mankind had fallen in this very particular, was the means of exposing the philosopher Copernicus to a savage persecution ; nay, what is more, we are even now told that the same ' spirit which made Galileo recant upon his knees his discoveries in astronomy, still compels our professors (in Spain) to teach he Copernican system as an hypothesis: [1]" besides, was it more unreasonable for a teacher of religion among the Israelites in the days of Joshua, to speak according to the popular belief of the sun's standing, than it is in these times with philosophers, who now-a-days talk of the *rising* and *setting* of the sun with as much familiarity as if the earth were always stationary, and the appearance and non-appearance of the ruler of the day, were affected by its revolution round the globe? But, Mr. Oswald, what will you say, if I adduce the argument of a learned prelate, now no more [2] , to convince you that the profoundest of all modern discoveries, one which has reflected such dazzling lustre on' the fame of our immortal Newton, is not very remotely alluded to in these very Scriptures, unphilosophical or unscientific as they may have been thought — I mean that of gravitation! Look only into the Book of Job, and you will find that the Almighty is there said to have

[1] Letters from Spain, under the feigned name of "Doblado." 1822.

[2] Bishop Newton: see particularly his Posthumous Dissertations, in one of which the Philosophy of Scripture is fully and ably discussed.

' stretched out the north over the empty place, and to have hung the earth upon nothing. ' Now,' says this writer, ' how can the earth be said to be hanging upon nothing, without some notion of the principle of gravitation?'"

" I can assure you, Dr. Freeman," said Oswald, " after what you have adduced, and the able manner in which you have illustrated these things, I am satisfied my objections have been advanced without proper consideration. The greatest obstacles have now, to my mind, been clearly removed; and with respect to those of minor importance, I conceive that many, if not all of them, may be accounted for as the exuberant product of Eastern phraseology. I am too much an admirer of the beautiful metaphors and figures of Scripture, to interpret them according to the strict letter, or to consider all terms, seemingly applied to nature, as unphilosophical: indeed, after what you have so ably advanced, I must honestly say, that I should now have considerable hesitation in producing any further instances of this kind, even if I could recal them, because I feel a persuasion that as I have not, hitherto considered these chief points in the manner I ought to have done, it is more than probable that whatever I could farther advance, is capable of as easy a refutation."

" I am entitled, Sir," replied the Doctor, " to no merit whatever, for the strength of the arguments I have now very briefly and very imperfectly adduced; they are only such as I have derived from authors who are deserving of your consideration. But the result of all I have gained from others, and from the deepest reflections of my own mind, is, that true philosophical knowledge is essential to the complete under-standing of the sacred volume, and that the greatest philosopher is best qualified to become the soundest divine."

" I now believe it," said Oswald, " and I am resolved to turn my mind to the fall consideration of the subject, the doctrines, precepts, and evidences of Religion. I know by experience, that men have the reputation of being considered scholars, whose advancement in polite literature is extensive, and whose taste, while it accords with the knowledge of the times, assisted by a readiness of talent that may indiscriminately, be applied to the various consideration of the sciences with tolerable success, gains them merit they do not deserve, unless there be blended with it the knowledge and practice of religion; I know also, and hope to feel, that however correct my actions may have been in a philosophically moral view, something more is required, and I am now well confirmed, from all that I have witnessed upon this extraordinary day, that, after all, Religion is ' the one thing needful.'"

This open and candid avowal, spoken with manly simplicity, brought a ready tear into Maria's eye, for it excited a feeling she could not conceal; nor could Oswald resist the acknowledgement of her sympathy by the warm pressure of her hands, while her father, a silent but not an inattentive observer of what passed, added — " My dear Sir, it is no slight gratification to perceive that, like me, you have yielded yourself vanquished by the combined efforts of these two assailants; and, like me, also, you must now subscribe to the terms of capitulation, acknowledging with Lord Bacon, that' a little philosophy inclineth men's minds to Atheism, but depth of philosophy bringeth men's minds about to Religion.'"

THE RECOVERY.

CHARLOTTE was the only unmarried daughter of widow Armitage, whose husband had left her children fatherless, and herself encumbered with a mortgaged property, and beset with difficulties, at the age of thirty-five. With a mind nerved to meet every misfortune, and convert it to the best possible use, Mrs. Armitage had brought up her children decently, industriously, and reputably. Her son, at an early age, by reason of his father's death, was unavoidably thrown into a situation far beyond his years and experience: and as an unpractised swimmer, who is suddenly carried out beyond his depth, for awhile buffets with the deadly element in a vain attempt to save himself; so James Armitage struggled with an overwhelming tide of difficulties, until the current of the trials bore him down. The nature of his business had thrust him forward into company, and that not of the choicest kind: but how few are there in trade who can select their customers, and deal only with those whose morals are as good as their pockets, and whose religious conduct will bear the test of Christianity? It is a most unfortunate circumstance for any youth to be placed in a situation of manhood, before either his principles are formed, or his education completed; and yet it is the error of the times, in the chain of education, to omit the links which connect childhood with maturity. The female no sooner arrives at her teens, than she sets up for all the privileges which formerly belonged to those only who had left them; and the boy, even in pupilage, arrogates all the prerogatives and pretensions of the man. Hence it is, that so many parents, Whose fond anticipations are drawn from the precocity of their children, are disappointed. Like forced fruits and shrubs, their sweetness is only for one season; time which should complete, destroys their mellowness. Thrown into this unfortunate situation by his father's death, James Armitage, though the ingenuousness and natural timidity of youth, joined to the workings of a good disposition, for a short time suspended the evil blast of corruption, fell, like too many others, into vices which, in their consequences, boded ruin to the little property belonging to his family. He married, unhappily for himself, one whose notions were extravagantly high, and whose mismanagement of his domestic concerns, for his mother and sisters had now left him, completed his destruction. In a few years she died, leaving him five pledges of their union. His mother and sister Charlotte, for his other sisters had entered into the pale of matrimony, returned to him, and became parents to his motherless babes. They had lived together about ten months from his wife's death, when his, sister was seized with an illness, which, though trifling at first, gradually assumed a decidedly alarming character. Previously to this, she had left the communion of the church, and attached herself to one of those dissenting meeting-houses which are now so thickly spread throughout the country. Though alienated from the fold of her father, she received a visit from Mr. Deacon, who, in the discharge of his duty, and through respect for her excellent mother, who remained faithful to the altar at which she was dedicated to God, called to see her at the time when disease lay heavy on her, and " the arrows of the Lord oppressed her sore." He found her strongly tinctured with the sentiments of a sect that assumes the title of Baptists, as if no other denominations of Christians had claim to that appellation, except themselves. Like another class of religionists, who in their self-sufficiency, by forming a Deity carved to the standard of their understandings, assume the distinctions of Unitarians, whilst at the same time they cannot fail to be conscious, that there is no body of Christians (a name they abjure) which is not as much unitarian in worship and belief as themselves ; and certainly which has not much better pretentions to Christianity than the disciples of Priestley or Lindsay.

There was something in the appearance of Charlotte that struck the Curate forcibly. The expression of her countenance was divided be-tween the interesting languidness of sickness,. and the varying unevenness of incertitude and anxiety. Her voice was tremulous, and her eyes wandered. Like an autumnal day, when gloom and sunshine in their contest for mastery, alternately possess the atmosphere, the ray of cheerfulness now superseded, now gave way to the cloud of melancholy. The bed of sickness is at all times an interesting object. To behold a fellow creature, struggling under the power of the chilliness of death, and hastening to leave a world, which will scarcely feel conscious of the gap, whilst the denizens of heaven are looking down with intensity of solicitude for the dis-encumberment of the soul from its earthly coil, is calculated to excite powerful emotions in the heart, which, whilst they proclaim " Thou too art mortal," bid us carry our expectations beyond the dark confines of this world, to that land of purity, peace, and unspotted pleasures, " where the wicked cease from troubling, and the weary are at rest" This feeling is considerably heightened, when the victim of death is young; one, who in the natural course of things, might have defied his powers for several years, and calculated upon many days of earthly enjoyment. This sentiment flashed through the Curate's heart as he contemplated the object of his attention. There was a timidity in her look, which marked an involuntary shrinking from his presence, which, however, was not so perceptible towards the close of his visit. He repeated his call for several days successively. By degrees she paid attention to what he said, and soon after expressed herself anxious to be instructed by him, and directed in the way of life. Mixed with her anxiety for his spiritual guidance, there still continued a tincture of schismatic expressions, which eventually were mellowed down to a more rational form. The approach of death, whether fancied or actual, frequently restores things to their true colours, and removes the film of prejudice and self-delusion. And though this is not an instantaneous effect, yet every day breaks down some obstacle, and gradually prepares the way for consummation. So was it with Charlotte Armitage. Lately initiated into all the enthusiastic and vacillating opinions and habits of her adopted sect, she had allowed herself to be carried away by the warmth of her imagination, or " a zeal not according to knowledge/" beyond the boundary of reason; but now, in the time of sick-ness, she began to see through a clearer medium, and her mind was regulated by more tempered principles.

On every occasion of his visit, the Curate laid aside the feelings that the person before him was a zealous sectarist; he viewed her only as a stray lamb — one who had been withdrawn from the fold of her first faith in the pursuit of an ideal purity, which had bewildered her reason, and benighted her comfort. His words were those of gentleness. Like the Almighty Father, who is represented in the beautiful discharge of his merciful dispensations, to carry the tender lambs in his bosom, and gently to lead the sheep which are unable to go without assistance, Mr. Deacon saw that a task of great delicacy was imposed upon him, and that it would require the full exercise of that liberal spirit which is the halcyon of his Church, to bring this wanderer back to ' the bosom of her Father and her God.' He did not, therefore, address her on her sectarian principles, but confined his observations to those points of practical faith, on which all Christians, how wide and varying soever their creeds on other topics, think alike — The imperfectness of human nature, the proneness to sin, and the necessary consequence of the atonement and mediation of the Saviour, together with the influence of the Holy Spirit, and the abundant mercies of the Godhead, were points on which he dwelt, as most essential to rouse mankind to " use all diligence to make their calling and election sure." He did not, however, treat these high mysteries in an abstruse or a meta-physical way, but confined himself to the plain facts, as developed in Scripture. By these means he gradually won her attention, and at length wholly reconciled her to his spiritual visits — an acquisition of no trifling interest: for, attention once won, what may not follow ? Her aversion from being visited by him or any Minister of the Establishment, gave place to a desire for his ministration. Her strength was much decayed, and her dissolution appeared at hand. — He spoke to her on the Lord's Supper.—

" Did you ever, Charlotte," said he, " receive the Sacrament?"

" No, sir."

" What, neither at the Church nor the meet-ing-house?"

" No, Sir: I was thinking about it when my illness began. Indeed, I have had serious thoughts about it a long time, but somehow I was always afraid."

" And why were you afraid ? "

" Because I never understood it."

" That must have been your own fault; for, had you attended to the different discourses you ? must have heard at Church on that important subject, you could not have failed to understand it. But do you understand it now ?"

" No, Sir, I cannot say I do," replied the sick woman; " perhaps you would explain it to me."

" Sir," said Mrs. Jameson, her sister, " I have never received it, partly from the same reason, but principally because I keep a shop in a neighbouring village, and am obliged to sell goods to my customers on the Sabbath-day morning. Now I cannot reconcile this with so sacred a thing as the Lord's Supper : for how could I receive with pure hands the holy bread and wine, when those hands just before have been busy in worldly traffic ?"

" You are right," said the Curate; " but I am surprised," he continued, " that you, who appear so sensible of the impropriety of it, should continue to do it. Remember you cannot serve two masters. Your traffic, in this case, is a service you are paying to one master, and your attention to religious worship is a duty you owe to another master. Now, who of these two is to be preferred, and who to be rejected ? Is the Mammon of unrighteousness to be honoured, and the God of purity and mercy to be disregarded ? I trust you will not ' halt between these two opinions.' If the Sacrament be your duty, then observe it. If the traffic on the Lord's day be your duty, then pursue it. One must soon end in the driving away of the other. Let, me, therefore, advise you to give up the latter, lest it should induce you wholly to neglect the former. For, ' what shall it profit a map, if he gain the whole world, and lose his own soul; or what shall a man give in exchange for his soul ?'"

" So then, you think I ought not to sell goods on the Sabbath ?"

" Decidedly not, and for this simple reason, because, as the Sabbath is the Lord's day, every thing done on that day, ought to be particularly the Lord's: every thing therefore that is not peculiarly his, is wrong, and ought not to be done. Buying and selling belong to the concerns of the world, and may lawfully be practised on the other days of the week, but on this day, they must be laid wholly aside, or else it cannot be kept holy."

"I feel all this," said Mrs. Jameson, and the tear started into her eye. " I will tell my customers that I will not attend to them on the morning of the Lord's day."

" Do, sister," said Charlotte, " and stay till Mr. Deacon has explained to me the Sacrament"

" In few words, then," said he, " I will point out to you the nature, duty, and benefit of this holy institution. The Sacrament of the Lord's Supper was ordained as a perpetual remembrance of his death, in token that we bear in mind, and are thankful for his dying for us, ' whereby alone we receive remission of our sins, and are made partakers of the kingdom of heaven.' It is our duty to observe it, because our Saviour Christ hath commanded it; and we are as much bound to perform it strictly and frequently, as we are to keep any of the moral commandments. ' This do, in remembrance of me,' were the words of the blessed Institutor of it; and they are consequently as binding upon us as any of the laws of Moses. As, therefore, we would not transgress any of the ten commandments, why should we neglect to observe the Saviour's last request, the Redeemer's last injunction. Surely, if they demand our observance, this is infinitely more incumbent on us, inasmuch as it is the only appointed way we have of evidencing our gratitude for all that the Messiah has done for us, and of showing in our actions the vital spirit of Christianity. For as man, by nature, is wholly unable to come to God, by reason of sin actual and original, and as that inability is removed by the great atoning sacrifice which the Saviour made for us, ' as a full, perfect, and sufficient sacrifice, oblation, and satisfaction, for the sins of the whole world;' and as this Sacrament, instituted by his command, continually sets this before us, as well to remind us of our corruption, as of his meritorious cross and passion: — so must it be the duty, the indispensable duty of all to partake of the ' blood of sprinkling, which speaketh better things than the blood of Abel,' if they wish to participate in the blessings which it purchased. It is, therefore, both our duty and advantage to observe this ' holy feast which Jesus makes:' — our duty, because the Saviour has commanded it, and our advantage, because every time we celebrate his death, we renew our interest in his merits and atoning love,' and come to him, for fresh supplies of grace to enable us to go forward in the holy way of that covenant, which ensures for us an admission into God's favour, and in which we show our interest every time we ' take the cup of blessing and call upon the name of the Lord.' And beside all this, the examination pointed out by St, Paul, cannot fail of producing good in us. For, in this, the ' faith that works by love,' will, whilst it helps us to rake into our hearts, and search out our many infirmities, fix our attention more strongly upon the 'things that belong to our peace,' and raise our thoughts to the contemplation of the enormity of sin, which is so great, that not only did the Saviour die to ransom us from it, but his continued mediation is still required, to atone for our imperfect doings: and this consideration will make us weary of our burdens, and compel us to confess, ' that after we have done all, we are unprofitable servants.' Thus will true repentance follow our faith, and hope encourage us to press forward, whilst charity, which ascribes glory to God, and exercises good-will to -man, will be ripened into joy, by the blessed influence of that Holy Spirit, which is sent to ' guide us into all truth.' And thus shall we find the heavenly comfort of that invitation of the Lamb of God, which he has addressed to all: * Come unto me, all ye that are weary, and heavy laden, and I will refresh you.' This general invitation he again presses upon us, when he says, ' Drink ye *all* of this."

" Oh, Sir," said Charlotte, " you have indeed made me feel it; and though I cannot fully understand it, yet, I hope before long I shall, through God's grace, both know and practise this duty, that I may obtain its benefits."

" And that you may the better strive for it," said the Curate, " let us pray to that good God, by whose grace alone you can receive power to do it"

So saying he kneeled down, and caused the others to follow his example. He then read those prayers which the Church has appointed to be used on such occasions. When he had concluded, Charlotte said,

".These were comfortable prayers, though they were taken out of a book."

" And why should they not be as comfortable and good out of a book, as in any other way?'

" I do not know," she replied; " but before, I never paid such attention: I dare say that is the reason why the Church prayers never seemed so good as the prayers in the meetinghouse, which are not written or printed."

" You are right," said he; " but I fear to exhaust you too much. — Good evening: think on what I have said, and God bless you !"

For two days the Curate was prevented from calling to see her. Late on the evening of the second day a person came to his lodgings, and requested that he would go with him to Mrs. Armitage's.

" Charlotte," said he, " is so very much worse, that they fear she will not outlive the night"

" Oh, Mr. Deacon," said his convert to him as he entered the room, "I am glad you are come: I seemed to want you so much; you talk and pray so comfortably, that I always feel happiest when you are here: but I am not afraid when you are away; only I like so much to hear you read or expound to me. I fancy I shall not live very long now, and I am thankful. you explained to me my duty about the sacrament: I have been considering about it, and reading and praying, and I seem to want it so much, that I think when I have taken it, I shall be more resigned to God's will."

" I am glad to hear your wish, Charlotte," replied the Minister, " and I hope you fully understand it, and have a sincere desire to communicate, for ' with such offerings, God is at all times well pleased.'"

" That I have," she replied: "I am too near dying to think of any thing that is not sincere and good. You may depend upon it, Sir, I am quite sincere: I have prayed that God would, through his grace, open my understand-ing and give me a willing heart to do his commandments, and particularly that he would enable me to receive his dear son's last and best gift. I now trust that he has heard my prayer; and I have reason to think, that when I sought, I found. — Oh, Sir, he is a good and gracious God ! — Mother, you are a good woman: you have always been steady in one religion, and have taken the sacrament in the Church; will you take it with me now ?"

" I will, dear Charlotte," she answered, " if Mr. Deacon thinks fit."

" I not only think it fit, but wish you to do it; for God only knows whether it may not be the last time you and your daughter may eat together in this world: therefore, together lift up your hearts to God, together perform his will, and by reverencing his command, show that you strive to ' walk worthy of your vocation.'"

The Paschal lamb was slain, — the body broken was figured, — the atoning blood was poured out: earthly elements shadowed heavenly things, and genuine religion, in this solemn ordinance, reflected its sacred influence upon these communicants.

Morning came, yet Charlotte lived. A week passed by and left her yet alive, but faltering on the brink of the grave. Not unimproved passed that week of grace: many were the hours devoted to spiritual instruction; and deep, and lasting, and beneficial, were the impressions received. Again she communicated, for she found it' sweet and pleasant to know the Lord;' and she seemed to all appearance to have seen the last sun rise upon her. So deeply was the Curate interested in the condition of his convert, that on the evening, when to all appearance she would not see the following morning, he resolved to remain and witness her last struggles. She talked of death, but with meek composure; she blessed her sickness, for it was ' the chastening of the Lord;' she joined with the Psalmist in saying, ' Before I was afflicted I went wrong, but now have I learnt the way of thy commandments;' she professed herself full of hope through the merits of her Redeemer, and gratefully acknowledged that it was through grace she had it. At times, however, Reason seemed, like a swallow that sits on the house-top sequestered and alone, to be on the wing: her imagination wandered, her fancy was active, and her faculties seemed engaged in lively contemplations. The progress of her disease, which had now reached its crisis, threw her into violent fits; and in these her senses seemed lost to every thing, except the consciousness of her situation, and a conviction of the happiness of being restored to the society of the Church. Fre-quently in these visitations she would say to those who were surrounding her in apprehensive uncertainty —

" I have been in heaven in my sleep; I saw all religions : the Church is the best way!"

And these latter words she would repeat several times together, sometimes adding, that the sect which had drawn her aside, and which still, in the presence of some of its members, strove to retain her, was very wrong. One of her sisters was married to a leader of this sect, and by her means they were still admitted to visit her. Grievous was it to her poor mother, for each visit they paid her was followed by some uneasiness: they were loath to lose her, and in their desire to keep her ' one of theirs,' they scrupled not at the means. These means too frequently had for their effect the discomposure of her peace, and the trial of her faith: but each successive day weakened their influence, till finding their endeavours vain, they at length ceased their persecutions. Many and pointed were the expostulations they received from her in those moments: and kind, and friendly, and christianly were the admonitions she gave them when her reason was collected. On this night of trial, she, one by one, requested to see her friends, and to each she applied instruction suited to his or her individual failing. To her brother she pointed out the vanity and wickedness of dissipation; to her sister, Mrs. Jameson, the error of sacrificing her sinful duties to Mammon; and to her other sister she expressed her opinion of the fault she was committing in the religious opinions she had adopted. Each and all of them she entreated to follow the Church, for she said — " That is the best way."

After this christian scene, Mr. Deacon was admitted. To him she related all she had been doing and saying.

" I cannot now agree with those people," she observed, "'who never say the

Lord's Prayer, and do not baptize their infants. I think they cannot be right."

" God only knows who are right and who are wrong," replied the Curate : " but the omission of the Lord's Prayer has no sanction in the Gospel, and is contrary to the express command of the Saviour."

" If they knew the comfort of this prayer," she replied, " they would not neglect it. I love it, and I never feel so much satisfaction now from any prayer as I do from it"

" That is,". said Mr. Deacon, " because it is the prayer of Him who knew all our wants, both bodily and spiritual, and because you now utter it faithfully."

" Shall I tell you, Mr. Deacon, why I like you and your Church ?" — He nodded. — " It is because you endeavour to make friends with, and pray for, every body. Now the people I was with, were always finding fault and ridiculing the Church, and saying that you were all shut out from heaven. I like you for your liberality, for Christ was liberal, and so is his religion. Will you pray with me?—I shall die soon, and then I shall not want your prayers." Then looking on her friends who, weeping, were standing round her bed, with a countenance beaming with more than human animation, like the last brightest effulgence of the setting sun, she said, " Weep not for me: I shall be happy soon in heaven; why should you mourn for me ? Be comforted, mother; we shall all meet hereafter; and then ' every tear will be wiped off every eye.' Mr. Deacon, bury me in the evening, just as the sun is setting. I have often thought that the duskiness of evening makes a funeral more solemn; — not that it matters to me; only that it may produce good impressions upon others. You will preach a sermon, not to praise me, but to point out to all my companions how ' good and pleasant it is to know the Lord' in life, ' and, oh! how comfortable in death.' "

These words were not uttered without a strong bodily effort, the effect of which formed a striking contrast with the heavenly placidity that played around her features. At length, exhausted with the effort, she sank, and was again seized with one of her fits; and violent was the struggle : she heaved to and fro upon the bed: life seemed contending, as if unwilling to quit its hold. To all appearance her earthly tabernacle was becoming distenanted; and her soul appeared to be winging its flight to its native home. The scene was imposing: her aged mother, in all the speechless torture of sickening uncertainty, now:hoping and then despairing, stood a mournful spectator. A female companion of her early days was watching in sympathetic sadness her beloved friend; and the good Curate was no unmoved observer in this interesting groupe: he breathed that pious prayer which the Church has appointed on such an occasion, and looked on his recovered lamb, as translated from worldly trials to heavenly joys. At length, reanimation circled through her veins, her cheeks flushed, her eye- lids moved, her lips attempted speech. Nature asserted her power, and Charlotte once more raised her head. With her eyes upraised to heaven, and hands clasped and resting on her breast, she feebly articulated —

" That was a bitter trial; the tempter struggled to make me his prey: ' but thanks be to God, that gave me the victory, through Jesus Christ, my Saviour.' "

After this she sank into a sweet sleep, during which she appeared occupied with heavenly things. Mr. Deacon resolved to continue in the house a few hours longer. Before the break of day she awoke, and,

" Oh, I have had a sweet dream," she said; " I have been in heaven; and I am now satisfied that I am in the right way. It has cost me much to know what religion is the right one: now I know, and I will never leave it. Oh, that people knew what I know, we should have no dissenters then. The Church is the right way. No body that wishes. to be religious need leave it, for it will teach them all they want." Here she paused: there was something in her looks of a seraphic cast . "Hark ! to the little birds, how sweetly they sing ! Is it morning yet ? — O yes, I see it is —and they are singing their hymn. It is pleasant to praise the Lord; even the little birds know that. Mr. Deacon, a little bird has builded a nest by my window; don't let them molest it Is there not something in the Psalms about the swallow building her nest ?"

" There is," was the reply. " Does not David say it builded in the Sanctuary ?" "Yes."

" And does not that prove," said she, with a ratiocination which could hardly be expected from her at that time, " that as the swallow finds shelter in the Sanctuary of the Lord, we find salvation and help from God whenever we seek for it?"

" Even so," replied the Curate; " and how truly has this been experienced in your case ! May you never forget it!"

" I hope I never shall. If I recover, and I now think I shall, I will always attend the Church, and do as you and good Dr. Freeman, that nice old man, teach me: and I will tell every body that the Church is the best way !"

Finding a favourable change, Mr. Deacon now took his leave, but instead of going directly to his lodgings as first intended, he was invited by the unusual serenity of the morning, to walk in the fields that skirt the town. " The sun was not yet risen on the earth," but his harbinger proclaimed his early approach. Rich streaks of inimitable splendour chequered the eastern horizon, and the frown which always precedes the immediate approach of day, either reflected from the sullenness of night, compelled to relinquish his temporary influence, or the last shadow of the ' rear of darkness thin,' gloomed on the hills. There was a pensiveness mixed with impressions of a more glowing character, that stole over him, and he sat down beneath an aged oak to contemplate the scene. There, as the sun disclosed his full orb, and the death-like stillness which had reigned around, began to teem with signs of busy life, his imagination bodied forth his inward aspirations in the following

STANZAS.

MORN'S earliest blush with frowning dyes Proclaims Night's empire done,
And soon the full-orb'd power will rise Of Day's creative sun

At such an hour, 'tis sweet to mark
Nature's unruffled state,
And hear the matin-hailing lark

Carol at Heaven's own gate: —

And view the pearls unmined by Night,
As sparkling on each spray,
They catch the morn's reflected light,
And glistening melt away; —

And list to voices which prevail
When noisy man's is still,
As floating on the dewy gale,
They breathe from stream or hill: —

In such an hour the soul expands,
And fearless dares explore
The vision of those viewless lands
Beyond Time's bounded shore.

The mind forgets its cares awhile,
The heart its pangs foregoes,
And, warm'd by Nature's peaceful smile,
Is lull'd to sweet repose.

Our thoughts the lapse of time retrace,
When Eden's bloom was young,
And Man, inspiring heavenly grace,
Heaven's songs of virtue sung.

Then all was like this prime of day,
All peaceful, all serene;
And Innocence with artless sway
Gladden'd each happy scene.

All voices join'd in sweet accord,

In hymns of grateful praise,
To hail Creation's mighty Lord,
In pure, and hallow'd lays.

The sun ascends — morn's freshness fades,
The spell of peace recedes;
Labour resumes his busy trade,
And Man his bustling deeds.

So, when the Sun of Knowledge rose,
Eden's rich treasures past, —
The soul no more with pureness glows,
Chill'd by Sin's withering blast.

The garden is a wilderness,
The wilderness a grave,
Han's, mind a chaos of distress,
But Heaven was rich to save.

For lo ! with healing wings the sun
Breaks forth with richest dyes,
The moral night's dark reign is done —
Hear, earth ! list, O ye skies ! —

He, who from chaos call'd the world,
And bade creation be,
From depth of moral gloom unfurl'd
The mind, and made it free.

This renovation of the soul,
This morn of happier time,
Makes former wounds of sorrow whole,
Atoning man's first crime,

And still his rays are shining bright,
To all who seek their power,
Infusing warmth and guidance-light
In life, or death's dark hour.

Oh! hail him then, with shouts of praise,
With loud hosannas sing,
High, high your swelling anthems raise
To Heaven's and Nature's King.

For, thro' the dim of future years,
So Faith illumes the eye,
Him, who the drooping spirit cheers,
I see forsake the sky,

And, clad in glory all his own,
Begirt with Mercy's sword,
Whilst Seraphs wait around his throne,
He speaks the vital word.

And the last morning flashes forth,
The graves give back their dead,
From west to east, from south to north,
Hell's power is captive led.

That morn shall set again no more,
But rise to perfect day, And grief
and sin on Eden's shore,
And tears, shall pass away.

No clouds the lovely scene shall gloom,
No terrors man affright,

Celestial blessings ever bloom,
A day without a night!

Each succeeding day brought returning health. Her disease had passed its climax, and the lately feeble and emaciated Charlotte began to assume her former looks. The Sun of Righteousness had spread over her his healing wings; and with her natural strength her religious resolutions grew more strong. At length she was so far restored to convalescence, that she was able to go out into the air. Her first visit was to the Church; and the satisfaction she derived from being so far favoured, as once more with amended spirits, and a more rational idea of religion, to re-visit the altar of her forefathers, was great indeed.

She remained firm to her recovery from schismatic errors, and everywhere proclaimed as well the goodness of her Maker, through the meritorious atonement of his dear Son, and the gracious influence of the heavenly Paraclete, as the blessing of belonging to the Established Church, which she simply but emphatically denominates " THE BEST WAT."

THE EXCURSION.

DR. Freeman found himself so much benefited by the little excursion he had taken, from the relaxation it had afforded his mind, that he determined to pursue the advantage, with the hope of laying up in store a supply of health that might last him for some time to come, and strengthen him for a renewed attack upon his professional employments. With this view he accepted the invitation of his friend, Duncan Stuart, to accompany him from his house in Northumberland, upon a visit to his relations in Scotland. Duncan was a young man of excellent heart and understanding, possessing an inherent politeness of manner that distinguished him in every circle; and however differing in age, a variety of interesting circumstances had cemented between these friends a deep-rooted and mutual regard.

They shortly commenced their journey, and leisurely made their way to Edinburgh; there having spent some little time, Duncan left the Doctor to himself, while he went over to the Fifeshire coast to pass a day or two with some of his relatives and friends. This interval, the Doctor intended to devote to a survey of the various objects with which the town abounds, and which are so highly deserving the attention of the stranger. As he was enquiring of th0 waiter of the hotel the way to Holyrood Palace,* the same question was put by another inmate of the house, evidently as great a stranger to the place as himself.

" Sir," said the Doctor, addressing him, " I conceive that it is possible you may be bent upon the same object with myself, and if so, I . shall be happy in accompanying you to a place which excites my attention, not so much, perhaps, from an expectation of seeing any thing striking, as from the desire of visiting the ruins of the chapel."

The stranger bowed, and lighting up a grief-worn countenance with an expression indicative of pleasure, they left the house together. As they walked down Prince's Street, the Doctor could not help remarking the very striking distinction manifested in the buildings and streets on the sides of the opening here between the Old and New Town. " Here," said he, " may, at a single glance, be seen not merely the difference of taste in separate ages, but the astonishing improvement in the knowledge and art of building in times not very remote from each other;—there you perceive houses carried to a height, which it tires the eye to measure, and from the windows of which it must be painful to look down; here, less lofty, more convenient, handsome and commodious, the eye rests upon these with pleasure; — there, the streets con-tracted and dark, exclude the light and air; here, broad and open, they invite the entrance of the sun and wind: — cleanliness and health seem to dwell in one, whilst dirt and sickness must prevail in the other. Then observe how frequently your attention is caught by some striking object; see that fine building; the bridge on the left; the church before you; above it, the castle hanging in the air; and beyond all, those lovely mountains."

" My eye," said Graves, (for that was the stranger's name,) " is now directed to the objects as you mention and point them out with a feeling and warmth of expression which make it evident that you possess taste for these things. Had I been by myself, I must confess, my mind would not have been arrested by these, certainly, fine objects. I am a spectator, now, from necessity, not from choice; there was, indeed, a time when I loved to gaze upon these novelties, and I could dwell upon the beauties of nature and art; but it is gone by, and she with whom I delighted to exchange all my thoughts upon such subjects is, alas ! no more; and I have lost all relish for unsubstantial and fleeting pleasures."

" I fear," said the Doctor, " that you have suffered from some heavy calamity; and yet youth is so much upon your side, that I should hope time would gradually efface what-ever has thus contributed to cloud your happiness."

" Never," replied he, " for I am deservedly wretched. — Excuse me for thus obtruding upon a stranger the expression of my feelings, which have thus inadvertently been betrayed. I have been here waiting for the execution of some business, and as this overplus of time is left upon my hands, I am compelled to beguile it by occupying myself in looking around me; and I feel happy that any circumstances should have thrown me into the society of one like yourself whom I conceive to be a Minister of our church."

" Sir," replied the Doctor, "l am what you suppose me to be, and I shall have pleasure during the little time I am here, to improve an acquaintance thus accidentally begun; and I would fain entertain the hope that I may be allowed to sympathize with you in your sufferings, and that I may be permitted to offer you the consolation under them which it may be in my power to give: and I hope to be better known to you as Dr. Freeman."

" Dr. Freeman," he replied, " I feel greatly obliged by your willingness to lend me such assistance as I have long desired to obtain, without having had the courage to solicit it; perhaps you will have no objection that we should dine at the hotel together, either in your room or mine, when I shall be glad to make my situation better known to you, -and solicit your consolatory aid."

" Gladly," rejoined the Doctor; " but we have been wandering from our directions; for to make our way to Holyrood House, we must turn back, and pass over the bridge into the Old Town."

During their walk thither, they were occupied in making remarks upon the closeness of the streets through which they passed, fully verifying the Doctor's former observations.

" This palace," said he, as he entered it, " bears some resemblance to that of Hampton Court; but it has undergone so many changes from the distraction and turbulence of civil commotions, that no part but the chapel, I believe, can claim any distinction from antiquity: we will, however, take a view of what it contains, and visit the apartments of the unfortunate Mary, said to be precisely in the same state as when she left them."

They followed, therefore, the conductor, who had accosted them upon their entrance, and then proceeded to the chapel, a beautiful ornamented Gothic ruin, used only as a cemetery.

" Here," said the Doctor, pointing to a mural tablet, " here is the memorial of one who died in early life *; it has been principally with the intention of visiting the soil which covers

* Miss Henrietta Elizabeth Hay.

her ashes, that I have been induced to view this consecrated spot It was on the death of the amiable and beautiful girl, whose name that tablet records, that an elegy was written by an accomplished female who styled herself Adeline."

" Can you, Sir," said Graves, " recall any parts of it ? if so, nothing would give me greater pleasure than to hear them:" —

Hail, awful dwelling o*f the silent dead,
Where the wild weeds of desolation wave!

Here the meek sufferer rests her drooping head
On the cold pillow of the peaceful grave.

To him that haunts this proud sepulchral dome,
Yon wandering planet of the midnight skies
Seems Love's pure torch, to guide the pilgrim home,
Where the lov'd treasure of his bosom lies.

O'er yon chill sod, to Love and Nature dear,
That shrouds the beauteous tenant of the grave,
Shall pale remembrance shed the bitter tear,
And from the dust, the form of beauty save i

Oh powers of Memory! it is yours alone,
While beams of Paradise the grave illume,
To bid the heart a transient rapture own,
And call bright visions from nocturnal gloom.

In vivid tints, like Heaven's aetherial bow
To sainted Virtue on the soul impress'd,
While Death's dim shades in faith's refulgent glow,
 Float like the shadows from the dawning East.

Yet shrinking Nature o'er yon sacred urn,
Shall muse on scenes of bliss for ever gone,
And o'er the ashes of the dead shall mourn,
While deep and loud congenial tempests moan.

When hapless woe corrodes the aching breast,
More dear the waitings of the winter's storm;
When sinks the moon dim in the darken'd West,
Then vernal bow'rs wear Summer's glowing form.

Oh, hear, ye winds, that sweep the vaulted sky
O'er yon grey tow'rs, oh, pour your cadence wild,
And bid the blast like dying Evening sigh, —
For there a father guards his slumbering child.

What though the storms that chill the changing year Wave their dark pinions
o'er the humid ground,
Yet silver dew, pure as an angel's tear,
Shall gem the wild weeds as they spring around.

No blushing bands yon mouldering arch entwine,
 Where the lone night-bird wakes his cries of woe;
But there the wreaths of new-fall'n snow shall shine,
Pure as the innocence that sleeps below.

O'er the green turf that wraps the blessed clay,
Shall the light wing of youthful fancy wave,
And chaunt at eve, beneath the lunar ray,
The dirge of sorrow o'er Eliza's grave.

Stranger, approach, if e'er thy bosom knew
The sacred influence of an angel's smile,
When thy lov'd hand dispell'd the chilling dew .
From the sweet face that cheer'd consuming toil;

Approach, for thou art consecrate by woe;
Oh come and gaze upon yon holy tomb,
While pensive Memory's vivid visions glow,
And her pale fires the shade of death illume!

During the recital of these stanzas, Graves had shed many a tear; indeed he discovered a feeling so acute at many of the passages as they recurred, that the Doctor was convinced something remained to be unfolded in his history that bore connection with the circumstances that had thus drawn forth his sympathy. They now ranged into the park, and thence surveyed the majestic rocks which overhung the plain, and after rambling about until dinner time returned to their hotel. During the whole morning, Graves had made few observations, but manifested a deep abstraction, which was only occasionally dissipated by the observations of his companion. After dinner the Doctor gave him an opportunity of entering upon his history, by saying,—" You cannot be surprised at my remarking how deeply one, so young as you surely are, seems preyed upon by a melancholy which no ordinary events can, I think, have generated. I have no. wish to gratify an idle curiosity by prying into the affairs of others, and it is from no motive of this kind that I repeat my willingness to afford all the consolation in my power to one who seems to stand so much in need of it,"

" Dr, Freeman," he replied, " I very sensibly feel your kindness, and I assure you it is with no ordinary emotions of gratitude that I accept your offer, convinced as I already am, of your disposition to benevolence. Know then, Sir, that my name is Graves—that I am the only son-of a gentleman of good fortune, who, with his wife and daughters, has been for some time residing on the Continent. As my health has always been delicate, I have been advised not to incur the risk which I might run from a change of climate, since my native air is, perhaps, the only thing that will ultimately restore it. My family have been absent now three or four years, during which period I have been left master of my own time, with a handsome allowance more than adequate to all my wants. After I had been thus separated from those most dear to me, I became a prey to dejected spirits, occasioned by the fearful notions I still entertain of religion; a subject which, without much advantage, has long engaged my attention. I verily believe, had I persisted in the study of it, I should have fallen a victim to a distracted mind; but I had the happiness to fall into the society of one who possessing good sense, fine feeling, and superior judgment, took an interest in my welfare, and finally evinced that regard for me which gradually ripened into affection. Oh! she was one without a parallel; one who could draw from the depths of sorrow consolation to refresh the most wearied mind. She possessed a cheerfulness which enabled her to throw a charm over all she said and did: her intelligence and vivacity could dispossess the most gloomy spirit. In her beloved society I passed most of my time; she constantly diverted the current of my thoughts; led me to the study of a variety of interesting subjects; took me, as it were, from myself; represented all things, and particularly religion, in the most pleasing point of view. With her I could have endured existence; without her, I have lost all relish for it We waited only for my family's return for the solemnization of our marriage, but alas! alas!— how shall I tell it ? —she died the victim of a rapid decline, and has left me infinitely more miserable than she found me!"—He paused to give way to his feelings, then, hardly stifling his sobs, he added—" I deserve to be miserable, for I have sinned the sin unto death."—

" I pray you stop," interrupted the Doctor, " and let me assure you that the bitterness of sorrow has obscured your mind, and prevented you from seeing the Author of all this in the light that you ought to regard him. We are all short-sighted mortals, and it is not only folly, but impiety to give way to a grief, the purport of which is to correct and amend, but not to break the heart Our attachment to this world would be too great, and altogether inconsistent with our transitory life, were we not to meet with sorrows and afflictions which gradually untie the knot that would otherwise bind us to the world, and which we find are designed to bring about what the poet has said:

Every sorrow cuts a string, And urges us to rise.

For, I myself have suffered misfortunes keener, and anguish immeasurably greater than you have: I have lost the wife of my bosom, ' in an hour when I looked not for it;' the child, the only child of my fondest affections, in the morn and pride of life;—my heart has been pierced with the sharpest arrows of affliction; I have felt, I have suffered, bitterly suffered, but l have never dared to complain; nor have I, though the storm has raged with unbridled fury, ever despaired, because I am well assured these events are under the guidance of Almighty Wisdom; under the con-troul of an all-gracious Power, which, breaking our unsubstantial happiness here, will strengthen and make it permanent hereafter. The arm that leans on God will never want support; the heart that is fixed upon him can never be long dejected. In all these respects we fall infinitely below him who has endured the consummation of sorrow to reconcile us to Heaven, and to bring us, through his sufferings, to a future glorious inheritance. That Redeemer who has suffered so much, calls upon us to follow him to glory through the paths which he has trodden; and to all, however wretched, however fallen, his invitation, extends; therefore, Sir, remember that it is your duty to shake off this weakness and infirmity of your nature, by striving to endure all things for him who promises in a short time to requite all your trouble."

" But." replied the unhappy man, " unfortunately these promises do not extend to me; for, as I have before said, I have sinned against the Holy Spirit, and for me there can be no redemption, for 1 have denied the Saviour both by word and deed in earlier life, and no renunciation now can cancel that abhorrent act; this is a crime which it is expressly declared can ' neither be forgiven in this world, nor in that which is to come.'"

" You, Sir," rejoined the Doctor, " are not the first person who has represented himself as having committed a *sin* of which. I .find no mention whatever in any, part of Scripture The offence which you designate the sin against the Holy Ghost is, by the Saviour himself, exclusively termed *blasphemy*; and it is one, let me add, which in these days it is impossible for you or for any other person directly to commit; and I am persuaded you have alarmed yourself in this case with an unfounded fear. To convince you of this, suffer me to advert to the circumstances under which the denunciation that you have applied to yourself, took place. Our Saviour, it will be remembered, had just cured a demoniac; but his enemies, instead of being convinced by the miracle, attributed the effects they witnessed to a co-operation with Beelzebub; that is to say, the working of miracles being constantly referred to the Holy Spirit, the operation of them was now perversely ascribed by them to the power of an evil spirit; they, therefore, in the most signal manner *traduced* or *blasphemed* the Holy Ghost, by imputing that which was the peculiar and indispensable proof of the presence of Divinity to the arts and machinations of Satan. Now, let me ask, have you yourself seen the Saviour cast out devils, and seeing him, have you declared that he has derived his power from Satan ? If you have not, then you neither have been, nor can be guilty of this blasphemy. There may, indeed, be a boldness of evil-speaking, a degree of wilful unbelief somewhat akin, or of the same species, but the precise degree of guilt cannot be incurred, unless under exactly the same circumstances. Or, as some have thought, this sin could only be committed by those, who, though eye-witnesses of all that the Saviour did and suffered, rejected, even after the visible descent of the Holy Spirit, against whom this deadly sin could be committed, the preaching and teaching of the apostles; and thus by obstinately refusing to admit the Gospel, they excluded themselves wilfully; and in despite of the most complete evidence, from all the benefits which it brought and still brings upon all those who ' hear the word of God, and keep it.' Such was the condition of the obstinate Jews; and that they experienced the most signal punishment, I need only remind you of the destruction of their Temple and City. In either of these points of view, you see that, as you neither witnessed the expulsion of the devils, nor the descent of the Paraclete, and as you do not deny the Gospel, you cannot be guilty of this sin."

" I readily grasp at the assurances you give me," replied Graves; " for it is impossible for me to describe what I have suffered from the opinions which your reasoning now induces me to think erroneous. There are times when I have driven it from my mind; but when the circumstances have ceased to operate which have had this effect, it has again recurred in all its force : but, surely, ' the wilful sin after baptism for which there remaineth no sacrifice,' is this especial blasphemy of which we speak."

" No," interrupted the Doctor, " for though all blasphemy in one sense is sin, yet is this particular crime designated by the Saviour and the Evangelists a *traducing* or *blasphemy*; but ' the wilful sin after baptism' alludes to a very different circumstance, — to an apostacy from the Catholic faith; a conversion from Christianity to Infidelity or Heathenism; but even this, as it is capable of being repented of, is not impossible to be forgiven, although it be so difficult as in a manner to be impossible ' to renew' the offender ' to repentance.' "

" The arguments to which you have alluded, Doctor Freeman," said his companion, " are such as demand very serious attention, and I shall not fail to devote time and consideration to a subject which is so vitally connected with my happiness: but, since we are upon the subject, permit me to ask, how you conceive it possible for a person like myself to dispel those gloomy thoughts which involuntarily and perpetually take possession of my mind, and retain dominion over it in spite of all my attempts to resist them? I cannot divest myself of fear when I consider that ' tribulation and anguish await every soul that doeth evil;' and I neither am, nor can be sinless; — these are points which I would fain, but still cannot believe; and yet it is said, ' whoever believeth not is condemned.' These, and a variety of other passages, show me how utterly impossible it is for one who carries his thoughts beyond this World, who here only lives that he may save his soul alive, to spare one moment from this great business of existence, or to feel any other than the most melancholy and fearful anticipations."

" Sir," replied the Doctor, " if Solomon could direct the sluggard to learn industry from the Ant, he would have sent you and other dejected souls' to take instruction from the Bee, which gathers honey even from the weed, while you gather poison, and even death itself, from the tree of life. Ascribe this disposition to the true cause; this dejection of spirit springs from the infirmities of the body, and the one cannot be elevated or enlivened until the other be removed. Your case requires the aid of the physician as well as the divine; the body and mind are so dependent on each other in the present constitution of our frame, that the infirmities of the one extend to the other. Religion is not then to be taxed with the imputation of exciting despondency and despair when its object is to inspire a hope which should ever be embraced with complacent gratitude and cheerful faith. Religion is not to be represented as enveloped in shade and darkness when it lives only in transcendent light; and the Gospel of Christ, that blessed anchor of the Christian's hope, has the direct tendency to inspire cheerfulness and not gloom: ' It resembles a fine country in the spring season, when the very *hedges* are in bloom, and every *thorn* produces a flower.' Depend upon it, if you can draw no consolation from your religion, it is on account of the maladies of the body, and till they be healed, it will be difficult to cure the soul, for the spirit of a man will sustain his infirmity, but ' a wounded spirit who can bear?

" There are, however, some remedies for the cure of both, which I may venture to prescribe. ' Live,' as the Apostle says, ' temperately,' and I would add, avoid intercourse with those who entertain the same gloomy apprehensions as yourself and particularly avoid those who would make you believe that the want of an actual, inward, and a sensible *feeling* of the assurance of favour with God, even in persons whose life and conversation are strictly correct and religious, is a characteristic of a forsaken and reprobate state. Many there are who think this, and of all articles of belief there are none more calculated to destroy peace and serenity of mind. Perhaps, of all things displeasing in the sight of Heaven,' there is nothing worse than despair, because it distrusts the tender mercies of God, and converts his justice and eternal goodness into tyranny and revenge. The despair of Judas drove him to close the gates of mercy upon himself, and effectually precluded all possible chance of his being restored, like the disciple who denied his Master, upon deep repentance, to a state *of* favour and pardon. Let me, above all things, rouse you against the admission of despair. I have known several of different habits and of retired natures, alarmed by fears which have * existed only in the imagination of those who have excited them: I have seen them thus robbed of all mental composure, desisting from those praiseworthy acts of social and religious duty, which contributed to their former happiness, till at length falling from one apprehension to a greater, they finally lost all self-possession, and sank into morbid insanity."

" But how," said Graves, " how are we to spurn from us those evil thoughts which, by whatever means, have already taken possession of our minds, and keep dominion over them ?" · " You may not, probably," replied the Doctor, " be able by yourself to dispossess them: consider them as trials of your faith and virtue; suffer them to assail, without permitting them to disturb your peace. Argue yourself out of them, and if you cannot drive them away by other means, frequent good company; promote social and friendly intercourse with those around you; keep your mind occupied by some rational pursuit or other, and in time, the calamity which it' is your misfortune and not your fault to suffer, will die away; and above all things, ' set your affections on things above;' let your mind dwell upon the all-atoning sacrifice of your Saviour; consider his* tears—remember his sufferings — ponder on his love, his pity, his mercy —grasp by faith the whole scheme of Christian redemption- forget not that your ' body is the temple of the living God' — and that you may, by the grace of God purchased for you and all mankind by Jesus Christ, when you ask for it, receive the consolation of the divine comforter, the assistance of the Holy Spirit I know there ate some who erroneously conceive themselves either delivered into the power of the Evil One, and deficient in belief or practice — or that the decrees of Heaven, having been passed against them, they are deserted of God, and cast away from his presence; — without considering that the Lord permits no one to be tempted above what he is able to bear, and with every temptation makes a way by which to escape. It is true that you and others may have failed greatly in your belief and practice, but if you feel this, why not make greater exertions to accomplish the one and pray Heaven to increase the other ? The confession of this failure is half its cure, for no one sensible of his deficiency will long abstain from an endeavour to repair it But as to any fear that the Almighty has passed any decree against you, or any other of his creatures, or that he will withdraw his favour from them; be assured God never for-sakes those who have not long forsaken him; and it is directly contrary to the nature of all his attributes to conceive that a God of justice, of infinite goodness and mercy, should predestinate any mortal being to eternal destruction by a decree passed from an eternity before he was called into existence, and for a purpose over which that creature had no power or con-troul. On the contrary, God ' would not that any should perish, but that all should turn unto him and live;' hence he says, ' why will ye die?' And our Saviour himself has assured us, that ' whoever believeth in him shall not perish, but have everlasting life;' only this belief must be manifested and proved by your actions, for ' as works without faith are vain, so faith without works is vain also;' and ' without holiness no man shall see his God.'"

" But," said Graves, " my misfortune is, that I do not possess this justifying faith, by which alone we can be sure of salvation."

" What," interrupted the Doctor, " do you not believe in a God and a Providence ? Do you not believe in the atonement of your Saviour ? That not for any of your own, but for his merits alone, you are made acceptable to God? Do you not believe in a future state of rewards and punishments ? Have you not been baptized in the name of Jesus, and received his Gospel, and participated in the Eucharist, and led by the guidance of Faith, endeavoured to frame your life upon his precepts and ex-" ample ?"

" Most assuredly I have endeavoured to do this."

" Then, Sir," continued the Doctor, " what is it that you mean by a justifying faith: do you suppose it to have a talismanic power; to be a charm which is to work a miracle for your salvation ? Do you suppose that it is to give you either an arrogant assurance, or an infallible certainly of your election in Christ Jesus ? If so, you may gain it from the presumptuous, and spiritually proud empiric, but no where from Christ and his Apostles."

" Sir," replied Graves, " these awful subjects upon which you speak with such decision and with so strong an appearance of reason, are such as I cannot canvass in the rapid manner in which they have now been proposed for my assent; but I shall turn these considerations in my mind, and weigh them deliberately; yet I must candidly confess that I apprehend they will fail of the effect you wish them to have; indeed, under my circumstances, it is not of much importance what may be my future notion of them; for, deprived of her with whom alone existence could have been tolerable, I have no expectation of happiness."

" Excuse me, then," said the Doctor, " if I say that this is unpardonable weakness, nay, that it is more, it is direct impiety. If the Almighty in his wisdom has afflicted you, for whatever purpose it may be, it is your duty to bear it with submission, knowing that a pious resignation to his will is one way to a happiness which shall have no end."

" It may be weakness," exclaimed Graves, " but call it not impiety; my sins are too numerous already; oh ! add not to the number of them. I am naturally of infirm health, but I am now particularly nervous; the loss I have sustained so recently has unmanned me, and I am supremely wretched. — Excuse me, Sir, excuse me, for I must retire," — and he quitted the room.

The Doctor sat stupified, not knowing what plan to pursue respecting one with whom he was so perfectly unacquainted; he, however, determined for the present to suffer the unhappy man to remain undisturbed by any further offer of his assistance. He had hardly composed his mind when his friend Duncan presented himself, to whom he directly told the particulars of all that had occurred in his absence. " There is something," said the Doctor, " in this young man which makes him an object of great commiseration: I am afraid I have spoken too openly, perhaps too unwarily to one possessed of a tenderness of mind such as he has displayed. Grief has taken very deep root within him, and his mind is shaken by despair — I endeavoured in vain to bring him in the morning to conversation; but though he listened to my remarks with apparent attention, it was clear that he was absorbed in other re-flections. I pity him from my heart! would that I could be of service to him; in the morning, however, I am determined to see him; — but tell me, Duncan, what has brought you back so unexpectedly ?"

" I found," replied Duncan, " that my friends on the other side of the water had been called suddenly from home; I have therefore returned, and, under these circumstances, propose that we should go on to Blair, whence I have this day received a letter inviting us to pass a little time at Athol-House, and I have a strong desire to show you the beauties of the country. You will, therefore, have an opportunity of seeing this place better upon our return, which must be very soon, and then I and the relatives whom I expect to find here, shall have much pleasure in showing you all that remains for you to see."

In the morning, the travellers rose at an early hour, and the Doctor, as soon as he was dressed, while Duncan was making preparation for breakfast, went in search of his unhappy companion, when to his surprise and disappointment he learnt, that he had quitted the house by break of day, and was supposed to have left the town without any intention of returning to it .

The Doctor and Duncan now took their de-parture from Edinburgh, and being permitted to drive thence through the beautiful grounds of Dalmeny, arrived at the Queen's Ferry. The water was calm, and there was no wind; they were, therefore, rowed over in little more than half an hour, and in their passage, looking back upon the country they had left, they were gratified by the noble views that presented themselves. Now proceeding onward, they were approaching Kinross, when, just before advancing to the town, they stopped upon the little bridge, which gave them a commanding view of Loch-leven and its interesting little islands. On the north west side is seen the one on which stand the turretted remains of that Castle which has held captive so many il-lustrious personages; among the noblest and most un-fortunate of whom, must be reckoned one whose memory, though stained with the imputation of criminality, has ever excited from her bitter persecution and suffer-ing, the sympathy of mankind.

From Kinross to Perth, the road runs for some miles through a cold, bleak, and hilly country, when, suddenly diving into a narrow glen, it follows the winding of a stream; and then, emerging into an even and fertile country, at length opens to the view the river Tay, (the Tiber of Scotland,) and the town of Perth. The travellers proceeded hence through a fine country, now following, and now leaving the Tay, that classic ground, which exhibits Birnam Wood, Dunsinane with the remains of Mac-beth's castle, and the Grampian hills; when, after many deviations from the regular road, again they approached the Tay, and passing over a fine bridge in perfect harmony with the Cathedral and other buildings behind it, and surrounded with every thing that can heighten the picturesque effect of the scene, they reached the beautiful Dunkeld.

On the following morning Duncan conducted the Doctor to the Cathedral, a fine, dilapidated building, the choir only serving as the parish church, while the capacious nave has neither floor nor roof. The country people were, many of them, at their devotions, preparatory to receiving the Sacrament, which is here administered bat twice in the year, when persons from all parts usually flock to it. Tables were set out for the reception of the numerous communicants in every direction, and as this is partaken of in the manner of a usual meal, at which the guests are served by their ministers, the duty continues for the whole day. " Sir," said the Sexton, addressing the Doctor, " at the last Sacrament this place was filled from one end to another, and though it rained incessantly the whole day, the people remained in the uncovered nave, here, from nine in the morning until the, same hour at night."

" Where," said the Doctor, turning to Duncan, " where shall we find instances of such zeal among ourselves ?"

Near to this building, within the pleasure grounds of the Duke of Athol, stand, rivalling the Cathedral in its height, two majestic larches, originally brought from Sweden as plants, which in the first instance were placed in the Duke's greenhouse, and thence removed to the place they now occupy, where they remain the parents of *all the larches in Scotland*. Again pursuing their route, first along the sides of the Tay, and then of a stream branching from it, along a picturesque and mountainous country, the travellers came to the celebrated passes of Killiecrankie, the key to the Eastern Highlands. Here the finest formed mountains, deep broad woods, rocks, precipices, and glens conspire to form a scene over which the eye roves with inexpressible delight; and here it was in the year 1689, when the Royalists had been routed by the rebellious army, that the brave Athol-men so amply revenged their master's cause. Beyond this stands Blair Castle, the highland seat of the Duke of Athol, amidst a country presenting hills of various hues and of the most beautiful outline, and immediately surrounded by ornamental grounds of prodigious extent. In front of the Castle stands in all its majesty the many-headed Bengloe, estimated at nearly 4000 feet above the level of the sea, while in the distance behind is seen the noble Schehal-lien with its snow-clad summit.

It is only for a few months in the year that the Duke here takes up his residence, during which time that hospitality, proverbially attached to the character of Scotland, is maintained in a state of splendour, to an extent that has no ordinary limit Here the same mode of hunting and killing the wild red deer, and the same boundless liberality prevails as in the days when James, and the Queen his mother, with the chief of his Court, honoured this family with their presence. On the day following that on which the Doctor and Duncan reached Athol-House, at an early hour in the morning, the sportsmen among the visitors were summoned from their beds to partake of a substantial breakfast, and to hasten to the Forest

Soon afterwards, the trampling of horses, the occasional barking of dogs, and the " busy hum of men," all proceeding from the front of the Castle, notified to the Doctor the gathering of the sportsmen. Slipping on his dressing-gown, he observed their proceedings from the window of his room, and a finer or more exhilarating sight had seldom arrested his attention. The sun had just risen on the earth, and was dissipating the dews and haze of morn, and playing around the sides of the noble Bengloe, whose lofty summits, clad in the snow of one short night, were gradually unfolding themselves to view. The freshness of the mountain air animated all the party, and raised alike their spirits and their hopes. The sportsmen, twelve or more of them in number, were here met by about twenty attendants, all in their highland costume, with arms, ammunition, and provisions — others were holding hounds in leashes, — others leading sumpter horses for the conveyance of the game. And now each visitor was mounted, and each, also, accompanied by a second attendant on horseback, while the noble and spirited Athol, surrounded by his staff of keepers, and greeted by the notes of the pibroch reverberating from the door of his Castle, led the way; the whole troop followed in his rear. Duncan, however, remained behind, and after the family breakfast, conducted the Doctor to the Falls of Fendar, which are within the pleasure grounds; and thence traversed some of the interminable walks among the plantations ; and beguiled the time by walking, riding, and exploring the country. On the next day they visited the celebrated Falls of Bruar; and here, upon entering the little gate which opens upon the path leading through plantations to the various places from which the finest views are seen, they perceived a stranger to have entered just before them, of whom they lost sight in a moment By the right-hand path, the Doctor, assisted by Duncan, leisurely and gradually ascended the summit; and as they crossed the bridge which stretches across the yawning gulf upon the heights, the stranger, who had taken the other direction, was on the point of being met by them, when suddenly turning about, he again as suddenly disappeared.

" This," said Duncan, " must be some love-striken swain, who is determined to enjoy his reveries undisturbed, and seeks concealment— but," continued he, pointing to the crags above, " you will observe that the stream which springs from the summit, after running and losing itself amid rocks and clefts, suddenly falls into this abyss, and continues its course until, as I shall presently show you, it descends another precipice, and rushes impetuously around, and through a natural arch, and then winding along its steep and stony bed, at length reaches the plain. You perceive too, that this lofty hill covered now with wood, presents many romantic scenes within itself, and exhibits from various points of its ascent, others at a distance equally picturesque and interesting."

Passing onwards over the bridge, they now turned down the path running on the left side of the water, until they reached a grotto erected upon a rock overhanging the stream, and from which both waterfalls are at once discerned. The noise and foaming of the torrent, directly over which the spectator stands, inspire an awe which gradually connects itself with the feeling of sublimity into which the mind is carried upon a calm contemplation of the scene. The darkness occasioned by the precipitous rocks rising to exclude the light while the hanging wood keeps off all approaches of the sun — the high dashing of the foam presenting a cloudy contrast to the moss-stained running water—in the perspective above, the upper fall presenting an image of the same, while over all, as if poised in air, hangs a rude picturesque bridge reaching by a single span to either side — these sublime varieties carried with them a charm to the Doctor's mind which long rivetted him to the spot; made him forget that busy world to which he seemed no longer allied; inspired new thoughts; prompted new reflections, all closing with a sense of the manifold wonders and beauties of nature, and of the goodness of the great God, who had thus diversified the surface of the earth, to give man something more than a bare existence upon it

The next day Duncan and the Doctor set out upon their return to Edinburgh, where they re-mained for a fortnight, and enjoyed ample time for surveying all the noble buildings and institutions with which this fine town abounds; and having seen all, again set out upon their return homeward by way of Melrose.

The Doctor had determined to visit this superb ruin according to the recommendation of the poet:

" If thou wouldst see fair Melrose aright,
Go visit it by the pale moon-light;
For the gay beams of lightsome day
Gild, but to flout the ruins gray."

Accordingly the travellers presented themselves before the Abbey about the same time that William of Deloraine appeared before it when he executed the Lady of Branksome's high bequest. The moon was high, riding with unclouded majesty in the heavens. " Here," said he, " we see in perfection what I have before so often observed and admired—the exquisite beauty of these buildings by a light, which, casting deep and strong shadows, is so finely contrasted with the soft silver tinges which illuminate the projecting parts —

' See yon broken arches are black in night,
While each shafted oriel glimmers white;
And the cold light's uncertain shower
Streams on the ruined central tower!'

But then we see but half if we do not get within the building, for the tracery of the windows Can only be viewed to advantage by looking through them at that orb which shines to-night with more than common brilliancy."

" Then," said Duncan, " late as it is, I will go and knock upon yonder wicket," pointing to a small house at a distance, " and call up the Monk of St. Mary's Aisle, and bring him or his keys hither, if either be producible'

After he was gone, the Doctor indulged in a short soliloquy. " Aye," said he, " Scott was right; this is fine and interesting. Memory here glances back through many a day gone by, and conjures up the history of many a dark deed of superstition, clad in the garb of Religion. The impression created by such imposing scenes is diminished by the remembrance, that in these places. Religion wore sable habiliments to conceal avarice, disappointed pride, blighted ambition, deep hypocrisy, and sleek gluttony. Happy, transcendently happy was that event which broke the spell, and instituted a more pure, rational, and spiritual worship, more con-sonant with the debasement of man, and the sublimity of his Maker." — Duncan now approached, and, by the clanging of the keys, notified that he was unaccompanied: he soon unlocked the gates, and as they entered — " Beautiful, beautiful!" exclaimed the Doctor, " how accurate is the poet's description! —

' The moon on the eastern oriel shone
Thro' slender shafts of shapely stone,
By foliaged tracery combined;
One would have thought some fairy hand,
Twixt poplars straight the osier wand
In many a freakish knot had twined;
Then framed a spell when the work was done,
And changed the willow wreaths to stone.'"

" Here," said Duncan, stamping his foot upon a large flag-stone, " here

' A Scottish monarch sleeps below.' But I will show you among what were formerly the cloisters, even by this light, some sculptured work, as sharp and fresh as if it were executed only yesterday, and I will convince you that

' Not herb nor flowret glistens there
But is carved in these cloister arches as fair.'"

Haying surveyed these objects of beauty, the travellers returned to the nave; and gently feeling their way, advanced towards the western extremity, that they might view the eastern window to greater advantage by felling farther back. In doing this they were surprised by a noise proceeding from a part so deeply shaded as to conceal the cause of it from their sight; but still advancing towards it, they could just discern the figure of a man making his escape through one of the ruined windows. "I trust,0 said Duncan, " we have not disturbed the wizard Michael Scott; yet none but he, or the fiends about his grave, would prefer making an exit through a high window, when the door is wide open. But there," he continued, pointing above the columns, " there are

> the cloister galleries small
> Which at mid-height thread the chancel wall,

among which these fiends were wont to sport and ' keep holiday.' "

A second survey at length satisfied them; the gates were again closed and locked; and while Duncan went to return the keys, the Doctor took a last view of the Abbey, when he

> " Could, home returning, soothly swear
> Was never scene so sad and fair."

And now, having taken some refreshment, they retired to their chambers; but hardly had the Doctor closed his eyes, before he was aroused by a person in the room adjoining him, which was so thinly separated from that which he occupied, that every movement in it was as distinguishable as if it were in the same apartment. He waited some time to allow this disturber of his rest to settle himself; but it was in vain— the unknown continued to pace up and down the room—occasionally sat down—again seemed restless, and gave vent to many a deep-drawn sigh, which not unfrequently lengthened into a groan. At length, accompanied by a blow upon his forehead, he exclaimed, " Wretch, wretch that I am!" The Doctor now felt called upon to rise, and quietly putting on his dressing-gown, he knocked at the chamber door. No answer was returned; but a second brought the stranger to it, who, gradually opening it, enquired who it was that interrupted him. What was the good Doctor's astonishment to find the person before him was the unhappy Graves, when suddenly taking him by the hand he exclaimed —" My unhappy friend, what, is it that makes you so restless and miserable ? You alarm me more by your looks, than by what I have already heard; for you carry in your countenance the marks of deep-rooted despair, and even agony; let me, let me assist you."

" Is it possible that it can be you, Dr. Freeman ?" he replied; and in raising his hands with the emotion of his surprise, he let fall a pistol which he had concealed.

The Doctor hastened to take it up:—"I fear, young man, I fear that you have been meditating upon an act, which it makes me shudder to contemplate: indeed, I feel convinced that I have come in a propitious moment, to save you from what I dare not think of—tell me, have I not saved your life?"

" I confess," said he, bursting into tears, " I confess that I meditated the deed to which you allude. Spare me, spare me, I pray you; do not spurn me, do not expose me, for in (truth I am a most miserable creature."

" God be thanked," exclaimed the Doctor, " that I should have been made in this instance an instrument of good! I pray you throw yourself upon the bed, and compose yourself, and suffer me to endeavour to alleviate your mind." He did so. " Now tell me," continued the Doctor, " what induced you to flee so suddenly from Edinburgh after our last conversation?'

" I will candidly tell you," he replied, " that when the agitation which you had witnessed in me had a little subsided, I endeavoured to recall all that you had advanced, but I could not; neither could I recall the reasoning which she who loved me had so often used. I relapsed again into grief which admitted of no relief: I felt myself abandoned; and at the suggestion of my agonized feelings, I went with a determination to put an end to my sufferings."

"Thoughtless creature!" interrupted the Doctor; " thus it is that he who is not fortified by the principles of true Religion in the time of calamity, instead of submitting to the stroke which the Almighty has in mercy and wisdom given, unheedingly and deluded flies, like the moth, to the blaze of the lamp,—from transitory disquietude, from sins which may be repented of, to unalterable and inevitable destruction. Like Judas, of whose despair I had forewarned you, you rushed, or strove to rush, down the precipice which would eternally have shut you out from heaven. Young man, rash, thoughtless, desponding, despairing young man, let me charge you in the name of that God whom, if you ever hope to see, you must here obey, to listen to that voice which he has uttered, and know, that 'he seeks not to destroy men's lives, but to save them;' that for this end he has given a religion which administers consolation to the distressed, and which binds up the broken-hearted. Trouble and sorrow are the unavoidable lot and condition of all mankind, and without which no one can be the disciple of a master who has promised a crown of never-fading glory to him that, for his sake, will endure all things. If you think by cutting short the thread of life —by impatiently returning the gift which God has made you—to avoid such distractions of mind as you now suffer, you are egregiously mistaken. You exchange them only for sorrow infinitely deeper; sorrows to which those you suffer here bear no comparison; sorrows infinite in duration, infinite in degree; and thus you make your ' last state worse than the first9 Besides all this, the deed is not only the most wicked, but the most base and cowardly, prompted by despair, the most mean and despicable of all incitements to human actions. And let me exhort you to consider further, that by such an act you cut off every hope of future reconciliation with Heaven. But however burdened your mind may be, you can be no judge of future consequences from all that happens to you at present. Are you not placed here for some express purpose ? a purpose which, whether you consider useless and unprofitable, it is clear the Almighty has required to be fully answered, or he would not have given you existence at all. He has called you into action, and demands the fulfilment of the ends for which your coming into the world was destined; but if you will not undergo the trial, if you will not submit to the restraints which he imposes, but will violently flee from his presence, and think to hide yourself in death, you from that moment become his adversary, the opposer of his will; and then consider how great and fearful a thing it is wilfully and deliberately to have offended your Maker,—" how fearful a thing it is to fell into the hands of the living God!'"

" Oh, Sir! you probe me to the quick—you rack me with agony—and I am, indeed, a wretch.—Enough—"

" But," interrupted the Doctor, " I have not said all that I intended to say; for I must ask you one question, which may probably carry more influence in bringing you to sober reflection than any thing I have yet advanced. You told me, I think, that the young lady, whose premature death has hurried you into this wickedness, was able to arrest your mental agonies by her cheering representations of Religion, and by the power she possessed of pouring the balm of consolation into your mind; now,, during her decline, did she not exemplify in her conduct the same resignation to the divine will that I have recommended? did. she not, knowing your bent to indulge despondency, warn you at her death against the danger of a relapse?"

" Most true, Sir;—your words are daggers." replied Graves.

" If, then, her example was so powerful, and her admonitions so strong, let me ask you, what ought to be the effect of the example and admonitions of our Saviour and God ? Surely if a mortal can convey instruction, the Eternal Redeemer can render that instruction infinitely more effective, supremely influential. Listen, then, to him, who invites you to cast your cares upon him — follow his example, who, in the midst of sufferings the most agonizing, and trials the most overwhelming, resigned him* self and his will into the hands of his Almighty Father."

" Your suggestions sting me to the quick," he replied. " All that you have described respecting my lost angel is true. How could I have so soon forgotten her example ? And, oh, how could I have passed by my Saviour's sufferings, and dared to repine, when I knew all that he underwent for our redemption? How blind, how infatuated have I been ! How dreadful would have been my condition had not you stood in the gap between my purpose and its accomplishment! Indeed you are my deliverer ; and as a proof how sincerely I appre-ciate your kindness, and will follow your advice, I declare, in a manner the most solemn, that I will strive never to harbour the notion of the deed again. Need I pray you, from a consideration of my weakness, not to divulge what has happened? Take with you those instruments (pointing to the pistols), for I already loathe their sight, and shudder at the approach I have made to a precipice from which you have matched me."

" Assuredly I will," replied the Doctor; " and it shall be my determination that they shall never be employed to shed blood: but I cannot leave you yet; I must see you safely in your bed before I retire again to mine."

" You are determined," said Graves, " to be my preserver; but do ,not distrust my promise because I have broken it before; no, be assured that you may now return to your chamber in full confidence of my safely. Before, however, you go, let me tell you, that you have already more than once stopped me in the attempt to perpetrate this horrid deed. When I left Edinburgh, I went in quest of some solitary place where I might execute my design with the least fear of interruption. It was myself whom you nearly encountered more than once on the day you visited the Falls of Bruar. — It was you that arrested me in the moment when I meditated throwing myself from the bridge on the heights into the chasm below; and when I visited the grotto with the same intention, I was turned from my purpose by finding that also occupied by you; and now it strikes me that, what is, perhaps, still more astonish-ing, it must have been you, who only a few hours since, again drove me from my purpose by entering within the walls of the Abbey, which caused me to make a precipitate escape from it."

" The will of Heaven be done !" ejaculated the Doctor. " The object of my excursion has been more than fully answered, even though I had not been gratified by what I have seen, and had gained no accession to my health, since I have been the happy means, under Providence, of snatching from the yawning gulf of self-destruction, one whose life I will still hope may be saved. I must complete the good I have begun; and therefore I beg, with'a determination to take no denial, that you will accompany me to my home, and remain with me for some time, that I may be the means of producing in you that thorough repentance which the crime you meditated requires, and that I may have the satisfaction to instil into your mind the principles of a faith that may give you resolution to run your course with patience; and by these means gradually bring you not only to the restoration of your health, but to the recovery of your mind; not only to a conciliation with yourself, but to a reconciliation with your God!"

Graves joyfully and gratefully accepted this kind offer until the return of his own family from abroad, which was shortly expected.— They shook hands, and separated for the night. On the morrow the party, thus strengthened, proceeded through Jedburgh, and over the Cheviot hills to Duncan's house; where, after remaining a week, the Doctor and his new acquaintance took their way to the Rectory,

EVANGELISM.

DR. FREEMAN had risen at a late hour after a restless night, and was partaking of his breakfast made for him by his friendly Curate, when the servant announced Mr. Vincent Trustwell and the Rev. Mr. Wiseman, who, after the usual exchange of compliments, took their seats, and entered upon conversation.

" I find you, gentleman," said Mr. Wiseman, " in the very place in which I left you, when some time since I came to solicit a favour which it. did not suit you to grant. The object of my present appeal is, to request that you, Dr. Freeman, will join with me and another clergyman in signing the testimonials of our young friend here, who is about to offer himself a candidate for holy orders at the next ordination of the Bishop. He makes the request of you,as having known him all his life, and as the friend of his family."

" These," said the Doctor, " are indeed strong reasons for inducing any one to do an act of favour for another; but indeed, in this particular instance, I regret to say, I must de-cline to interfere; and I regret it the more, because, after what has happened, it may seem that I am actuated by feelings of hostility in-. compatible with my profession, and inconsistent with the conduct of one who ought to be forward in assisting another about to become a brother minister of the same Gospel: but, Sir, though I do not condemn Vincent for adhering to those principles which, upon full and mature consideration, he conscientiously approves, yet I cannot lend my name to sanction the dissemination of such as my judgment leads me to think erroneous. There are doubtless many others who think differently, and he can have no difficulty in obtaining from them what I feel I am not at liberty to give. Indeed, I am sorry, knowing what are my opinions, that you should have occasioned me the distress of refusing what, upon consideration, you could hardly have expected me to grant."

" Sir," replied Vincent, " nothing but the desire to please my father, which I am certain this would have done, and perhaps would have been the happy means of reconciling him to my entering the Church, could alone have induced me to make this solicitation; and I am grieved, not so much upon my own account as upon yours, that you should bear such enmity to the feelings and motives by which I am actuated to obey the strong bias of my conscience."

" Vincent," interrupted the Doctor, " you entirely mistake me. I bear no enmity whatever towards those sincere Christians, whose views of religion you have embraced: it is not for me to say they are wrong, and God forbid that I should charge them with the imputation of folly, when the charge may probably be as justly urged against myself; but so long as my unbiassed judgment convinces me that any of the doctrines you hold are not warranted by the Scriptures, so long I must consider it my duty to combat the growth of your sentiments among those committed to our professional care: and much more is it my duty to give no support to those who would propagate them."

" Doctor Freeman," said Mr. Wiseman, with considerable earnestness, " I am grieved that one so respectable and so zealous in the cause of Religion should entertain such feelings towards those who, like myself, have upon conviction embraced what, I will persist in saying, are the true orthodox opinions of our Church, if its Articles and Formularies may be taken as a standard by which to measure them. Doctor, you are only one of those who would attempt , to fix the odium of some vituperative epithet upon such as aim to preach the doctrines of the Gospel faithfully; of those who designate that portion of the clergy to which I belong as ' Evangelical,' using it as a term of reproach."

" For my part," said the Doctor, " I conceive the term *Evangelical* to mean something of or belonging to the Gospel; and *Evangelists*, to imply in the primary signification, the writers of that Gospel; when, therefore, I speak of the Evangelical world generally, I mean nothing more than the Christian world, whether they be Churchmen or Dissenters. The term, in a secondary sense, has been assumed by, not given to, a portion of the Clergy of the Established Church, as a mark to designate them from their less serious, but, let us hope, not less pious brethren. If therefore it can be considered as a **vituperative** epithet, it is one for the use of which we are not responsible. For my own part, I look upon it, when applied particularly, as an invidious distinction. We are all, I trust, evangelical. At all events, I know, ' woe is *me* if I do not evangelize.' I deprecate the use of this word, in a partial sense; because whether applied ironically or presumptuously, it has a tendency to weaken ' the very bond of peace and all virtues.' In like manner, devoted as I am to what I consider the true view of Religion, as developed by our Church, I think, that the word **orthodox** has been invidiously applied, and to the detriment of the Gospel. Why should you or I assume the title of Evangelists, to the exclusion of others, who, in the absence of outward professions, have perhaps more claim to the character than we have ? And why should you or I plume ourselves upon strict orthodoxy, when God only knows who may safely bear that title ? Let us not strive about names — rather let our contention be, who best may c do the work of an evangelist,' and who best may ' hold fast the form of sound words,' not only in self-profession, but in teaching and practice. The charge, therefore, of our throwing odium upon you is not just; and infinitely less so is it to suppose any real Christian can be capable of holding up to contempt an authorised minister who preaches the doctrines of the Gospel *faith-filly*?

" There is another cause of complaint, too, that I have to make against your party," said Mr. Deacon; " and it is, that whenever we make a statement of doctrines in which you do not coincide, you endeavour to persuade yourselves that it is a species of persecution levelled against you, and you too eagerly take consolation in the received notion of it, by giving out that ' the offence of the cross has not yet ceased;' a notion which every fanatic, from the earliest age of the Church to the present day, has not failed to apply to the conduct of those with whom he differs."

" Well, Sir," replied Mr. Wiseman, with some warmth, " we will leave theoretical discussion, and come to practical; and here I shall have sufficient evidence, which may be corroborated by my friend, of your being at least so far defi-cient in true evangelism, as not to enforce its doctrines to the utmost advantage in times of the greatest necessity. Dr. Freeman, it has lately happened, that, at the particular and urgent request of some few of your parishioners, I have been sent for to give them that spiritual food, which they have not at all times received, either from your hands or from those of your Curate; and from what I can judge from these instances, I am constrained reluctantly to declare, that a very unfavourable impression is made on my mind, of the manner in which this very im-portant branch of ministerial functions is here discharged."

" Sir," replied the Doctor, " I admire your Candour more than your politeness; but do not mistake me, I am not offended: I have no ob-jection to grapple with an open enemy, because I have some chance of making out the real motives by which he is actuated; and I had rather receive advice in a plain unvarnished form than in a manner calculated to produce a counter effect Before, however, I proceed to ask you in what respect our deficiencies lie, allow me to ask upon what grounds you presume, as a Minister of the same Church, without our permission, to interfere in the discharge of duties, which by episcopal authority are solely vested in ourselves ? But not to press you on a point to which you can give no satisfactory reply; in what respect do you consider our duty of visiting the sick and dying improperly discharged?'

" I consider," said Mr. Wiseman, " the visitation of the sick in our calling to be something like the attendance of a medical man; it is, of all other cases, that most likely to call forth our talents. Now in the instance to which I more particularly allude, and of which I have seen some account written by yourself, Dr. Freeman, you seem to have adopted a new and imperfect mode of treatment. By your publication of it you seem desirous that it should be looked upon as the model upon which you have formed, and by which you practise your visitations. For such, at least, is the case with Physicians; the accounts they give of their cases are always supposed to be set forth for the benefit of others."

" Sir," interrupted the Doctor, " I must deny the parallel When a Physician publishes an account of a cure, he has in view the probability that such a publication may add to his feme, and consequently to his practice. Now the Divine who draws up a plain statement of events connected with any portion of his ministry, tan have no such object. He looks not for more extensive employment, for his own parish opens a field sufficiently extensive for the range of his individual parochial labours; at least I think so, Mr. Wiseman, though it appears some of those of your party do not The Divine, therefore, in a sketch like that to which you allude, and which could never have been intended as a formulary, because it is from its very nature ex-tremely imperfect as to the *various degrees* of instruction which must necessarily be adopted in practice, differs widely from the Physician: and your parallel goes off in a tangent. You will nevertheless, Mr. Wiseman, perhaps favour me with a sketch of your plan."

" I am of opinion, Doctor, that on such oc-casions you ought to enforce the total corruption of human nature, and consequently the necessity of justifying faith, and sanctifying grace, and all the unspeakable benefits arising from the great doctrine of the Atonement."

" Sir," replied the Doctor, " to conceive it possible that any one, who has declared his belief in the two last Articles which you have mentioned, the doctrines of Sanctifying Grace and the Atonement, should not insist upon them upon such occasions as these, is so great a want of charity, that I should be tempted to regard it with indignation, did I not feel assured that it is impossible for any generous or charitable mind to entertain it. I am well aware that the visitation of the sick is one of the most arduous and difficult duties imposed upon our profession: I am aware that not all men are fit for it; it is one which, in a parish like ours, is so diversified, that no one can conceive the variety of cases that occurs in it, and the diversity of remedies to be applied to them. At one time we have to combat with hardened impenitence; at another, to temper and regulate the wild visions of inflated enthusiasm; at another, to awaken the self-righteous from their deceitful supineness; not unfre-quently to vindicate the justice and mercy of God from the charge of partial grace and personal favour; and sometimes to dissipate the gloomy terrors of moody nervousness, or the dark forebodings of unholy infidelity. These, with many other cases of corrupt nature, are continually calling for our intervention; for the exercise of the best powers *of* our mind. To suppose, therefore, that it is possible to discharge it *in* a manner strictly consonant with the tenour of the service for the ' Visitation of the Sick,' which we always carry with us, without the strong enforcement of the sanctification of the Holy Spirit, and the blessed doctrine of the Atonement, must spring not from any real grounds of objection, but from the desire to expose us to contempt. *And* how can you conceive it probable, that any of our body can converse with any person on the nature and duty of the Sacrament, without distinctly and fully dwelling upon the atoning sacrifice of which it is so lively a remembrance ?— and among the benefits to be derived from its worthy reception, it is next to impossible, that the sanctification of the Spirit can be omitted. But with respect to the doctrines of the total corruption of human nature and justifying faith, other considerations have weighed upon us not always to insist upon them. In the first place, I do not believe that theScriptures express the former; and the latter, I think, is misunderstood."

" If, Sir," ejaculated Mr. Wiseman, " you were to deny the doctrine of the total corruption as developed in the Scriptures, you could not, as being that which is maintained by the Reformers, or by the Articles and Formularies of our Church."

" The Articles !" said Mr. Deacon; " I can no way see in the articles this doctrine, excepting, indeed, ' Man is *very Jar gone* from original righteousness, and is of his own nature in-*clined* to evil,' can be construed to mean total corruption. It may be the infirmity of a darkened understanding, but I cannot construe (quam longissime) *very far gone*, into *wholly gone, totally gone*; nor can I see how ' *inclined to evil*' means *wholly evil, totally evil*."

" Nor," said the Doctor, taking up the subject, " can I discover in the thirteenth Article this desideratum of those who maintain your opinions, Mr. Wiseman; unless, indeed, ' works done before the grace of Christ and the inspiration of his Spirit are not pleasant to God,' may be twisted to mean total corruption; or, ' we doubt not but they have the nature of sin,' may be shackled with the same deplorable signification. They who ground their opinions and principles upon the Formularies of the Church, would do well to imitate the caution and guarded manner of the Church: otherwise they may run into expressions which are not easily defended, and bring, instead of reverence, odium upon the ' witness and keeper of holy writ' "

" Do not, however," rejoined the Curate, misunderstand us. We do not mean to assert, that by nature man can do any work acceptable to God. No; all the acceptance of his imperfect works must be through the merits of the Saviour. But still, we are of opinion that actions ***morally*** good may be done by unregenerate mortals; whilst, to be ***religiously*** so, they must spring from the principles and doctrines held forth in the Gospel. At least, I cannot discover any other way of understanding this important subject."

" As to your inability to discover the doctrines of total corruption in the Scriptures," replied Mr. Wiseman, " I am at a loss to conceive how so many parts as bear upon this point can be misunderstood. Has not Christ himself said, ' Out of the heart of man proceed evil thoughts, adulteries, fornications, murders, thefts,' with the whole catalogue of human passions and vices ? and this is a passage which can be regarded in no other light than that of a general description of the whole human race."

" I admit," replied Mr. Deacon, " this to be true, and that man's nature is inconceivably corrupt; yet if the heart be the seat of all human vices, it is, also, that of every virtue, for ' with the heart man believeth unto righteousness;' and that it was not so totally depraved as to be incapable of any degree of good affection, we learn from our Saviour's parable of the Sower, where some of the seed is represented as falling upon good ground, in allusion to those who ' yet possessed an honest and good heart;' and hence it is that the produce of the seed varied, some bringing forth thirty, some sixty, some an hundred fold. Now, if the grace of God be without variation or change, and given equally to all, this difference could arise only from the different degrees of honesty or goodness of the hearts, before they were quickened to the bearing of fruit by the vegetating influence of the Spirit, which we are not told was given to one more freely or liberally than to another. And in conformity with this high authority, our Reformers, in the opinion of Dean Tucker, ' supposed not only the possibility of the existence of good works, prior to our justification, which a Calvinist can never do consistently with his genuine principles; but also required the ***actual pre-existence*** of them as necessary conditions, though they ex-cluded them as meritorious causes.' "

" The allusions to this total depravity are endless throughout the apostolic writ-ings," continued Mr. Wiseman. " St. Paul complained of the evil disposition of his nature being at continual warfare with his desire to obey the will of God—that the flesh is at enmity with the Spirit, and the mind with God."

" But all this," continued the Doctor, " carry it as far as you will, ***quam long-issime***, still falls short of arriving at entire, total depravity; and ***inclined*** cannot mean ***compelled***, but rather a disposition towards, necessarily implying a means of doing or not doing. And you will not forget that' incline' as well as ' quam longissime' are the words used in our Article. But independent of such a doctrine representing man as incapable of co-operating with the Divine Spirit for his good (which Spirit he cannot, without making a virtuous effort, attain [3]), the argument advanced

[3] A heathen, or unregenerated man, can certainly re-strain himself on many occasions: he can do many good works, and avoid many bad ones; he can raise his under-standing to know and consider things according to the light that he has; he can put himself in good methods and good circumstances; ***he can pray and do many acts of devotion,*** which though they are all very imperfect, yet none of them will be lost in the sight of God, who certainly will never be wanting to those who are ***aoing uhat in them lies to make themselves the proper objects of his mercy, and Jit subjects for his grace to work upon.*** — BP. BURNET

against it by St Paul himself, though it has not unfrequently been urged, has never, I think, been answered, and to my mind it is perfectly conclusive—for, ' when the Gentiles which have not the law, do by nature the things contained in the law, these having not the law, are a law unto themselves: which show ***the work of the law written in their hearts;*** their conscience also bearing witness, and their thoughts meanwhile accusing or else excusing one another.' Now, if human nature were ***totally corrupt,*** they who were not blessed either by the moral law of Moses, or the brighter effulgence of the Gospel, could do no act but what was corrupt and wicked; and yet it seems ' they do by nature the things contained in the law,' such, probably, as reverencing the Deity, honouring their parents, abstaining from stealing, adultery, murder, or bearing false testimony against their neighbour: how, therefore, can they be totally corrupt ? And if they are not, why should we be so, since we are from the same common stock, and partake of ' the fault and corruption of the nature of every man that naturally is engendered of the offspring of Adam ?' Now in respect of the corruption of human nature, may we not draw some such parallel as this:—A body may be infirm and incapable of healthy action, in consequence of some sickness; but will you say, that because one part is affected which incapaci-tates the whole man, that the whole man is sick; that is, as much disordered throughout as the particular part affected ? I mean, in plain terms, a man may be incapable of action in consequence of the lameness of a particular limb, whilst his other members, though at present useless, partake not of that lameness: so may it be in respect to total corruption."

" Besides," observed the Curate, "if human nature be totally corrupt, it can have no free will. Now, that man has the power to judge between good and evil, is manifest from the tenour of exhortation contained in the Scriptures, the Fathers, and the Formularies of our Church. ' I set before you life and death,' said God by the mouth of Jeremiah. — ' We conclude,' saith Augustine, ' that free will is in man after his fall' —' Wherefore men be to be warned that they do not impute to God their vice or their damnation; but to themselves, which by free will, have abused the grace and benefits of God' — is the language of our Church, as contained in the Article on Free Will, explained in 'The Necessary Erudition of a Christian Man' "

" But, Sir," observed Mr. Wiseman, " the total corruption is strongly maintained in the Homily of ' The Misery of Man'—"

" In the Homily of the Misery of Man !" exclaimed the Doctor; " you surely will not insinuate that we have not read it The word *corruption* is not to be found in it, unless that word which pervades the whole, and which is the sum of the argument, means corruption, I mean the word *imperfection.* And that total corruption in your sense is neither expressed nor meant, I dare boldly assert, and will maintain against the whole assembly of Geneva Divines, that choose to range themselves against me. Let me recommend you to read it again; but do so impartially, and you will think with me that misery may exist without excluding all happiness, and imperfection without being totally corrupt."

" How comes it then," said Mr. Wiseman, " that our Saviour has said, ' Without me ye can do nothing ?' And the Apostle teaches us, that ' we are not sufficient of ourselves, as of ourselves, to think any good thing.'"

" We do not say that we can do any good thing that is acceptable to God, without the grace of God helping and preventing us," replied the Doctor; " but we do say that we may do things morally good. We may, for instance, ' cease to do evil,' and thus shall we be more inclined to ' learn to do well.' And though this is neither pleasing nor acceptable to God, inasmuch as it does not spring from a true motive, yet it certainly is not offensive; but rather that habit or inclination of mind, which, like the soil on which the seed fell that brought forth fruits as from a good and honest heart, is, from its ceasing to do evil, disposed and fitted for the reception of that grace, by which alone it can do all those good things prepared for those to walk in who shall finally attain, through the merits of their Saviour, everlasting life. Now, what need would there be for a helping grace, if human nature were so totally corrupt, that the preventing grace, alone, gives life? which, by your hypothesis, it must do; otherwise there is something of life before, some sparks of it at least, which though unable of themselves to rise into a blaze, are ready to ignite when the vital application is made. But if all the effects of this preventing grace are absolutely and independently its own, without any co-operation on the part of the receiver of it, how do we read in the Article of 'the Grace of God by Christ preventing us, 'that we have a good will ? and working *with us, when we have that good will?* ' And what need, then, of the helping grace? But we know that the helping grace is necessary; and if necessary, then the preventing grace is not absolutely effective, which it must be if corruption be total; because, then, all men must be equally corrupt, otherwise preventing grace must be partially given. Now, as God is no respecter of persons, so neither can his grace be partial; and, consequently, the different effects of it must be the result of the different readiness of mind (as among the Bereans) with which that grace is received and employed. A thing quite inconsistent with total corruption, but in perfect unison with the scope of Scripture and Scripture characters. What distinguished Saint Paul above other persecutors? Was it not from the zeal, though exercised in ignorance, which he displayed in the execution of what he erroneously conceived his duty, but which, when the quickening influence of God's grace directed it, distinguished him *more* as a Christian advocate than it had before signalized him as a Christian persecutor ? His zeal was not changed by regeneration; it was only directed by the bias of proper principles to higher and more exalted objects. A striking example that his readiness And disposition required only the preventing and helping grace to give it distinction and utility: as he himself confesses, ' *I* laboured more abundantly than they all; yet not I, but the grace of God which was ***with me!*** Thus, Sir, I cannot understand how you prove from Scripture the total corruption of our nature,"

" If you will permit me to show you these things neither from Scripture, nor pur Reformers," said Mr. Wiseman, " let me prove them to you from experience, from inward feelings, and from history; let me —"

" All this," interrupted the Doctor, " is perfectly unnecessary. I grant that you may demonstrate, from the infirmities of our nature, the continued disposition to evil, a disposition which is stronger in some persons than in others; but you can deduce from this no argument for the absence of every spark, however latent, of good. Experience shows us what we feel, and what we may expect to find; and history may unfold all that has actually passed. The picture is dark and dismal, though not quite so black as you would represent it; and it is such as must operate upon our minds, and excite in them all gratitude, praise, and thanks that a merciful God, by the mediation of his blessed Son, should vouchsafe to raise us from this wretched state of degradation to an inheritance in glory, on the easy conditions of faith and obedience."

" Rather," said Mr. Wiseman, " upon the *sole* condition of faith *alone;* for it is only this justifying faith that can save us: for that is the doctrine of Scripture and of our Articles."

" Surely," said Mr. Deacon, " you will hardly go so far as to say that faith is the in-strument, without admitting that good works are the conditions, of justification. — To use the argument of Bishop Home, I say, — ' if faith can of itself avail to justification, it must be either as it is an assent to the Gospel truths, or a reliance on Gospel promises; for I know of no other notion of faith besides these two. Now, that faith as an assent to the truths of the Gospel cannot justify, is agreed on all hands; else were the devils justified, whose faith, or belief of the truths relating to him who is to be their Judge, makes them tremble, which is more than it does to many who profess to have it And then as to faith as a reliance on the Gospel promises, those promises being conditional, every reliance must be a delusion which is not founded upon a conscience witnessing the performance of the conditions; and a reliance that is so founded is the result of works wrought through faith. It undeniably follows, therefore, that faith cannot justify but as it worketh by love; and, consequently, that works are a necessary condition of our justification.'"

" None whatever," replied Mr. Wiseman; " for, in the words of Bishop Burnet, I beg to say, that" justification is the admission of a man into the favour of God by a mere act of grace, or upon some consideration not founded on the holiness or merit of the person himself.' No, Sir, when God justifies a man, it is by forgiving him his trespasses, and accepting, esteeming, and rewarding him as a righteous person, although he is not really such."

" As far as this goes," said Mr. Deacon, " I see no objection to it But do you consider, that works in this justification are not even of any indirect avail ?"

" None, Sir," he replied; " the *procuring cause* of this and of all other mercies, is the *death and mediatorial* work of Jesus Chrisct; and the impulsive cause is the mercy of our Saviour; for, in the language of an old writer, ' we are justified declaratively by works, instrumentally by faith, really by God.' "

" Right again," replied the Curate; " but as this justification is declaratively by works, the only evidence of a true faith, and as we are told, that we shall be judged according to our works, surely our works cannot be excluded as conditions (I do not say causes) on which that justification is made effectual to salvation. How else do you reconcile the two Apostles, the one speaking of justification as the result of faith, the other as the result of good works ?'

" How?" asked Mr. Wiseman; "in the same manner that I stated in our former conference. St. Paul, jealous for the free grace of God in Christ, disdains all merit in man; inasmuch as he cannot be justified by the works of the law, for they are; *necessarily* imperfect. St. James, finding that some had *abused* St. Paul's statement, and had ' turned the grace of God into licentiousness,' pleads for a corresponding practice and holiness of life. The one speaks of justification as in the sight of God, the other regards it as in the sight of men."

" I think," said Mr. Deacon, " that, in answer to this explanation of yours I adduced the arguments of Mr. Young, for showing how the Apostles were to be more naturally and logically reconciled, by explaining, that the one spoke of a first justification which takes place at baptism, the work of faith, through the secret operation of the Holy Spirit; the other, of a final justification at the day of judgment, the conditional reward of works."

" Sir, the elaborate work you allude to I have, since we met, procured, and I have given it the most attentive and dispassionate consideration; and I am constrained to declare, ingenuous as it is, it is fraught with inconsistency, and, I think, error. To speak candidly, I consider the notion of a first and final justification altogether papistical, and that the author's reasoning amounts to this, viz. that our final justification, or the attainment of everlasting salvation, is to be by the *merit* of our own works; a conclusion deducible from your own words also, and not unfrequently from your practice."

" Sir," said the Doctor, with a degree of warmth unusual with him, " such a doctrine, and. the imputation of holding it, I abhor as much as I value our salvation by our Lord Jesus Christ; and it is one that I am perfectly astonished any persons should hold, as it is to me so plainly subversive of the whole Gospel. God forbid that we should ever in the slightest degree countenance a doctrine which would rob us of every hope! I am the more surprised at this imputation, and the more grieved at it on your account, because you profess to have given the work the most attentive and dispassionate consideration; and yet in both the text and notes of it, there are passages which, with every mind not darkened by the thickest mists of prejudice, must free the author, and such as, like ourselves, embrace the same opinion with him, from all possible suspicion on the point in question : permit me to read the passages to which I allude." Then taking the volume from the shelf he continued; " ' And now can it possibly be necessary that we should put in any caution in favour of the orthodoxy of our doctrine ? If men were disposed to judge favourably, or rather, if they were not resolved to judge unfavourably in controversies of religion, such caution would be utterly unnecessary. Can it possibly be imagined or insinuated that I have done any injury to the great Christian doctrine of Justification for the sole merit of our Lord and Saviour Jesus Christ by faith, and not for our own works and deservings ? Salvation by Christ only, and no merit of our own righteousness, is so vital to Christianity, and so pervades the Gospel system, that surely one party ought to conceive it impossible that the other should not hold it' Again: — ' But how much better had it been to have left them (good works) as he found them, placed in their true and natural order, by Christ and by St Paul, in the Christian oeconomy: as a *condition* not required towards our *first* but indispensable towards our *final* justification! By repentance towards God, and faith towards our Lord Jesus Christ, we become, though heathens and sinners before, admissible to all the benefits of Christianity: but once admitted into that holy covenant, we come under the obligation of being new men, and leading a new life; a pure, a holy, a Christian life. ' We are God's workmanship, created in Christ Jesus unto good works, which God hath before ordained, that we should walk in them;' and these are required of us as a *condition,* not of meriting, but of obtaining the inheritance already purchased: as a *condition,* I say; if injunctions and penalties can make them a condition ; injunctions the most weighty and authoritative, the declarations and commands of our Lord and King; penalties the most awful and tremendous, the loss of heaven and the endurance of endless unmitigated torment.' [4]—Your imputation, therefore, I consider as springing

[4] See three Sermons by the Rev. Thos. Young, Rector of Gilling, 2d edition, p. 153 & 250.

from your own groundless suspicions, and not from any real foundation of them; and should you or others in future be inclined for one moment to harbour the preposterous notion that any one can entertain the belief of the merit of our own works for the attainment of eternal salvation, much less that any authorized teacher of Christianity can insist upon it, before you are so uncharitable as to express, or even to insinuate it, call the precaution of the judicious Hooker to your remembrance: ' The more dreadful a thing it is to deny salvation by Christ alone, the more slow and fearful I am, except it be too manifest, to lay a thing so grievous to , any man's charge.' "

" Notwithstanding all you have urged," said Mr. Wiseman, " I cannot admit of this double justification; it certainly was not recognized by our Church in the time of Elizabeth."

" Stop," said Mr. Deacon; " we read of a first and final justification, in a book entitled ' The Necessary Erudition of a Christian Man,' a work coeval with the Reformation, and which may be looked upon as a fair oracle of the opinions of the Reformers, for it was the production of Cranmer himself. It happens that I have the very extract which I made only a few days since, now in my pocket—yes, here it is: —' And this justification whereof we have spoken (viz. the Justification of Baptism) may be called the *first* justification; that is to say, our first coming into God's house, which is the church of Christ, at which coming we be received and admitted to be of the flock and family of our Saviour Christ, and be professed and sworn to be the servants of God, and to be soldiers under Christ, to fight against our enemies, the devil, the world, and the flesh: of the which enemies, if it chance us, after our baptism, to be overthrown and cast into mortal sin, then is there no remedy but for the recovery of our former estate of justification which we have lost, to arise by penance; wherein, proceeding in sorrow and much lamentation for our sin, with fasting, alms, prayer, and doing all such things, at the least, in true purpose and will, as God requireth of us, we must have a sure trust in the mercy of God, that for his Son our Saviour Christ's sake, he will yet forgive us our sins, and receive us into his favour again; and so being thus restored to our justification, we must go forward in our battle aforesaid, in mortifying our concupiscence, and in our daily spiritual renovation; in following the motions of the spirit of Christ; in doing good works, and abstaining from sin and all occasions thereof; being armed with faith, hope; and charity, to the intent we may attain our *final* justification, and so be glorified in the day of judgment with the reward of everlasting life.' —Now, Sir, here is the doctrine you oppose; and if you will be at the pains to consult the opinions of our Reformers on this point, you will find it handled,. in the same sense, in different ways. Hence the Homily of Faith begins with this sentence, ' The *first* coming unto God is through faith, whereby we be justified before God;' and it concludes with these words, ' And at the length,' as other faithful men have done before, so shall you, when his will is, come to him (mark here the *second* coming, by the faith that worketh by love), and receive ' the end and final reward of your faith,' as St Peter nameth it, ' the salvation of your souls.' If, however,' you quarrel with the words *first* and *final,* as meaning two intrinsically separate and uncon-nected things, I would say that this double meaning is not designed, any more than when, talking of a journey, we speak of setting out, and arriving at our journey's end. Now, what we call the first justification, which takes place at baptism through God's grace by faith, is nothing more or less than the beginning of our Christian profession; and as in going a journey, we cannot expect to reach the end of it unless we travel the way appointed, so likewise we cannot expect to reach the end of our Christian profession, that is, the consummation of our justification, namely, the award of salvation, unless we fulfil by growing in grace, the conditions of our first or commencing justification,. which conditions are understood under the general title of good works, or the result of that true and lively faith, which enables us, under God's grace, purchased by the Saviour, ' to make our . calling and election sure.' And hence it is, that the author of the Epistle to the Hebrews makes their partaking of Christ depend upon ' holding the *beginning of our confidence steadfast unto the end.* '

" And here," said the Doctor, opening a volume which he had taken from the book-case, while his Curate was reading and making his observations, " here we have testimony of the same belief in the writings of that profound theologian, Dr. Isaac Barrow, who, not a century after the time of Elizabeth, declared, that ' The Justification of which St Paul discourseth, seemeth in his meaning, only to be that act of grace, which is dispensed to persons at their baptism, or at their entrance into the Church, when they openly professing their faith' (by themselves or their sponsors), ' and undertaking the practice of Christian duty, God most solemnly and formally doth absolve them from all guilt, and accepteth them into a state of favour with him. That St. Paul only or chiefly respecteth this act, considering his design, I am inclined to think, and many passages in his discourse seem to imply; in several places justi-fication is coupled with baptismal regeneration and absolution.' " [5]

" And, upon reference, if I were so disposed," replied Mr. Wiseman, " I could adduce authorities as great for the support of our argument, in addition to the testimony of Bishop Horsely, who says, ' Justification by faith,' (meaning faith alone) ' is the very corner-stone of the *whole* system of Redemption.' "

"And so it is," added the Doctor; "and probably we should all think so if we were to

[5] See Sermon on Justification by Faith.

give definite meanings to the terms we employ; I grant you it is by *faith alone,* if you adopt such a signification of the word *faith* as that given by Jeremy Taylor, who says, ' Believing is the least thing in a justifying faith; for faith is a conjunction of many ingredients, and faith is a covenant, faith is a law, and faith is obedience, and faith is a work, and, indeed, it is a sincere cleaving to and closing with the terms of the Gospel in every instances in every particular," [6] In fact, our notions on this subject do not differ so widely as they may seem. If I acknowledge with the Church, that in the first instance we are accounted righteous before God, only for the merit of our Lord and Saviour, and that his righteousness is proved only to be fully. imputed to us, by our perseverance, in good works, which constitutes the second, final, or consummation of justification, we are not, perhaps, so widely at issue; because the latter evidently means the justification which Christ will, on the judgment-day, pass on all those who have obeyed his voice and followed the way of his pilgrimage on earth, as we read in the Article of Justification, as given in the edition of 1536, and which I know runs thus: — ' For

[6] Fides formata, or Faith working *by* love.

although acceptation to everlasting life be con-joined with justification, yet our good works be necessarily required to the attaining of everlasting life; and we being justified, be necessarily bound, and it is our necessary duty to do good works according to the saying of St. Paul.'—But, Sir, we have carried this point far enough: let us change the subject; and do not imagine that, because I differ in religious opinions with you, I at all undervalue your well-known zeal, or that I do not appreciate the sincerity of your intentions; I regret only, that by the fair and full exercise of our talents, we should not, beginning our career together, arrive at the same conclusions in our ministerial course." " Doctor Freeman," said Vincent, " I have not felt myself at liberty to accompany Mr. Wiseman in the subjects you' have discussed, from the sense of my want of such experience as those here have had, and from' being, at present, not professionally concerned, although my opinions upon these points are all made up, and are, I believe, at variance with yours ; there is, however, a subject on which I may venture to touch, and on which I feel authorised in making an appeal to you and to Mr. Deacon. You have yourself frequently attempted to guard me against what you call gravity and seriousness of deportment; and I know you have deprecated the appearance of any tinge of melancholy in the religious characters of others with whom I am intimately acquainted; and *I* fear not to say with respect to Mr. Deacon, that he has applied stronger terms, without considering that those who are so unfortunate as to become the objects of his virulent invectives, may possibly differ from him in their notions of cheerfulness of manner, and liveliness of spirit. What you denominate the former, they may perhaps regard as frivolity of disposition; what you denominate the latter, they may regard as levity of demeanour."

" Vincent," said the Doctor, " it would have been better had your prudence prompted you to have continued silent altogether, for you speak without proper consideration. It is true, we deprecate gloom and despondency in those to whom it has not been given by nature, and who have brought themselves to believe that they ought to **assume** it, of which there are now-r a-days so many; but it is impossible for an ingenuous mind to conceive us so devoid of feeling, as to be capable of showing a contempt of it in those who manifest it in their real religious characters; and much less in those to whom it is to be attributed as the infirmity of nature. You seem disposed to confound joy and mirth with frivolous levity or actual dissipation, as if it were impossible to maintain them within the bounds of innocence and virtue. It is not my opinion, but that of thousands, that no true joy can be evil —' nullum malum gaudium est.' Habits of overflowing mirth and hilarity, I readily grant you, are not adapted to our profession, nor indeed to any description of persons; and both extremes are to be avoided, as well one as the other."

" If' said Mr. Wiseman, " you will take the advice of such a man as Bishop Horne, you would be convinced that there is every outward and inward motive for seriousness; and that, of all creatures, Man has most reason to be so."

" It may be his advice in some cases," replied the Doctor, " and I believe it is; but few I think have adduced stronger motives for cheerfulness than that great good man has in his admirable discourse upon ' A merry heart doeth good like a medicine;' indeed,; there is one passage in particular which has ever struck me as decisive of his full opinion on the subject: ' Whether,' says he, ' we consider the name, the nature, or the end of the Gospel, its Author, its. doctrines, its duties, or the spirit which accompanies it, every way it is a dispensation of love and peace, consolation and joy; so that a good Christian, of all men, has most cause to be cheerful. *Some have gone so far as to affirm that it is impious in such an one to be otherwise.* "

" The opinion," rejoined Vincent, " of that primitive and heavenly-minded clergyman, George Herbert, may surely be quoted as carrying the strongest and wisest recommendation ; and he says, ' the country parson is generally sad, because he knows nothing but the cross of Christ, his mind being defixed on it with those nails wherewith his Master was."

" Yes," interrupted Mr. Deacon; " but even he. cannot be considered the advocate of that determined gloominess of character of which we speak; for I think he adds that, ' Nature will not bear everlasting droopings,' and that men ' shun the company of perpetual severity.' No, Sir, the Doctor has sufficiently explained that our animadversions are directed against those only who think it their duty to assume an unnatural moroseness; for I must maintain, that among persons naturally inclined to a lively expression of feeling, many in the present day, carried away by what they term religious impressions, suppress the harmless manifestation of outward happiness, and smother their mirth lest they should be thought less serious than they would otherwise be reckoned. It is im-possible to enter any where into society without observing this; and it is a species of dissimulation in the young, among whom it chiefly prevails, that deserves, and shall receive, my animadversion. I can, with as much feeling as yourself, appreciate the characters of those who exhibit the tinge of melancholy as the effects of a strong and sincere impression of religion, and my heart is as susceptible as yours in commiserating those who are so from infirmity. I can venerate a Herbert, I can pity a Cowper!"

" But," continued Mr. Wiseman, " we are not enemies to pleasure, and even to mirth at some seasons, although our pursuit of them lies in objects very different from those in which you seek them; we are only studious not to forget God at any time: we would blend heavenly thoughts with worldly pursuits."

" If it were necessary," said the Doctor, " I could show you to what wild extravagances this principle of blending things serious and gay, has led those, who, though not of our Church; claim distinction from their uniform gravity of deportment: but my concern is alone with those of our Church, with those who profess themselves adherents of it, and who censure their brethren for a participation in public and other amusements, which, they maintain, however guarded by propriety, are not merely injurious to their spiritual welfare, but repugnant to the principles of our calling in Christ. I still hold, without the fear of a rational contradiction, that whatever may be our stations here, we are nowhere forbidden to taste the joys, or to use the treasures, which the Almighty has so bountifully showered upon us. We are nowhere taught that to reject his favours will please the Deity, or that insensibility is a social virtue. — I am not the advocate of dissipation, idleness, or levity; but I maintain that a life of solitude is more the life of a Savage than a Saint, and the nobler faculties of the mind and heart are wasted upon a being, who takes no opportunity of bring-ing them into energy and practice. It was never intended that we should forego all that was designed to gratify and delight us, but ' so to use the good things of this life as not to abuse them. It is excess only that produces injury; we are to remember that ' the Lord made us, and not we ourselves:' as the creatures of his power he might have enjoined upon us laws harsh in construction, and difficult of observance; but is this at all the case ? No: he has given us a law ' whose yoke is easy, and whose burden is light,' and has hardly left a corner in our hearts for disobedience to work in; for our duty and our interest are so closely interwoven, that what we would not do from our love of God, we are prompted to perform from love of ourselves.

' The religion of a Christian does not require him to be gloomy and sullen, to shut his eyes, or to stop his ears; it debars him of no pleasure of which a thinking and reasonable man would wish to partake. It directs him, not to shut himself up in a cloister alone, there to mope and moan away his life ; but to walk abroad, to behold the: things which are in Heaven, and Earth, and to give glory to Him who made them; reflecting at the same time, that if in this, fallen world, which is so soon to be consumed by fire, there are so many objects to entertain and delight him, what must be the pleasures of that world which is to endure for ever, and to be his eternal home.' "[7]

"And pray let me ask," interrupted Mr. Wiseman, " how are we to draw the line of separation between harmless pleasure and the excesses of it?"

" I answer," said the Doctor, " whenever the indulgence of any pleasure or amusement 'leads us to temptation,' or is calculated to endanger our virtue, shake our faith, or unfit us for the exercise of religion — there we are to stop; that is the Rubicon, beyond which perseverance is not innocent, and begins to be criminal." " How then," said Mr. Wiseman, "can any one who has promised by baptism to ' renounce the Devil and all his works, the pomps and vanity of this wicked world, and all the sinful lusts of the flesh'—— how can any one be considered as acting up to the spirit, or even to the

[7] Bishop Horne's Sermon on ' Life a Journey.'

letter of these stipulations, or to the spirit of our Liturgy, who enters into the: scenes of pleasure and amusement, where the pomps and vanity of this wicked world are pre-eminently displayed ? Or how can any one be said to renounce ' all the sinful lusts of the flesh,' who resorts without scruple or hesitation to those plac-es of public amusement where he is most likely to meet with objects, the natural tendency of which is to excite; and inflame the passions, and to banish every thing like, serious thought and reflection from the mind ?' .

" Sir," replied the Doctor, " you draw your conclusions too rapidly; I must deny that all amusements have the ***natural tendency*** to excite
and inflame the passions, unless in gross and vitiated minds: and the same fear that would operate to drive me from the place of a harmless and rational' amuse-ment, might as reasonably prevail to prevent my passing through the streets to avoid all intercourse with the vulgar and lowly, that I may. chance to meet on my, way. There is no more reason for my contracting contamination from the one than the other. And when you say these pleasures have the tendency to banish every thing like serious thought and reflection, I only admit the truth of your affirmation, with this limitation, that if this banishment of grave consideration were a perpetual or general one, or operated to the exclusion of all good thoughts and religious im-pressions, I should think as ill of it as you can; but as it is only temporary, I view it in a different light, as necessary relaxation. In the same manner as the night interposes a refreshing change to the continued brightness of the day; for if the sun, which is the organ of life in the natural world, were always shining in brilliancy, his splen-dour and heat would be found too oppressive for the works of creation, constituted as they now are* And hence arise the utility and divine contrivance of the agree-able vicissitude of light and darkness, by which, while the former is the fountain of good, the latter is required to give it full effect by its re-laxing interposition; and that very interposition not only serves for such relaxation, but con-tributes most ef-

fectively, by the powerful in-fluence of the sun, **hidden** but not **unfelt,** to promote
the object obviously intended by the great Artificer of the Universe in dividing the
day into light and darkness, the year into sea-sons, and in diversifying the face of
nature with hill and plain. Carry the same idea with you in your consideration of
religious things contrasted with innocuous amusements, and you find the analogy
close, and favourable to that relaxation, innocent and inoffensive, for which we
contend. Though God is not always seen by our bodily, neither our mental eye,
yet even in the midst of blameless enjoyments, whatever they may be, the grateful heart will dilate with satisfaction. His power will be felt, and man's feelings be
therefore attuned to livelier bursts of praise, and turn more devoutly to the contemplation of serious things'. Indeed, if the evil consequences of pleasures and amusements, such as I allude to, were as certain as you represent them to be, it would be
infinitely better to fly to the cloister, and to renounce the world altogether. And
respecting what you further adduce against innocuous amusements, whether public
or private, being such as are at direct variance with the vow at baptism, and many of
the petitions to heaven in our admirable Liturgy, I have only to give you the answer
which the good Bishop Horne, serious as he was, and would have had others, has
made; 'As to the world and the flesh, jollity and pleasure, if we are commanded to
renounce, to mortify, and to abstain from them, it is by way of friendly , caution,
lest they should endanger the health of our minds, or bring on a relapse,' I repeat
it, excess is ever to be avoided, and is the only criterion by which to measure the
extent of harmless pleasures; and how it is immediately to be discovered, I have already given my opinion. But, Sir, Solomon has shown, that life is not to be devoted
to one uniform tenour of grave and serious deportment and thinking; he has shown
that the vicissitudes of the seasons and all earthly things teach us to enjoy what we
have, as well as what we industriously labour to obtain; for ' to every thing there is a
season, and a time to every (rational) purpose under heaven; a time to weep, a time
to laugh, a time to mourn, and a time to dance.' And that our joy as well as sorrow
may be manifested in outward social actions, we learn' from the Gospel; in which,
at one time, we see companies drawn together to sympathise with the distressed;
at another, to rejoice with the glad. Martha and Mary are attended by the Jews in
their lamentations upon the death of Lazarus. We find much people of the city of
Nain mingling their sorrows with the grief of the disconsolate widow who had lost

her only son; we find, also, the fatber of the prodigal represented as making a feast with music and dancing, to celebrate the return of his son: — we see more—we see bridegrooms making nuptial feasts; Pharisees and Publicans giving entertainments, at which, even the Saviour condescends to present himself; and though his only object was to call sinners among them to repentance, yet we can hardly conceive he would have made use of . such means if they had been such as were opposed to his principles; he would not thus have done ' evil that good may come,' had it been his intention to inveigh against such practices, or to prohibit entirely such customs. On the contrary, John, he says, came with all the characteristics of rigid austerity; and, with many, it was the cause of his rejection: He, Christ himself, came ' eating and drinking;' that is, in cheerfulness, avoiding no outward manifestation of joy; and it operated equally against his reception. And if the ministers of the same Christ, by disposition, or in. conformity with their principles, can conscientiously walk in the serious austerity of the Baptist, let them not revile their brethren, who, actuated by their inward feelings, put on the cheerfulness and manifest the social disposition of their Master. To insist, as you and your party do, Mr. Wiseman, that *no* worldly pleasures can be innocent, is the assumption of a dogma which, in my humble opin-ion, can neither be exclusively established nor defended. No, Sir, it is the excess of these things that it is to be inveighed against; it is when men become the ' lovers of pleasure more than the lovers of God,' that they are to be stigmatized as sinners: but do not say that the occasional gratifications of moderate pleasures are denied by Religion, because you feel no wish to enjoy them; do not prescribe your imagi-nary notions of good and evil to us, and say, ' That is the standard by which your are to be measured.' Our dispositions and feelings are different, and allowance and indulgence must be made for these distinctions. Do not, however, misunderstand me: once for all let me say, and I beg it may be considered applicable to all I have ad-vanced, that my defence of rational amusements is con-fined to such as are in them-selves strictly innocent, and not trifling; and, individually, I would rather curtail the disposition to enjoy them fully, than be conceived to sanction a latitude verging upon the limits of that sober seriousness of thought which should ever characterize the sincere Christian. But I am persuaded that if you were to regard the intentions more than the actions of mankind, you would find more religiously good than you are, at present, disposed to allow."

" I would make them," said Mr. Wiseman, " much better than they are, by de-
nouncing from the pulpit all such idle, unsatisfactory, not to say ungodly, practices;
by incessantly preaching the awakening doctrines of the Gospel, which might be
insisted upon more frequently than they are, and with much more benefit than the
subjects, I think, on which you generally expatiate."

" This," said Mr. Deacon, " is the renewal of the old objection against our
preaching morality. You seem to have forgotten what we formerly advanced on
this subject, and therefore I must repeat, that our discourses are equally directed
towards instilling faith and obedience: we urge one as much as the other; and for
doing this, without dwelling upon the highest possible example of the Saviour and
his Apostles, we have the authority of Bishop Taylor, who thus, instructs the clergy
— and to his advice we should all be disposed to listen: ' In your sermons to the
people,' says this great and learned divine, ' often speak of the four last things, of
death and judgment, heaven and hell; — of the life and death of Jesus Christ; — of
God's mercy to repenting sinners, and his severity against the impenitent; — of the
formidable examples of God's anger poured forth upon rebels, sacrilegious, oppres-
sors of widows and orphans, and all persons guilty of crying sins: — these are useful,
safe, and profitable; but never run into extravagances and curiosities, nor trouble
yourselves or them with mysterious secrets, for there is more laid before you than
you can understand, and the whole duty of man is, ***to fear God and keep his commandments.*** Speak but very little of the secret and high things of God, but as much
as you can of the lowliness and humility of Christ.9 Need I say, that this advice is
a short sum-mary of those inspired lessons given by St. Paul to Timothy and Titus:
lessons so full of Christian doctrines and Christian morality, and so urged that he
who preaches one to the exclusion of the other, neglects, however ***popular*** his sermons may be, the plain injunctions of Him who spake by the Spirit of God, and who
tempered zeal with knowledge, and faith with, practice. I wish for no other guide
for our ministration, no other direction for our ad-dresses-—"

" It seems then," interrupted Mr. Wiseman, " that you consider the moral precepts and the doctrines of the Gospel as things entirely inde-pendent of each other;

as if you thought the end. of preaching to be answered by giving your congregation, sometimes an ethical disquisition, and sometimes a doctrinal discourse; in short by your urging morals as much as doctrine — a practice against which the Homilies of the Church are at direct variance."

" And so, Sir, am I," answered the Doctor. " Indeed, Mr. Wiseman, this is not ingenuous. Can you conceive it possible, that even those of our body, whom some of your party designate as moral essayists, can from the pulpit enforce any article of morality, excepting on the grounds of its being in correspondence with the practice, with the injunctions of Christ, and with the great object of our salvation through him? Can you suppose, which is equally just and liberal to imagine, that we can inculcate the cold maxims of Heathen philosophy, — that we can lay down the precepts of Plato and Socrates,— and leave out all reference to the scheme of Christianity? It is impossible you can misunderstand us when we say, that we preach as well doctrines of faith as obedience; that we mean to be understood as selecting for our discourses sometimes the discussion of a doctrinal point, urging it as a matter of belief, at other times the discussion of a moral subject, as a matter of Christian obedience. Why should you impute notions and actions to us which you cannot but know we disclaim? Why should you be so studious to misunderstand and to pervert, unless it were with a motive I will not impute to you ? It is this, and this only, that gives me offence; I will freely and amicably converse with you upon any point in which we may differ, but let us do it in perfect good will and charity. If I have directed any animadversions against you, or the party to which you belong, on the articles of practice and belief, they have not been made upon imaginary grounds, the objects of my own cre-ation, but such as I have actually found to exist. If I have ever brought against any who differ from me a charge which has no other foundation than bare supposition, I would not only recall it, but make all the restitution in my power. I would not be dogmatical, I would not be thought infallible; on the contrary, I too well know my own peccability not to be assured that there are many things in which I might profit by your advice, or by that of others. Human nature, though, perhaps, not ***totally corrupt,*** does not always discover its own errors. It is, therefore, kind in any friend to point out the faults of others, provided he does so from a good spirit; as Cicero has said in the language of Ennius:

Homo, qui erranti comiter monstrat viam,
Quasi lumen de suo lumine accendat; facit:
Nihilominus ipsi luceat, cum illi accenderit.

And as a greater than. Cicero has also said —' Let all bitterness and wrath, and anger and clamour, and evil speaking, be put away from you, with all malice. And be ye kind to one another, even as God, for Christ's sake, hath forgiven you.'

" Come, Sir, let us not carry this conversation any further. I assure you, I regret, very deeply regret, that our opinions should be at all at variance; and I grieve for it the more, because 'a house divided against itself cannot stand.' Before you go, give me your hand; and do me the justice to believe me sincere, when I say, I have the strongest disposition to admire the sincerity of your intentions, and the warmth of your zeal in the cause of your sacred profession. If I do not agree with you in all particulars, it is from the honest conviction of my mind that I am not at liberty to do so, and not from the most distant wish to underrate your opinions, or to overvalue our own; and I know this to be the feeling of my good friend here, whose actions, I am sure, will ever follow the dictates of his heart, and will lead him to give you now, with myself, the right-hand of fellowship."

Here the conference closed, and Mr. Wiseman and Vincent took their leave.

GRACE.

" MY good friends," said Mr. Deacon, on entering the drawing-room of his friend Mr. Eustace, who was now married to his beloved Marian, " I sincerely hope I find you well, and truly happy."

" My dear Sir," said his friend, " your appearance increases our happiness; we have not seen you for some time. Where have you been? We thought you had forgotten us, and are almost disposed to call you to order. But, however, sit down, and let us enjoy your company."

" I readily obey your summons. My time has been much occupied of late in visiting the abodes of sickness, and administering to the wants of. some of our suffering flock. The increasing infirmities of my worthy Rector necessarily impose upon me additional duty. He is, I am sorry to say, daily growing weaker; and though his active mind abates nothing in its exertion for the good of his fellow-creatures, yet it is too evident, that unless a favourable change takes place, we shall, ere long, have to lament the loss of our excellent pastor and most benevolent friend. The little time which my clerical duties leave me, I must devote to him who is superior to all complainings, but who daily requires the increased attentions of his friends; and though .1 cannot avow to him these sentiments, because in his feeble state it might affect his shattered nerves, I contrive by little stratagems to be with him as much as possible, taking care to engage his attention, at one time, by the relation of any bright events of a cheering nature which shine across our ministerial paths, and at another, by discoursing with him on topics, light, yet interesting. By these means I contrive to while away with him many an hour that otherwise would hang heavy on his hands; and the satisfaction and instruction I derive from his society, afflicted as he is, more than rapay me for what other people might think time heavily spent There is something in his appearance and conduct at present, to which all his past actions appear but as foils. It is delightful to mark his placidity,—his cheerfulness, struggling with bodily anguish, and the eye of hope which irradiates his countenance. I never leave him without feeling ' the Divinity stirring within me,' and encouraging me, with whispers of holy impulses to cling fast, more steadily, to that beautiful system of heavenly love which thus can cheer the drooping, still the poignancy of bodily pain, and raise the corrupted affections of the soul to the bright expectations of purer joys and unruffled pleasures. You, my dear friends, have felt the influence of God, speaking through the medium of his word, and felt his grace inwardly, silently, unostentatiously, and imperceptibly producing within you a composure that has sustained you under events the most distressing, and trials the most seducing. You have felt all this; to you I need not, therefore, dilate on the subject. Your own experience is a volume that requires no comment. But I am sure you will feel deeply interested in the declining health of our good pastor.—You, Madam, in particular," (addressing himself to the mother,) " from your long knowledge of his character and many excellencies, joined to your similarity of years and approximation of suffering, will feel another chasm rent in your worldly prospects, and be still more convinced that this earth is not our home, and that nothing can so sweeten the hour of age, and soften the approach of death, as the retrospect of a life spent in the simple . and sincere performance of religious, social, and Christian duties. This, through the grace of God, supplies an armour invulnerable to every worldly dart, and proof against the insidious attacks of sin and death combined."

" All this we feel and acknowledge," said his friend Eustace; " and we hope that in hours like these, and under dispensations so trying, our hearts will, as they now do, responding in sympathy, feel the proof, and experience the truth of your correct observations.—But, my good friend, there lies my Marian's Album; have you no contributions to bestow, nothing in your own good style with which to enhance the value of your other favours in the same way? I know you have; your self-satisfied looks, and that air of pleasing composure, indicate that you are both disposed and able to be charitable."

" I am sure Mr. Deacon requires no im-portunities," observed Marian; " for in your absence, my dear Eustace, his subscriptions were frequently voluntary, and at other times we had only to ask and to receive."

" My dear Madam," he replied, " your good opinions go before my deservings; — I am, nevertheless, happy to be prepared to answer your requests. Here is a rough draught of a little sketch with which I last night amused myself. 'Tis yours, if it be worthy the trouble of transcribing. And I can only say, may you never experience the trials it depicts, or be exposed to the sufferings it faintly describes. Of this I am sure, that though as a human being you are liable to the same casualties, yet, as a Christian, whose faith is well-tempered and sure, you will never so far set your affections on things below, however happy your present state, as to allow them not only to supersede ' those which are above,' but to drive your reason adrift, and leave you a blank in creation. But here they are; and that you may the more easily decipher them, I will first read them." So saying he drew out the following

LINES.

THE thickening shades began to fall
On the old church's eastern wall,
And vesper's broad, retiring light,
Glared from its windows deep and bright,
And glancing on memorial stone,
That told of mortals long since gone,
'Twixt dark and clear impresse'd a gloom,
Which warns mankind, that in the tomb
Each age and rank, degree and form,
Fattens the banquet of the worm:—
And as the gales of evening pass,
Rustle the wavings of grass;
Whilst under the dark yew-tree's shade,
The brighter tints of splendour fade.
'Twas at that hour, when nature wears
A hue most soothing to man's cares, —
Enough of day remained to show
The busy deeds of hearts below,
And night's obtruding, sombre vest,
Awed living things to pause, and rest;
'Twas at that hour, so mild, so still,
Inspirer of the sober mood,
That Anna sought the sacred hill,
In dark, unconscious solitude.
Seest thou that stone with carvings rude ?
In chronicles no tale of fame :
A babe of undistinguish'd name
Lies there entomb'd. Oft o'er that scene
A mother weeps whose plaintive moan
Figures the cheerless' lot o£ those

Who sink beneath life's weight of woes.
Survey her form; behold her eye,
Now fix'd on earthy now raised on high-
Now glazed with blankoess -now like stars
Flashing portentous signs of wars!
That stone hath pillow'd oft he* head,.
When sense and feeling both are fled,.
And thro' intensity of grief
Her eyes refuse their soft relief;
And still she moans, in accents wild,
" My boy! my boy 1 oh where's my child?"

She, once the darling of the green,
Beneath the aged yew is seen,
When wheels the evening bat hit flight,
And village hinds have said, " Good night."
Happy her early years pass'd on:
But, oh ! those days of bliss are gone;
And they, who once her cares beguiled,
Her husband, and her darling child,
Howe'er beloved, have run their race-
And now what fills the vacant place ? —

Alas! her reason's eye is blind;
With them are buried sense and mind;
She walks, unconscious who may gaze;
And as thro' lanes and fields she strays,
Her moan is still, in accents wild,
" My boy! my boy ! where is my child ?"

Her husband plough'd the briny wave;
Gentle in peace, in action brave:
In love, in friendship, who so true ?

The favourite of a hardy crew.
But what avails the manly form ?
What, skill to battle with the storm ?
What, Friendship's heart, or Honour's meed;
Prompt to direct, or act the deed ?
He fell: and Victory's laurels wave
In clustering wreaths above his grave.
His child was Anna's only joy,
The only tie that bound to life;
And he too died,—the darling boy!
Mother no more,— no more a wife!
Without that only stay of Hope,
Which can alone with troubles cope,
Her Reason, on Grief's ocean tost,
Waver'd — return'd — and then was lost.
Had she but known, how gracious
God Entwines compassion with the rod,
And joys the broken heart to bind,
To pour relief in Sorrow's mind,
To raise the orphan, and to cheer,
And wipe from widows' eyes the tear,
And by Religion's aid decrees
A med'cine for restoring ease
To hearts that truly seek to Him;
Her mental eye had not been dim,
Nor would she moan, in accents wild,
" My boy! my boy! where is my child?"
For turn, ere fades that lingering ray,
And a true Christian's grief survey,
Behold yon altar! there is one
Who likewise weeps for treasures gone;
Yet Hope is hers — that soother kind,
The halcyon of the troubled mind,—

That Hope which in Religion lives,
And joy, and balm, and comfort gives,—
That Hope which soars on eagle's wings,
And thro' the future's darkness springs,
Points to the world beyond the skies,
And whispers, " Lo! the dead shall rise!"—
She, the poor Christian's steadfast friend,
Still cheers him onward to his end,
And in each hour of dark distress,
Prevents, or makes his sorrow less.
So felt Eliza—she had known
Pleasures; but they, alas! were flown:
Rank, fortune, and those joys that warm Domestic scenes with purest charm,
Her path with choicest flowers had strew'd,
And claim'd, and won her gratitude.
But trials came — infections spread —
Her children sleep among the dead.
Years have roll'd on, and she has been
Distant from that grief-stirring scene,
And other spots her hand has blest;
Caressing all, by all carest.
Once more she comes to mark the place
Where 'sleep the dearest of her race;
And now she by the altar bends,
Whilst tranquil Peace her steps attends,
And trust in Heaven her bosom arms
From 'whelming grief or vain alarms,
And deep the sacred truth she feels,
Which Sorrow's withering touches heals: Tho' dark is life, and full of gloom, "
We all shall meet beyond the tomb."

The prayer is done — the vow is paid —
The tablet is again survey'd: —-

The tear falls fast — the heart beats high,
And the breast labours with a sigh.
One moment's pause — the trial's o'er!
Calm, tranquil, placid as before,
She traverses the gloomy aisle,
And quits the venerable pile;
And as she onward bends her way,
She casts one glance upon the ray
That now its latest gleam has thrown
On the rude church's western stone,—
And thinks, though light forsakes the skies,
Its glory soon again shall rise.
Then feels assured the time will come
" When friends shall meet beyond the tomb."
And there the maniac's grief will cease,
And troubles soften into peace;
And hush'd shall be the rending sigh,
And tears no more shall gem the eye,
And griefs shall probe no more the heart,
And friends shall meet, no more to part.
Weep not, poor suffering child of grief,
Be this thy med'cine and relief;.
Know that above, is blissful state,
The widow'd hearts with joys dilate:
'TIS this that all thy grief shall cure,
And give thee patience to endure
And when thou moan'st, in accents wild,
"My boy! my boy! oh where's my child ?"
Think that thou hear'st the Christian say,
Who feels Religion's purest ray,
 " I know the glorious time will come
When friends shall meet beyond the tomb."

When he had read these lines he handed the rough copy to his friend, who having commented upon them, was proceeding to make observations on the comfort of religion under all circumstances, when he was interrupted by the introduction of Alexander Trustwall and his brother Vincent, the former of whom had lately paid a rather marked attention to Miss Eustace. The usual compliments were passed, and something like a mixed conversation prevailed, when Miss Eustace observed to Alex-ander, that Mr. Deacon, had favoured her sister with some original lines, and as be was himself a poetaster, she wished him to read them. He did so; then, having first obtained permission, handed them to his brother, who perused them, and observed, that as for the lints, they might be good, but he was ftp judge of poetry: the sentiment was what he looked at, and the lesson designed to be inculcated. "I do not exactly see, Mr. Deacon," he continued, " the moral you wish to convey. I see, indeed, that you make the difference of the conduct of the two females to arise from religion. Do you mean to infer, that one was comforted under her affliction by grace, and the other was rendered inconsolable from want of it ?"

" It was undoubtedly the grace of God," replied Mr. Deacon, " which enabled Eliza to see love in the heavy dispensation of her Maker, and to submit to the trial, as ' one who had a hope.' Without that grace she would not have been able to do it; at least, not in the calm, patient, resigned, and Christian-like manner she did: it was probably the want of this heavenly quality which rendered the other character liable to the extremity of wretchedness which overwhelmed her reason. Her affections were wholly set upon this world: she had not mixed with the comfort and delight of domestic emjoyments, with which there is nothing earthly to be compared, ' the one thing needful,' which is the heart of real happiness. I suppose that the difference of their lives, subsequent to their trials, arose from these considerations: one was religious; the other, though neither immoral nor wicked, was not so."

" Do you think, then," said Vincent, " that the poor creature, whose senses were darkened by her trials, could have resisted them, and borne them as patiently as the other female ?"

" Cæteris paribus, certainly," replied Mr. Deacon. " Some difference will arise from the bodily constitution. There are such things as nerves, and these affect, in some measure, the operations of the mind, and consequently the soul, to which the mind is, as it were, the inlet I have no hesitation in saying, that had the poor woman, in the summer of her health and happiness, been laying up, through the instrumentality of true religion, provisions against the. winter of suffering, her subsequent condition would have been different: if it were not so, that is, if she had made the proper use of the comforts and supports of religion as held to her and to all mankind in the Gospel of the Saviour, she would not, under God's grace, have ' had her understanding darkened' by the terrible visitation of affliction. The word of God is rendered of none effect, when it say, ' God is faithful, who will not suffer yon to be tempted above that ye are able; but will, with the temptation also, make a way to escape, that ye may be able to bear it,' if the gifts of Heaven be not properly used. I affirm, therefore, that the grace of God did not help her, as it helped the other, because she did not strive to avail herself of it so much as the other did, allowing, as I said before, that they were on a level in point of sensibility and affection."

" So, then, you think the grace of God depends upon ourselves, and not upon God ?" observed Vincent

" Not wholly," replied Mr. Deacon; " but in a certain degree. The receiving does, but not the giving. Do not, however, misunderstand me; I acknowledge, fully and unequivocally, that the grace of God is a free gift, because the bestowing of it depends wholly upon God. He can give it to whom he likes: but at the same time I believe, as far at least as I am able to understand the language of Scripture, that he does give it to none but those who ask him. And here, as we have fallen on the subject, and as I believe there are sane shades of difference between us on this doctrine, I would fain take such an opportunity as the present for considering the matter; but however interesting this might be to us personally, it cannot be so to those around us, who can have no great desire to hear a dry point of theology discussed; so, Vincent, with your permission I will meet you elsewhere to settle this dispute."

" By no means," exclaimed Eustace; " we will not permit you to indulge in a private combat;. I assure you, that we are all deeply interested in this matter, and would fain have our notions set aright, for it is one of vital importance; and I am equally sure, that Marian and my sister feel as much concerned in the understanding of it as I do myself."

" Indeed," continued Marian, " since the subject has arisen from the lines you have given me, I feel a great desire to have the sentiments they express defended by your arguments and opinions."

" Well then," rejoined Mr. Deacon, " since it is your desire that Vincent and I may fairly and candidly understand one another, I will state my idea of Grace. I know that misrepresentations frequently are made from casual observations, or isolated sentences; and people are apt to run away with a belief founded upon such vague grounds, when, if they would be at the pains to investigate, they would find that something very different was really intended from what they were led to believe. On this principle, then, I would observe, that the necessity of the grace of God arises primarily and solely from our original sin. Before sin entered into the world, when man was in a state of innocence, he was in favour or in grace with his Maker. When, however, by the subtlety of the tempter, our first parents traingressed the only prohibition that the goodness of God had made, they lost that favour or grace, as far as it regarded their own exertions, irretrievably. The purity of their minds became corrupted; their thoughts inclined to evil, and their actions (alas ! how unlike their first state) were contaminated by a sinful taint. The consciousness of their transgression, although it exposed them to punishment, yet proved that their corruption was not total; that, however far they were gone from original righteousness, there were yet latent some sparks of former purity. In this state, then, of conscious guilt, in which, although they saw the sad condition to which they were reduced, they could find out by themselves (however desirous) no means of extricating themselves, the goodness of the Almighty, who always tempers justice with mercy, ' pitied their lost estate,' and appointed a way of reconciliation; by means of which they, who were now out of favour, might, upon certain conditions required of them, be brought again into it That way was the promise of the Messiah, which, for 4000 years, proved the beacon of hope to all who looked up to it with the eye of faith. At length the Saviour came! The beacon flashed out the Sun of Righteousness, not merely to give light to direct the path, but warmth to influence all who would travel on it. By the coming of the promised One, in whom patriarchs, kings, people, and prophets, had delighted, the offence of our first parents was atoned; and instead of the imputation of sin to all who are of their nature, which excluded them from the grace or favour of God, there now is offered to them the imputation of the righteousness of Jesus Christ, which brings them back to favour."

" So far, Sir, our sentiments accord," said Vincent

" But, permit me to ask, how is that righteousness imputed ?" said Marian Eustace.

" To all who name the name of it, by bap-tism," replied Mr. Deacon.

" How, Sir !" exclaimed Vincent, " do you say that the new birth takes place at baptism?"

" I do" Sir," he continued; " because it is the doctrine of the oracles of life and our Church. And, indeed, looking at Grace as I have explained it, I do not see how you can deny it, because, as the child from its natural parents draws in the principles of corruption, and as the Saviour came to obviate these principles, surely the means that he appointed to distinguish who are his should be conferred as soon as possible."

" You surely are not disposed, Mr. Deacon," said Vincent, " to advocate the doctrine of the Church of Rome, respecting baptism. The opus operatum' cannot be defended on scriptural grounds, else were every action after bap-tism necessarily good and acceptable to God."

" By no means," replied Mr. Deacon; " by no means am I an advocate of that tenet. But still, as the Saviour himself has said. ' No man can enter into the kingdom of heaven, except he be born again of water and the Holy Ghost ;' and 'Whosoever believeth and is baptized, shall be saved;' and as our original sin is derived in our natural birth from Adam, so also is the remedy of it to be obtained from the means appointed by the Saviour, which is the Mew Birth of the soul, or the bringing it into that state of grace or favour before God, in which further grace may be obtained to enable it to go for-ward even to everlasting salvation. I think one part of the old Article on Baptism runs thus: ' By the sacrament of baptism they (infants, innocents, and children,) obtain remission of their sins, the grace and favour of God, and be made thereby the very sons and children of God.' And in the Article of Baptism, as it now stands, this doctrine is most unequivocally and plainly asserted in these words —' It is a sign of Re-generation or New Birth' — and in the service of Baptism how, except in the sense I am advocating, do you understand, ' being dead unto sin and living unto righteousness ?' These expressions all show, clearly enough, what our Reformers wished to be understood by Baptism; and the expressions of the ancient Fathers are even stronger. On these grounds, then, of Scripture and the Articles of our Church, I contend that I am justified in asserting, that the New Birth, or the birth of the second Adam, which is appointed as the means of taking away the bad and deadly effects of the nature of the *first* Adam, is conferred in baptism. Thus, then, grace is first obtained in baptism; and thus obtained, man is endowed with the capability of ' working out his own salvation,' on certain conditions, which He, who won the grace, has prescribed for the performance of all those who look unto Him for peace, for pardon, and ever-lasting life."

" I rather hold," replied Vincent, " that the New Birth of which you speak, and which is the gate to everlasting life, takes place at no stated or definite time, but is the work of an instant, as if a new creation were taking place; and that it works effectually to salvation, when once it is bestowed. This, by an act of special grace, is the infusion of a spiritual action upon the soul and its operations, which gives it new views, new ideas, and a totally new mode of life."

" I cannot agree with you, Sir," said the Curate. " The tenour of Scripture warrants no such conclusion: if it had, our Reformers would not have overlooked it. The scrupulous exactness with which they sifted every tenet, the jealous care they exercised over every thing that related to the religion of Jesus, and the deep, inquiring, experienced piety which warmed their hearts, under a feeling of God's grace, which perhaps approaches nearer to direct inspiration than any thing we know of, since the influence of the tongues of fire ceased, would sure have detected this principle you speak of, if it were to be found in the Oracles of God. I grant you, that certain persons, such as Saul of Tarsus, could fix the time when his conversion began; but this extraordinary instance, together with others, of a conversion which . may be dated, and which, for wise purposes, God was pleased to bring about, must be looked upon rather as an extraordinary, than an ordinary effect of the operation of the Holy Spirit Yet, Sir, if you will consider, you will invariably find that the New Birth, or Regeneration, always took place at baptism; and that though the persons thus regenerate could date the time of their introduction into the Church, yet they were by no means admitted by an act of special grace, and certainly were not considered in a state of ***certain salvation.*** They were then, as now, only admitted into the favour of God, and this admission put them ***in the way*** of being wholly reconciled to Him, through the merits of the Saviour, upon the performance, on their parts, of the conditions entered into at their baptismal covenant Now, Sir, can you, can any one, rationally assert that you know experimentally, the very moment when your regeneration took place ? or can you safely assert that this special act of favour puts you, beyond doubt, into the inheritance of bliss immortal? I am rather inclined to think, as our admission into the visible Church takes place at baptism, and by faith ' we are accounted righteous before God;' and as this is the free gift of God, bestowed before we can have any claim to his favouar, that the continuance or increase of that favour depends upon stipulations which he has a right to exact, and we ought to be desirous to perform; — stipulations that require not unsinning obedience, for as man is naturally imperfect, so must his actions necessarily partake of his nature; and as Christ Jesus alone was perfect, so did he fulfil or keep the whole of them, that we, through his perfections, might be accounted perfect, and have his righteousness imputed to us through the grace of God. — I cannot, therefore, see any ground for allowing a special grace; that is, a grace which works effectually, and brings man to salvation without any exertion of his own, or without any possibility of losing that state of favour into which he was once brought. No; the effects of grace are, like every other dispensation, progressive; for, says the Apostle, ' By the grace of God I am what I am; and his grace bestowed upon me was not in vain; but I laboured more abundantly than they all; yet not I, but the grace of God which was with me.' Now here, the word ' grace,' three times repeated, has a different signification in every place. In the first, it is understood to signify the free love and favour of God; in the second, the effects of that love and favour received thankfully, and used actively and sincerely; and in the third, the consequently continued assistance and help of Him ' who can will and do of his own good pleasure.' And this is excellently developed in the Collect thrice used in Easter week, in which the word 'special' is used; yet its signification is very different from your acceptance of it, because it is supposed only to prevent, or go before; then comes ' the continual help,' and afterwards, the 'good effect.' In which we cannot but mark the progress of grace as set forth by St Paul himself, and as designed by God, and experienced by all ' who so pass through things temporal that they finally lose not the things eternal.' What then are the grounds for your special grace ? Even St. Paul himself (which is a special case) felt no such assurance; at least he did not think it expedient to avow it in himself; else why should he have confessed — ' Not as though I had already attained, either were already perfect; but I follow after, ***if that I may apprehend*** that for which also I am apprehended of Jesus Christ. Brethren, I count not myself to have apprehended; but this one thing I do, forgetting those things which are behind, and reaching forth unto those things which are before, I press toward the mark for the prize of the high calling in Christ Jesus.'[8] And if we consult the general scope of his Epistles, we see no ground for such a belief. Else why should he exhort his converts, who had been admitted by baptism into the covenant of Christ, and who were called holy, and beloved, and elect, to ' let not sin reign in their mortal body, that they should obey the lusts thereof?' He encourages them to ' work out their own salvation,' — to ' grow in grace,' and ' to come boldly to the throne of grace.' If they needed such exhortations, why should any of us pretend to a favour, which the immediate disciples of the Apostles were not allowed to claim ? The doctrine of special grace is only another name for personal election; than the idea of which nothing can be more repugnant to

[8] Let those who at one time would make man a mere machine, and totally incapable of doing any thing, even in co-operation for his own salvation, ponder this passage; which is so ***agonistical,*** that there can be no doubt the Christian's exertions are absolutely required in the great contest for immortal life, as the put-

ting forth of his strength was necessary for the champion of the Olympian Games. The Scholar immediately sees the allusion, and the Christian applies it to its true purport—the glory of God, and the striving for honour, glory, and immortality!

the spirit of the Gospel, nothing more subversive of Christian exertions, and nothing more derogatory from the atonement of the Saviour. We know it not. The ordinary effects of the Spirit of God exclude all idea of this speciality. Consult any page of Scripture — canvass every tax that refers to grace — expatiate on the Christian scheme of redemption, and ponder on the doctrines of the Gospel,—there you will find one broad and general principle pervading the whole, that all mankind are sinners by nature, and can only be brought to God by the atoning merits of the Saviour, ' in his own ap-pointed way;' — but nothing of peculiar or special favour. Surely St. Paul might have expected that his converts would possess as much grace as any: yet if we take the example of the Galatians, who were planted into the Church of Christ by him, and who had received the Spirit of God, so that they once had walked well, but afterwards fell away by the false doctrine of evil teachers, so that he asked them ' who had bewitched them?' we shall have no great reason to suppose that we possess a grace which they had not ' I do not put you in comfort,' says the venerable Latimer, ' that if ye have once the Spirit ye cannot lose it.' — ' Quench not the Spirit,' says St Paul; and again, he exhorts his followers not to ' receive the grace of God in vain.'—Now, if we may believe the truth and extent of all this, surely we have no reason to flatter our vanity that we shall have the benefit of an act of special grace, when those who possessed higher and more glorious privileges than we do, and who probably were much our superiors in faith, hope, and charity, were excluded from it."

" Notwithstanding all that you have ad-vanced," replied Vincent, " those whom God justifies, he glorifies; and a person once admitted into this state can never wholly fell away . from grace."

" For instance," said Alexander, " when David had committed the sin which cost Uriah his life, was he in a state of grace ? If so, grace was no more grace, but sin, black and deadly."

" I do not say that such an act was the re-sult of grace; certainly not; but still he was not out of grace," replied Vincent.

" Had he died at that very time," observed Marian, " would he have been admitted to salvation ?"

" He could not have died at that time," said Vincent; " God reserved him as a chosen vessel, and would not let him fall away, but gave him grace to return to virtue."

" In God's hands are ' the issues of life and death,' and he can do with us what he pleases," rejoined Mr. Deacon: " we may not question his decision, nor judge what he performs. But yet, it hardly seems consonant with our nature, or the general providence of God, for us to suppose that we may presume upon this special grace, to prolong our life till we have repented of our sins, and are brought again into a state of justification. Upon your principle, a person may commit any sin, however grievous, and yet be in grace. Now I prefer the exposition advanced in the Article entitled ' Faith,' ascribed to that much-maligned, but excellent man, Cranmer — ' They who after the knowledge of God fell into sin advisedly, as they that commit murder, adultery, and other abominations, and so fall from faith as it is taken in the second acceptation, and be therefore *out of the state of grace and favour of God for the time,* yet do not these men fall from faith as it is taken in the first acceptation.' And if the Apostle's doctrine be any criterion to guide our judgment, the contrary is the case. Every act of sin is described as an alienation from grace; and the fruits of the Spirit are the only marks that we are ' alive unto God, through Jesus Christ.' Now, the fruits of the Spirit are love, joy, peace, long-suffering, gentleness, goodness, faith, meekness, temperance. And they that are Christ's have crucified the flesh with the affections and lusts: when these, then, are absent, there is no grace; but when these abound, then does grace abound as the only efficient cause. ' That as sin hath reigned unto death, even so might grace reign *through righteousness* unto eternal life, by Jesus Christ our Lord.' And besides all this, I need only mention the evidence given by Bishop Latimer on this very point, when he says — '

David was written in the Book of Life: but when he sinned, he, at the same time was out of the Book of the *Saviour of God,* until he had repented, and was sorry for his fault.' [9]

[9] Sermon on the third Sunday after the Epiphany, p. 312. ed. 1607.

" St. Paul also talks of a newness of life," observed Mr. Eustace; "by which he must mean a life of holiness, in contradistinction to a life of sin; that we may be ' dead unto sin, but alive unto God, through Jesus Christ our Lord."

" But I still hold," said Vincent, " and consider that you have not offered any reason to refute it, that ' whom he justifies, him he glorifies.' I consider that as we are justified by faith, through an act of grace, God will, in his due course, by his grace bring those whom he has justified to a state of glory, pure, undefiled, and that fadeth not away."

" If you mean to say," replied Mr. Deacon, " in the words of St Paul, that 'being justified by his blood, we *shall* be saved from wrath through him,' I will agree with you.' But if you mean to say that justification is eternal life, I must admit it with some reservation, viz. the justification which God's final sentence shall award at the last great day. Now this justification depends upon our performance, by the grace of God, of the conditions required of us at our entrance into the sonship of adoption, by faith through the meritorious atonement of our great High Priest When a Christian, (which title implies admission into God's grace by baptism,) goes forward in the way of God's commandments, mortifying the evil and corrupt affections of the flesh, and striving to do all things to the glory of God, there is no doubt, that God will glorify him, whether he be considered by man as elect or non-elect, whether under common or special grace. And in this sense will God glorify those whom he justifies. Because, as no one can be justified without God's grace, so neither can any one be glorified, but by the same grace of God working with his will, (and hence the different effects of Grace in different characters, resulting from the different exertions of individuals,) and inclining his heart to the performance of the fruits of the Spirit: inasmuch, as these two glorious privileges and blessings are gifts which God alone can bestow, and which he confers liberally, freely, and without any restraint As no one can order the ways of Providence, so must we consider that every good and perfect gift of which He is the author, (and there is no good and perfect gift, of which he is not the author,) springs from his abundant good will to man, which is so exceedingly rich, that glory, and honour, and immortality are offered to all, without respect of persons, without money and without price."

" True, Sir, ***offered*** to all; but can all to whom they are offered accept and lay hold on those offers to their great and endless comfort ?" asked Vincent.

" All do not receive it," said Mr. Deacon; " but I believe all may receive it who strive for it, as the Saviour has said, ' Ask and ye shall have; seek, and ye shall find; knock, and it shall be opened unto you.' So thought one whose opinions are valuable, — I mean the venerable Latimer. ' Whom hath He (the Saviour) saved? His people. Who are his people ? All that believe in him, and put their whole trust in him, and those that seek help in and salvation at his hands; all such are his people.' "

" I am inclined," continued Vincent, " to think, that they only receive to whom God gives: those whom He, by his foreknowledge, has predestinated, as chosen vessels of his grace, and love, and redemption. This is pretty strongly asserted by St. Paul, when he says, ' Whom he did foreknow, he also did predestinate to be conformed to the image of his Son, that he might be the first-born among many brethren. Moreover, whom he did predestinate, them he also called; and whom he called, them he also justified; and whom he justified, them he also glorified.' How, Sir, do you get over this ? This, certainly, is strong for a particular grace or election by the grace of God, of those whom God shall choose, or has chosen, to immortal life."

"If you take this passage by itself," said Mr. Deacon, " it would, perhaps, be very difficult to avoid your conclusion. But if you will consider the general scope of the Christian redemption, the promises and privileges of the Gospel, and the peculiar circumstances under which the Apostle wrote this Epistle, the direct contrary will be the result of your unbiassed judgment If predestination be the foreknowledge of God, no one can deny the doctrine; but if it be the eternal purpose of God to choose out personally, and individually, this person and that person to be *saved irrespectively,* and to exclude this person and that person **unconditionally** from the participation of the benefits of the precious blood-shedding of the Lamb of God, I cannot, for one, assent to such a view of the dispensations of God, Because when we consider that 'Jesus Christ came into the world to save sinners,' and that all are sinners, we may restrict the benefit of his coming to those only whom God has predestinated to life; otherwise they who are not predestinated are not sinners, because the Saviour did not die for them. The Saviour is ' the Lamb of God that taketh away the sins of the world.' Of what world, I would ask ? Of the world elected and predestined before there was a world? Surely not: but of the world, or the people in it, which were suffering the punishment of Adam's transgressions. And who are they? All, all mankind. And how are the benefits of his precious blood-shedding imputed to them ? By faith, when the knowledge of all this, and of the conditions annexed to the receiving of them, is manifested to men; that is, when, by the ministry of the word, they are called, by faith, to justification, and having received this justification, they, through the ' grace of God working with them,' and the ' Spirit of God bearing witness with their spirits, render the obedience due to these holy assistances, and rest all their hope of eternal life on the sole merits of Him 'who died for their sins, and rose again for their justification.' When they thus proceed in virtue and godliness of living, they are said to ' glorify their Father who is in heaven,' and also ' to be glorified in him.'"

" But how with respect to God's foreknowing and predestinating them? How do you give an explanation on that point?' said Vincent

" By referring you to Timothy, who says, ' God hath saved us, and called us with an holy calling, not according to our works, but according to his own purpose and grace, which was given us in Christ Jesus, before the world began, but is now made manifest by the appearing of our Saviour Jesus Christ, who hath abolished death, and hath brought life and immortality to light through the Gospel:' hence it is evident, that the foreknowledge of God of those whom he calls, justifies, and glorifies, consists in his purpose of grace of sending into the world his Son Jesus Christ to be the propitiation for the sins of the world, that 'as in Adam all die, even so in Christ might **all** be made alive.' That as he died for the benefit of all who would come to him, so all who accept the condition on which the imputation of his merits is offered to them in the Gospel, by believing on Him, and by acting in conformity with that belief, 'may not die, but have everlasting life.' Thus, then, the Gospel-scheme of redemption, which brought 'life and immortality to light,' was purposed, and foreknown by God, to the end that many should be saved, the making known or preaching of this Gospel being the calling of God; the accepting it by faith, the justification of God; and the fulfilling the conditions by obedience, the glorifying of God; and all this through the ' exceeding loving kindness of Him who hath called us out of darkness into his marvellous light.'"

" However, Sir, this may be," observed Vincent, "there is one passage in John, in which our Saviour says, and his authority must be decisive on this point, that no one can come to God except he is chosen by God, and appointed by him. 'All,' says he, 'that my Father giveth me shall come to me.' And again: ' And this is the Father's will which hath sent me, that of all which he hath given me I should lose nothing, but should raise it up again at the last day.' How understand you this ?"

" Not as you do," answered Alexander. " I remember to have seen an ingenious observation on this very text. The Saviour is speaking of the bread of life, or himself. Which bread of life is sent by the Father, and not one part or tittle of it shall be lost As the Father sent it, it remained with him how to distribute it Those who received this bread, that is, the doctrine and merits of the Saviour, and made the proper use of it, are those whom He will on the last day raise up. That none of this bread might be lost, it was offered to the Gentiles as well as to the Jews, when the latter had refused to accept it"

" It may be so," observed Mr. Deacon; " and by considering two questions, we may also form an opinion contrary to Mr. Vincent's. The first question is, who or what are those, or it, which the Father gives? David supplies something like an answer in the 2d Psalm: 'Ask of me, and I shall give thee the heathen for thine inheritance, and the uttermost parts of the earth for thy possession.' The Father is said to give, because, as the Saviour confessed he came not to do his own, but his Father's will, he is, as the Father, the author of every good and per-fect gift \ and as man by himself could not come to Christ by his own unassisted endeavour, and as the grace of God, assisting him, enables him, in the spirit of 'the honest and good heart,' to come to the Fountain of Life, by means that are offered to him as well as to others, whether they come or not; so is that ability supplied by God: and God, therefore, is the giver of it, whether as received by Man or transferred by Christ. The next question, which indeed we have been all along considering, is, whether the Father gave the Saviour a certain number, who should be saved unconditionally ? Now, this is decidedly at variance with the spirit of the Gospel, and the whole scheme of redemption. It could not be unconditionally, because Judas was one of those given to the Saviour, and yet he fell away. I take it, that the plain meaning of this passage is, that of all those whose ' honest and good hearts,' by the secret, strong, though resistible, grace of God, predisposing them, received the message of salvation as first declared by the Saviour, and then by his Apostles and Gospel; not one of these, thus ' set in order,' or ' ready,' by the Spirit working with them, should fail to come to Jesus, and by believing on him, miss the chance of attaining everlasting life. And why ? Because the promises of God are sure — He cannot lie. Whatever rewards he has proposed, he will confer: and whatever punish-ments he has denounced, he will execute. But in both instances, though it is his pleasure rather to reward than punish, yet he does neither, except according to the deeds of the person thus rewarded or thus punished. Hence they who work well and have striven to ' make their calling and election sure,' are the persons who are appointed for happiness, whilst they who have neglected the means of salvation are appointed for misery. In no other way can I understand Elec-tion and Reprobation; for in no other way, as far as I can comprehend, are these doctrines set be-fore us in the rich treasury of the Scriptures. God has appointed the means, and without his appointment of than, no one could come to life: but these means are plain and ordinary; they compel not, they force not, they are not irresistible: on the contrary, they who duly employ them are said to be drawn by God; and when thus drawn, that is, thus disposed and willing to avail themselves of the appointed means, they eat the bread of life, that is, May hold' on and 'keep' the good way prepared by God, through the unsinning obedience of his Son; and hence they ' will be raised up at the last day,' to share in the glory purchased for them by the Saviour, as they have shared in the 'way of his pilgrimage upon earth.' Instead, therefore, of establishing the personal or partial election of a certain part of mankind to salvation irrespectively and uncondition-ally, it proves, rather, the infinite mercy of God in giving the means of coming to the capability, and the justice of the Son in paying the deficiency of our nature, and the instrumentality of the co-operation of the Holy Spirit in sanctifying those who have faith in this article, and evidence that faith by works of love."

"Come, come, gentlemen," said Eustace, " if I may judge by myself, you have buried us in the profundity of your reasonings; and we see no way of getting to the day-light of explanation again : we have lost our clue, and cannot follow you in the rapid manner you would conduct us onward, and therefore, as you have usurped the female prerogative of talking, you must now make the 'amende honorable' by listening to Marian, who has this morning received a piece of music, that will, I think, be found calculated to give us a notion of Christianity, by its real harmony." "Only on one condition, if you please," said Marian.

"And what is that?"

" That Mr. Deacon would just briefly point out in what way the grace of God enabled one of the characters in his lines to be so superior to the other."

" In doing this," rejoined Mr. Deacon, " my friend Vincent will, I hope, find nothing that jars with his opinions, which, as he has con-scientiously formed them, I respect; as, I trust, for the same reason he does mine.

" ' Set your affections on things above,' said the Apostle: this, by the grace of God, was obeyed by Eliza; it was neglected by Anna. The one, in her attachment to the blessings of earth, felt that this world was not her home, and set her heart upon the place where her best treasure was. When, therefore, afflictions came, the tem-pest descended, but shook her not, because her hope was founded on a rock—the Rock of Ages. This she did by the agency of God's grace, given to her through the merits of the Saviour, and rendered efficacious by her humility and obedience to his commands. You may easily suppose the contrary picture: poor Anna rested all her hopes of happiness upon earthly tilings, and neglected, through love of this world's goods, to remember her Creator, who had given her such dear and interesting objects. When, therefore, these were removed from her, she was like the Philistine temple: the pillars were taken away, and she fell a pitiable ruin, because her foundation was in sand. I will not take upon myself to say how this grace is communicated; whether it is to the soul, and conveyed by the same kind of channel that the air is to the body. This God only knows. It is enough for us to judge by its fruits; and to be thankful, that though sin has abounded, does abound, and will abound, the grace of God has abounded, and does and will much more abound."

Here the discussion ended, — the music was introduced, which finally gave way to other topics of conversation; when the party separated.

THE PENITENT WOMAN.

THE Virgin's offspring, from the Godhead sprung, The Prince of Peace, of whom Isaiah sung,
 The great Messiah, and the Lord of Man,
 Who vow'd Salvation ere the world began,
 Came not from Heav'n an earthly throne to fill,
 Or reign despotic with a Tyrant's will;
 But to reclaim the sinner from his way,
 And urge redemption while it yet was day ;
 To bless his creatures with religious light,
 The deaf with hearing, and the blind with sight;
 To free the tongue from ev'ry captive string,
 That so the dumb might speak aloud and sing;
 To heal the lame, rear up the palsied head,
 Instruct the simple, and awake the dead: —
 Such were the objects of His gracious plan,
 And works of wonder for rebellious man!

This great Physician of the wounded soul,
Whose love and mercy knew no fix'd controul,
Sought not alone for those of high degree,
As objects suited to his charity;
His blest redemption was design'd for all, —
E'en for as many as the Lord shall call.
Here then behold the source of heav'nly light,
So good, so gracious, so supremely bright:
For lo! more splendid than the dazzling sky,
He comes,—the glorious Day-spring from on high!
Oh! hail with transport its benignant gleam;
Catch its reflection from that living stream,
Where may the sinner quench his thirst, and lave
His blackest sins beneath the crystal wave.

As the lone wand'rer, at the close of day,
Catches from far the taper's glimmering ray,
Which lures him onward with its feeble light
To seek repose and comfort for the night, —
A female Penitent, oppressed with shame,
Won by the light of truth, to Jesus came;
By pinching want and poverty undone,
Led on by vice, her youthful race was run:
Too soon, her heart, misguided, fell a prey
To Satan's wiles, and Hell's tyrannic sway.
Yet He, who scans with knowledge unconfined
The latent virtues of the human mind,
And views the faintest and the fairest form
Amid the shadows of the darkest storm,
Could well perceive, and, seeing, well admire
The lively faith his blessings would inspire ;
Could well expect, and hoping, well foresee
The love that yet might spring from misery;

For though polluted by seductive crimes,
Her mind though tainted by corruptive times,
She could discern, howe'er unused to scan,
God's holy finger from the hand of man.
Forlorn, the pilgrim halted on her way;
Wearied with sin she made her God her stay.

And now behold the Messenger of love
Breathing the spirit of his Sire above,
Placed at the table of an earthly host
Whose outward splendours were his proudest boast;
And mark proud Simon's high indignant air,
His sordid spirit and repulsive stare,
When at the feet of his complacent guest
The poor and sinful woman stood confest!
A box of ointment in her hand was borne —
With face averted, and her tresses torn,
Her eyes bedimm'd with many a gathering tear,
And bosom heaving with awaken'd fear,
She came to Christ, and, reckless of the crowd,
Fell on her knees, and, mourning, wept aloud.
Uncheck'd the sigh, and not the tear supprest,
She clasp'd her hands, and smote her aching breast,
With suppliant looks, that spoke an earnest pray'r,
She wash'd his feet, and wiped them with her hair.

As when the traveller, thro' the rainbow's hues
Some chance of guidance from the tempest views,
And hopes the sun its hidden light may send
To cheer him onward to his journey's end, —
So gazed the sinner thro' the varied dye,
The tear-drops, hanging, cast on either eye,
Trusting the mercy of her God would show

Some happier prospect to her hopes below.
'Twas then that Simon, to the Godhead blind,
These vain surmises ponder'd in his mind:

" Is this Messiah ? this the promised ' ROOT,'
" The stock from which ' The BRANCH' is now to shoot ?
" Can this be He, of whom the prophets tell, "
Whose word alone should shake the pow'rs of Hell?
" It cannot be,—for our Messiah knows
" His faithful subjects from rebellious foes ; "
And long ere this had known the tainted part "
Of that vile sinner's vitiated heart;
" Much less had suffer'd her polluted grasp, "
'Presuming thus, his sacred feet to clasp."

These silent dictates of his erring mind
Were not, though secret, to himself confined;
For He, whose knowledge hold's supreme controul,
E'en o'er the breathings of the inmost soul,
Observed the taunts his knitted brow exprest,
And dark suspicion lurking in his breast;
With piercing aspect gazed upon the man,
And thus, in dignified rebuke, began, —
" Simon, behold ! — and then he turn'd his eye,
Survey'd the sinner, and exchanged the sigh, — "
Simon, behold! — Behold this woman here! "
Mark her mute anguish, and that silent tear;
" When first I enter'd this thy splendid hall,
" Thou didst not prostrate at my presence fall,
" Nor e'en didst offer the refreshing wave,
" My parched feet, or e'en my hands to lave;
" But this sad mourner, tho' opprest with fears, "
Here, on her knees, bedews them with her tears;

" Nor had she mourn'd, nor sought me sorrowing here,
" Had not repentance drawn the sorrowing tear.
" I came to open wide Salvation's door
" To those who promise to transgress no more;
" And tho' by waves and worldly tempests tost,
" I seek the sinner, and redeem the lost !"

Oh ye whose hearts can feel another's woes,
And trace the fountain whence compassion flows,
Who, while ye gaze on anguish and despair,
Can bless the wretched, and enforce his pray'r,
Oh! hail repentance and amending grace,
Forget the trespass, and the crime efface.
Here view the sinner, bending to the rod;
And there behold your Saviour and your God!
That Lord of life, that Victor of the grave,
Whose aim with mortals is the will to save;
Whose mercy pleads where justice must reprove,
And calls the wand'rer by the voice of love —
" Woman, rejoice! for in the Courts of Heaven, "
Thy sins, though many, freely are forgiven;
" Thy faith hath saved thee, and shall now restore "
Thy mental peace. — Depart, and sin no more!"

Mark her retiring — mark the bitter sigh,
The heart's repentance cheer'd by victory!
Religion now, with soft persuasive voice,
Becalms her grief, and bids that heart rejoice;
If, then, we see Messiah loves to spare
The contrite sinner, and accept her prayer;
If He primeval nature can restore,
And grief exchange for joys unknown before;
Shall man presume to draw the veil aside,

Remove the screen, and now those sins deride ?
Shall man, presumptuous man! that guilt reveal,
Which Heaven is pleased in mercy to conceal ?
No:— let us learn forgiveness to display,
And what we ask of God, to Man repay!

Oh blest be He! that heavenly King above,
Whose works are mercy, and whose words are love,
Whose kind compassion, with his grace combined, '
Sent forth his Son, the Saviour of mankind!
That blessed Son, of whom the prophets spoke,
Whose lighter burden, and whose easy yoke,
Upheld the wonders of his godly might,
And with the Gospel flash'd immortal light.

What, tho' the pride of man conceives offence,
That He should come such blessings to dispense ?
What, tho' the people whom he came to save
Vain hopes imagine, and so madly rave ?
What, tho' no gorgeous robes his limbs enfold ?
Shall we, like them, our steadfast faith withhold ?
Like them, suppose no sov'reign power can be
Without eternal proofs of majesty ? —
Give place, ye sceptres, and ye vainer things,
The praise of courtiers, and the pomp of kings!
Hence, ye vain symbols of a monarch's right,
From temp'ral weakness turn to heavenly might;
Behold the tokens of the Saviour's power,
Then raise your hands, and bless the awful hour!
Here, in the multitude around, we trace
The' sick restored to all their former grace;
The maim'd are whole; the tortured body stands
Freed from the torments of infernal bands;

Lepers are cleansed; and oh ! our God be praised!
The proof of future life, — the dead are raised ! —

Christians and Men, who fear not hence to go,
To realms of glory by the paths of woe,
Know that in regions of the saints above,
All harmony prevails, all peace and love;
While man's frail nature, in the world below,
Is tempest-tost 'midst wretchedness and woe;
Hence let the paths of righteousness be trod,
And seek, first seek, the kingdom of your God,
And learn from Christ's persuasive words to share
Pleasures, the fruits of watchfulness and prayer;
But lest, frail mortals, his august career
Seem too refined for imitation here;
Lest his consummate virtue seem too high,
And man's united efforts to defy;
Take from the suppliant, trembling in his sight,
A simple pattern, to direct you right;
Behold how He, who while he shows the way
Thro' boundless mercy to the realms of day,
Proves to mankind the blessings He has giv'n,
And makes this sinner guide our steps to heav'n.

Oh! blest be He, who rides in glory high
Upon the cloudy chariot of the sky;
Thro' tracts unknown, and pathways unconfined,
Stalks on the storm, and walks upon the wind:
And yet not heedless of the speck below,
Extends the hand whence plenteous blessings flow.
By his consent the great Redeemer came,
And here on earth proclaim'd his mighty fame;
By his decree the son of Joseph rose,

A prince superior to his kingly foes;
By his acceptance, Christ upon the tree
Held Sin in chains, and set its captives free;
And thus to man, to sinful man, was giv'n
Peace here on earth, and bliss supreme in Heav'n!

See, see how high those glorious orbs appear
', Exalted far above this bounded sphere! —
To such an height God's mercy will extend
To every mortal fearful to offend.
Behold the rising of yon orb of light,
And view its setting at th' approach of night;
So wide the space Messiah has unfurl'd
'Twixt Sin and Death, destruction and the world.
Opposing good to every evil plan,
" He smiles benignant on the race of man"
Who shall describe the pleasure of his mind,
When she, whom Satan had in bonds confined,
Led by contrition, sought his proffer'd grace,
And read forgiveness in her Saviour's face ? —
With what benevolence he hail'd her tears,
Assuaged her sufferings, and allay'd her fears;
And told her frailties, only to display
Her firm repentance, and its gentle sway;
So much he loved in adverse lights to paint
The Sinner, thus contrasted with the Saint.

Woman, for ever blest! by God approved!
By Saints regarded, and by Angels loved, —
'Twas then, fair mortal 1 that thy op'ning mind,
Good, though debased; corrupted, but not blind;
Prompted by feelings of thy earliest youth,
Hearing, embraced the sacred words of truth;

Owning the wonders of Almighty pow'r,
Thou stoodst a penitent that self same hour!
Woman, for ever blest! to thee were giv'n,
E'en while on Earth, the lesser joys of Heav'n:
The streams that flow'd upon thy Saviour's feet;
The balmy incense and the ointment sweet;
The hands then clasp'd to urge the fervent pray'r;
The head that hung to wipe them with its hair,
Were all expressive of thy wond'rous love,
And purchased ransom of thy soul above.

Woman, for ever blest, beyond compare,
For ardent love and soft engaging care;
Where'er the Sun of man's redemption shines,
'Where'er the wicked for his frailty pines;
Where'er salvation and the cross unite,
To show the glories of the Gospel's light:
There shall the tale of this great deed be told,
And with thy sin thy virtues shall unfold.

Long as mankind, by inspiration led,
Shall know that Christ will surely raise the dead;
Long as repentance shall a joy impart,
And bring forgiveness to the contrite heart;
So long, oh woman! shall the world declare,
Thy faith and love, thy penitence and prayer.
All they who mourn shall moderate their grief,
And ask of Heaven its solace and relief;
Sinners, abash'd, shall leave their former ways,
And seek their Saviour with a song of praise,
While e'en the righteous shall attempt to vie
In equal proofs of pure fidelity;
And looking only to reward above,

Shall learn to imitate thy ardent love.
Know then, ye mortals, Christ is ever near,
To yield you courage in the hour of fear.
Could ye on wings of mighty cherubs fly,
And reach the joyful mansions of the sky,
There, on his throne, th' Almighty would ye see, Array'd in all his glorious majesty! —
Could ye submerge to realms of endless night,
Still would the Lord appal your darken'd sight.
Or if on pinions of the morn ye fled
From these terrific dwellings of the dead,
And sought the limits of the farthest sea,
There too, the glory of the Lord would be;
There would his mercy and his love appear,
To wipe the eye, and chace away the tear.
Where'er ye fly, where'er in sorrow roam,
The voice of Christ still calls you to his home;
" Be of good cheer, your sins are hence forgiv'n,
Come share with me eternal joys in Heav'n!"

The contrite sinner, with availing sigh,
Regards her Saviour's soul-subduing eye;
And hears with rapture his inspiring voice
Invite the sad and mournful to rejoice:
" Come unto me, all ye who lowly bear
" The stress of poverty, and weight of care;
"Come unto me, all ye with grief opprest,
"And I, the Lord, will give you peace and rest.
"Oh take my yoke, and learn of me to know,
"That Heav'n is enter'd by the paths of woe.
"Behold how I in meekness can sustain
"A heart made lowly by continued pain;
"And if I suffer, happy should ye be

"To bear such evils as are borne by me.
"Then let not worldly cares distract the mind:
"Be calm, be patient, constant and resigned;
"For inward joy shall ev'ry ill repay,
"Such as the world ne'er gave nor took away.
"Come unto me — my ways shall lead you right,
"My yoke is easy, and my burden light!"

MATRIMONY.

MR. LORRAINE and his daughter had now been returned from their tour about two months, during which time they had received frequent, though short, visits from Arthur Oswald, who was now the avowed and accepted admirer of Maria. Preparations were making for their nuptials, and the day was fixed. All who knew the amiability of her disposition were profuse in their best wishes and congratulations. Among her female friends no one was more sincere in her tributes than Miss Trustwell; and of her male acquaintance her pastor, the good Doctor, was not the least interested in her prospects, which promised so much, both of domestic happiness and public consideration:—he had seen the passion in its bud, and hailed its expansion; he had pledged himself to join their hands, and give them the benediction of the church. He took, therefore, a lively interest in the proceedings, and was frequently referred to for his guiding counsel in the matters now under arrangement'

" My dear young friend," he would say to Miss Lorraine, " my strength seems declining; and I cannot engage, as I have been wont, in the ministration of my ordinary duties, yet I hope from the altar to bestow on you the pious blessing of our common mother; but should I not, be assured that my heart yearns upon you, and, as the venerable Patriarch said, ' Yea, and you shall be blessed.'" The remembrance of his own child, prematurely snatched from him, awakened his thoughts; and he sighed: even at such an hour, when in the decline of life, affection, the affection of a father, nature's purest throb, and Heaven's own reflection, stirred within him!

The day drew nigh,—the joyful lover came; —a select few were met around Mr. Lorraine's hospitable board, and friendship, love, and affection, enhanced the feast There was no envy, — the apple of discord was banished from the dessert,— the olive of peace, and the myrtle of love, entwined in clustering wreaths, shed their genial influence; while hearts meeting hearts, not in " dreams Elysian," but in tempered, chaste, and holy communion, diffused the " sunshine of the breast."

The glowing conversation of the accomplished Oswald, now dilating on passing events, -and now embellishing the more sterling topics of art and science, formed an interesting contrast to the mild demeanor of his lovely fair, who united all the winning softness of her sex with some of the most solid acquirements of human intellect,—that whilst all acknowledged the bright prospect it held out, they simultaneously felt—" Happy, happy, happy pair !"

The evening passed, not as is general in mixed assemblies, which depend for their interest on meretricious events, but in the enjoyment of pleasures which will bear the test of reflection, and the party separated with increased respect for one another, and an additional cause of admiration and thankfulness for the comforts and embellishments of well-regulated society. It would tend greatly to the improvement of many, who place all their ideas of pleasure in sensual pursuits, and mistake the corrupted inclinations of their nature, (rendered still more vitiated by their own depravity,) for the gift of God, and therefore to be indulged in, to witness scenes like this; where the good things of the world are used as Heaven in-tended ; where reason is tempered by religion, and wit subjected to the guidance of intelligence, and the sublime acquisitions of the human mind made subservient to the noblest purposes which either dignify man or show forth the glory of God. There, under the direction of Religion, " whose ways are pleasantness, and whose paths are peace," rational beings used their reason, not for a cloak of licentiousness, like too many, alas ! in these our days, but for the manifest and noble purpose of fulfilling that voice of God, which announced to a sinful world the rising of the Sun of Salvation, whose beams irradiate and warm all " those who sit in the valley of the shadow of death."

On the following day, Oswald, seizing a fa-vourable opportunity, made his way to the Rectory, with the view of enjoying a little private conversation with the Doctor. He had the good fortune to find him alone and disengaged.

" My dear Sir," said the lover, as he entered the library, " I am particularly glad to find you unoccupied, as I am desirous of consulting you upon a matter of conscience, and I know your disposition to combine the character of the friend with that of the divine. You know that not many months ago, I was, in respect of Religion, a reasoning infidel; and that Heaven, in its due season, has enabled me to throw off the film of prejudice, and to open my eyes to a better understanding of the ' things that belong to my peace.' Need I say how much your counsel aided the circumstances which Providence has thrown in my way, to make me pause in the pursuit of a system which I vainly fancied right? The charms of my dear Maria wrought upon me like a spell; the sweetness of her disposition, the amiability of her actions, the tenderness of her affections, all modulated and attuned by the hand of Christianity, carried conviction to a heart, that bowed to her influence with gladness, and that now vibrates with gratitude, because, in receiving her silken chains of reciprocal attachment, I have thrown off a yoke which must ultimately have crushed me to the ground.

" Whilst my heart glows with the feelings of love, I cannot suppress the tribute of thankfulness, that whilst thousands are madly pursuing where desire leads, and, in the spirit of infatuation, submitting to the corrupted dictates of their inclinations, as implicitly as if the voice of passion were the voice of God, I have been enabled to own the influence of a better and more holy guidance. Though I have used my endeavours to make myself conversant with all that a ' Christian ought to know to his soul's health,' yet from the short space of time that I have been able to bestow upon my religious duties, as enforced in the Word of God, and in what I consider the best comments upon it, the Formularies and Doctrines of your Church, there are necessarily many things in which I am greatly deficient. From the time since my union with Miss Lorraine was fixed on, I have been much occupied in making arrangements that have in some degree abstracted me from more serious considerations. There is one topic on which I am anxious to have your guiding counsel. The office of Marriage, as performed in your Church, may be, and, I dare say is, founded on the best principles. I have not had sufficient leisure to canvass them; and as I am a Christian only upon conviction, I beg you will give me such information as you can on this subject, more particularly as to-morrow I am to be an interested party in its celebration. Do you consider Marriage as a civil or religious obligation? I know that in Greece and Rome it was a matter of policy rather than any thing else, and was regulated, not, only in its performance but its obligations, by the magistrates. In both these countries, Marriage was instituted as much to repress wild and irregular passions, which, as numbers increased, tended to gender dissentions and dangers, as to promote civilization. The gods were reverenced in some measure, particularly by the Greeks, in this ceremony; but when we consider how this reverence was made instrumental to designs political as well as moral, we cannot infer much from that. I speak now as one who is yet a stranger to the grounds of this institution, merely for the sake of having the benefit of your opinions, which, I am well aware, will be raised upon the best foundation. Do you then, I repeat, consider Marriage as a civil or religious obligation ?"

" To answer your question satisfactorily," said the Doctor, " I must first know what sense you attach to these words,—civil and religious."

" By the former," continued Oswald, " I un-derstand something that is more properly under the management and direction of public officers, appointed for the internal government of a state or people, built upon moral rectitude or the general advantage: by the latter, I understand that which appertains to the worship due to the Great Supreme, distinct and separate from worldly considerations, and worldly customs."

" I have, then," said the Doctor, "no hesitation in asserting that Marriage is a religious obligation; and for this reason, because it was instituted by God himself."

" Yes, Sir," interrupted Oswald, " and so was the abstinence from theft, idola-try, fornication, and covetousness. Are they then reli-gious obligations ?"

" Only," replied the Doctor, " when they are the result of religious motives. I consider it possible for a man, without any regard for the honour or glory of God, through a sense either of their intrinsic comeliness or from an idea of their being advantageous to him in his worldly dealings, to do these things, and in so doing he would be morally good; but he could not be said to have been actuated to perform them from religious considerations, though the actions themselves are enjoined by God himself. Marriage, I consider, rests for its obligation upon a somewhat different footing. The duties you allude to are written in the law of nature; so too, you may say, is Marriage. I say, No, at least not as understood by Christians. Natural duties are simple acts interwoven so closely in our daily experience, that they constitute the connected and multiplied succession of the various events of our life. But not so Marriage— instituted by God when he gave to Adam the woman, whom he had previously taken from his side, to be a help meet for him — it receives additional sanction from the allusion to the sanc-tity of it, to be found in different parts of the Scripture. The moral actions to which you allude received their obligation as laws from the sinfulness of man; whereas Marriage was ' instituted by God in Paradise, in the time of man's innocency!' If they then be pure, how much rather the obligation of this ought to be considered as binding upon man, since it was ordained for him, when his mind was untainted, his passions unknown, his life innocent, his peace unruffled, God for his director, and angels his companions. As it was an institution of innocence; so, when perfect innocence was lost, it was designed as a remedy against sin, and for the mutual comfort, support, and endearment of those who, following the impulse of the best affections, ' reverently, discreetly, advisedly, soberly, and in the fear of God,' take this ' holy estate' in hand. The sanctity of this is more strongly enforced by the representation St Paul makes of the union between man and woman being typical of the ' union between Christ and his Church,' and the ' union between the head and the members in a natural body.' Now there is nothing in civil polity, however grounded on the basis of morality, which can bear any analogy with so. sacred an union, as Marriage does to the Church of Christ Because, before civil policy existed, and before the sin of man called out for the promulgation of laws, the fulfilment of which constitutes morality, Marriage received, even at the very dawn of creation, the sanction of Heaven and the blessing of the great Artificer of the Universe. Who then shall, say that Marriage is a civil dealing ? Or who, still more audaciously perverse, shall presume to deny altogether the obligation, the necessity, the holiness of this primitive institution ! You must remember what the immortal poet has said, —

' Hail, wedded Love ! mysterious law, true source
Of human offspring, sole propriety
In Paradise, of all things common else!
By thee adult'rous lust was driv'n from men,
Among the bestial herds to range; by thee
(Founded in reason, loyal, just, and pure)
Relations dear, and all the charities
Of father, son, and brother, first were known.'"

" Enough, my dear Sir," said Oswald: " I see sufficient to quiet any scruples I had of the purity and obligation of Matrimony. Give me next your ideas of the construction and general nature of the service, as performed in the Church."

" Our service is modelled upon that of the early Christians, who are said to have received it from the Apostles themselves. The contracting of the parties, the performance of the ceremony in the Church, the blessings pronounced by the minister, the praises and thanksgivings offered up to the throne of Goodness,— all, all, performed as they are in the spirit and words of Holy Scripture,—must, in those who have any sense of religious feeling, produce an effect full of goodly instruction."

" I admit," replied Oswald, " there is much solemnity in the ceremony, and, I dare say, it is modelled upon the best usages. Perhaps, if I might trespass still further upon your valuable time, you would enter rather more minutely into the different parts of it"

" In the first place, then," said the Doctor, " you will observe, by referring to the service, (here Oswald took up a Prayer-book,) that the parties, having first obtained due permission from the Church, and being placed before the altar, which on this, and every other occasion, in which it is used, may truly be called, the Altar of Love, they are informed of the nature, institution, and duties of the obligation they are about to take upon them. They are then, in the most solemn and impressive manner, called upon to declare most sacredly, that there is no impediment why they should not be joined to-gether. Their free consent and willingness are then respectively asked and declared, in language and terms so plain and intelligible, that the meanest comprehension may understand them. These terms are carefully selected from Scripture, and surely no one can make any objection to them. Then comes the giving away of the spouse by her father. This is also founded on the most established custom. God, the common Father, gave Eve to Adam; and in all nations the authority of the father, or of his legitimate successors, was necessary to sanction the transfer to the husband of the power and influence hitherto exercised • by the natural guardians. In this is acknowledged the husband's superiority, and the wife's consequent dependance upon him. In the same way that Christ is the head of his spouse, the Church; and the husband is accordingly bound to be as tender, as watchful, and as affectionate to his bride, as the Saviour is to his Church. Then is given that symbol of eternity, that seal of fidelity, the ring. And here I must remark, that as all things are under the disposal of the Most High, and as every thing we do. ought to be done to the glory of God, so is the ring first laid upon the Prayer-book, to show that we acknowledge our Almighty Father as the Giver of all goodness, and to submit ourselves in this to his gracious Providence to bless us in this ordinance, which in this part especially binds us in an indissoluble knot The ring is returned to the man, and he puts it on the finger of the bride as a token and pledge of union, and pronounces a few words, which bind him most solemnly to perform the duties required of him, as a Christian and a man. He pledges himself to pay due attention, honour, and love to his wife; for such is the meaning implied in the term *worship*. ' He made man a little lower than the angels, to crown him with glory and *worship,*' says the Psalmist. In which place ' worship' means nothing more than honour.' This word, it appears, was on the point of being altered in the time of Charles II. for the word ' honour,' which, thus understood, would imply respect founded upon love. 'With my body I thee worship,' conveys, therefore, no idea of personal idolatry, which would be quite inconsistent with the spirituality of the Christian faith, and could not be uttered without blasphemy. It is to be understood as meaning only an acknowledgment, that as their union is founded in affection, the woman is to be honoured by the man in such a way as is most consistent for him to conduct himself towards her, ' giving honour to her as to the weaker vessel:' not looking upon her as an indifferent object of his esteem, but as one who is now ' bone of his bone and flesh of his flesh;' one whom he ought to love, as Christ loves the Church; one for whom he ought to have as great regard as he has for his own members; because, says the Apostle, ' he that loveth his wife loveth himself: for no man ever yet hated his own flesh, but nourisheth and cherisheth it, even as the Lord the Church.' After the man has thus pledged to pay ' honour where honour is due,' he further engages to impart to her a due share of his worldly substance, for the same reason that he promises her his personal attention and love: and this he confirms in the name of the blessed Trinity, by which he entails upon himself an obligation, which he may not break, without perjuring himself before that God, who created woman to be his ' help meet,' and gave him ' all things richly to enjoy.' The minister next prays for them, and supplicates that God before whose altar they have pledged themselves, and whose name they have invoked to ratify their vows, to give them grace to perform their promises, and live as becomes those who are not two but one, and who in this new character are daily reminded of the interest they have respectively in the Bridegroom, whose marriage-feast they one day hope to partake of with oil in their vessels, and decked in the marriage garment They are then publicly declared to be ' man and wife together, in the name of the Father, and of the Son, and of the Holy Ghost.' The blessing of Almighty God is then imprecated. The remainder of the service, whilst it reminds them of the honour and glory to be given to God, and thus operates as a check for them not to ' set their affections on things below,' sets forth their respective duties, with admonitions and exhortations that breathe the language of Holy Writ, and are calculated to encourage the genuine spirit of Christianity, 'glory to God, and peace and good will to man.' I have thus cursorily gone through this solemnity, that you may consider whether there be any thing unsatisfactory, or any point you wish to be farther amplified ?"

" None, Sir, I assure you," replied Oswald.

" I have then only to say," observed the Doctor, " and that I do in truth and sincerity,' may you experience the full extent of the Spartan's confession—' I have left the worse and found the better.' "

Oswald extended his hand,—a warm pressure bespoke his thanks; and with looks full of ani-mated intelligence, and beaming with purest affection, he said, —

" I trust you will feel yourself able, my dear Sir, to perform the ceremony, as Maria attaches so much to the hope she entertains of being married by one whom, of all others, she so highly venerates; and, permit me t6 add, that, with a regard not less strong, though not so long established, I entertain the same feelings on this, as on every other point with her,"

" My dear friend," replied the Doctor, " I am well assured of the sincerity with which you speak your own and your Maria's sentiments. Believe me, no ordinary impediment shall prevent my having the gratification of uniting your hands as firm-ly as you have your hearts: I hope I may answer for my ability to do this, as the time fixed upon is so very near at hand."

This promise was made good, for the following morning found the Doctor in the full habiliments of his order, ready at the altar to receive the happy pair. Here their whole demeanour evinced a sense of the obligation they were taking upon them; there was every mark of polished urbanity becoming their station in the world, unmixed with ostentation, and unclogged by parade. Whilst Oswald's coun-tenance spoke ' unutterable things,' and Maria's was suffused with the lovely blush of maiden innocence, there beamed from each the pure ray which emanates alone from hearts that feel and acknowledge religion as a governing principle; — hence, when called upon to give their troth, there was no affected shyness, no froward indifference ; they looked, they manifested the simplicity of innocence, height-ened by the consci-ousness of feelings which are neither elated by triumph, nor depressed by difficulties. In them was fully pourtrayed the picture so beautifully sketched by Thomson: —

" O happy they! the happiest of their kind!

Whom gender stars unite, and in one fate
Their hearts, their fortunes, and their beings blend.
'Tis not the coarser ties of human laws,
Unnatural oft, and foreign to the mind,
That binds their peace, but harmony itself,
Attuning all their passions into love;
Where friendship full exerts her softest power,
Perfect esteem, enliven'd by desire
Ineffable, and sympathy of soul;
Thought meeting thought, and will preventing will,
With boundless confidence: for nought but love
Can answer love, and render bliss secure.'

Oswald felt the reality of what Campbell has so glowingly bodied forth in his bright dreams -of Hope: —

" And say, without our hopes, without our fears,
Without the home that plighted love endears,
Without the smile from partial beauty won,
Oh! what were man ? — a world without a sun!"

The party, accompanied by the Doctor, now on their return to Mr. Lorraine's house, were met by Mr. Deacon on his way to the Vestry, followed by three other couples, votaries of Hymen, who having accomplished the three weeks' probation which the publication of their banns required, impatiently awaited the legal union of their hands. These were accompanied by their respective friends, dressed, like themselves, in their best attire; but with a total contempt of all harmony of colour, and a laudable disregard to the quality and structure of their garb. They were of a description so common, that their examples might serve as specimens of those who daily resorted to the altar for the same purpose. The first couple that presented themselves was an elderly decent-looking man, clad in a stout, striped, buff-coloured waistcoat, very thick corderoys, and - an upper garment, that might either serve as an ordinary or as an extraordinary coat, according to the state of the weather. His bride was a fleshy, red-faced, middle-aged woman, who had long been his house-keeper, attended by a sheepish-looking man, as old as the bridegroom, and who appeared either as if he had already entered into the state of matrimony under similar circumstances, or meditated doing so: while the companion of the bride resembled in form, figure, and countenance, the bride herself. The next couple was a simple-looking youth, of vacant appearance, with a many-coloured silk handker-chief tied around his neck, terminating in a large projecting bow, the ends of which were affixed to his neck by a large gilt buckle that had formerly been the appendage of a square-toed shoe. He was accompanied by a ruddy-faced female of large dimensions, who carried in her countenance a gaiety of heart, and a thoughtlessness of every thing beyond the present moment: they were attended by others, both young and old, who contemplated little more than the pleasures of a day to be devoted to festivity. The last couple were of a very different cast; both young, and both very serious: they seemed as if impelled by uncontrollable circumstances to take a step which neither contemplated with satisfaction, and this opinion seemed confirmed by the demeanor of those who attended them. As soon as the preliminary enquiries had been made, these were led out together by the Clerk, and assembled around the altar, who, when he arranged them in due order, returned to attire the Curate, and to usher him to his station. Before, however, the solemnity commenced, the Clerk whispered into the ears of the several brides the necessity for taking off their gloves: this was an operation of some difficulty, for from the degree of nervousness ; and the fever of the frame often excited to a great extent in these trying moments of existence, the long cotton-gloves which are buried in the profundity of the sleeves of gowns and spencers, from their obstinate tenacity to the flesh, can only be re-moved by the dint of persevering exertion, and at the expence of divers inelegant distortions of the countenance. During the time spent in these preparations, the up-per part of the Church had been filled by all those vagrant persons who, at such times and at no other, repair to witness a ceremony for which they have no rever-ence; but impelled by curiosity and worse motives, they come to put to confusion those whom, in the excess of their idleness, they wish to annoy. Over these the Sexton kept a partial controul, which was only made perfect by the appearance of the Curate, who, from his firmness of conduct, never sub-mitted to any interrup-tion in the discharge of his ministerial functions. The nature and object of the sacred institution being read, the Curate advanced towards the first couple, who, to his separate questions touching their mutual consent to be joined, received answers from both in a sort of half whisper, as if afraid either to hear their own voices, or to make them audible to others. The same was now repeated to the second couple, who returned their answers in a stifled laugh, which called forth an admonition from the Curate. And when the same questions were put to the third couple, the eyes of both were cast down in profound dejection, until they declared their assent in a deep-drawn sigh, and by casting their eyes upwards, to the great detriment of their eye-balls, which had well nigh disappeared altogether. The feeling Curate, struck by their manner, paused until they recovered their ordinary appearance, when he quietly asked them if the marriage now about to be solemnized had their entire concurrence, and was free from every sort of restraint ? They simply replied, " We are agreed;" and at this moment the Clerk, catching Mr. Deacon's eye, told him by a very intelligent, but silent signal, to proceed. He therefore returned again to the first couple, and thence to the others, to receive and give their hands, and to direct them in giving the troth by a mutual stipulation. The youth and his giddy bride here received a second admonition, accompanied with a threat to proceed no further in the service, but upon the express condition of their manifesting a behaviour more suited to the occasion, and to the place in which they were assembled. This rebuke was conveyed in a manner so serious, that it created evident discomfiture in the parties; while the bride's maids on the one hand, and the bridegroom's com-panions on the other, taking the alarm, twitched and elbowed their friends into something like apprehension, and all proceeded on reverently: . The decent-looking man was now called upon to produce the ring; but for this he referred to the bride, who, after some rifling of her pocket, began to empty the contents of it into the hands of her maid, in search of the precious trinket. She gradually disburdened herself, by first taking out a large bunch of keys; then a black spotted handkerchief, a huswife, a pair of scis-sors, a brass thimble, and a pincushion; then various pieces of ginger and sealing-wax, a quantity of brown paper, a lot of halfpence, and a nutmeg-grater; and, at last, a little red-coloured wooden box, the lid of which being unscrewed with a noise that set the Curate's teeth on edge, she drew from a motley collection of silver money the valuable token, which the object of her affections now took and placed upon her hand; but whether from fear or confusion, or from the heat of the weather, her fingers, which resembled a bunch of overgrown radishes, were so swollen, that it required all the robust violence of the bridegroom, and all the silent-suffering patience of the bride, to submit to the operation of having this symbol of eternity fixed upon the root of that finger which it seemed destined never to quit The youth was next called upon to perform the same; when he began to feel first in one pocket, and then in another. He now turned both waistcoat-pockets inside out; next those of his trowsers underwent . the same scrutiny; and here alarm and con-fusion seized both, while it was all the Curate could contrive, by a more than ordinary austerity of manners, to keep the spectators quiet. Again were the several pockets rifled, and even those of the coat were submitted to the closest inspection. The Curate was about taking off a mourning ring from his own finger to lend to the now disconsolate pair, at the same time that the Sexton was feeling in his own pocket for the key of the Church door for the same purpose, when a little brown paper packet was suddenly discovered on the pavement, near the place where the party stood; this was triumphantly recognized, and after divers undoublings, and the unpeeling of a nest of wrappers, the lost treasure was found. But here another difficulty arose, from the circumstance of the bride having had the misfortune to lose that finger to which the wedding-ring is invariably appended: one, therefore, had been procured to fit the corre-ponding finger of the other hand; when the father of the bride submitted, that the marriage not being solemnized according to the very letter of the Rubric, might not be considered altogether valid. This objection was at length overruled by Mr. Deacon's ordering the token and pledge to be placed on the little finger of the left hand, for which, however, it was unfortunately too large; and the difficulty did not even now seem likely to be surmounted by this adaptation, until the worthy Curate, to satisfy the prejudices of all the parties, (for all of them now took an interest in the affair,) read that portion of the Rubric which directs that the ring should be placed on the fourth finger of the left hand; then telling the bridegroom to count four, reckoning the thumb as the first, he came, in the existing order of things, to the little finger as the fourth, on which the ring was hung, being previously bent out of its circular form that it might retain its hold. And now the last couple, having all things in readiness, performed the same act, accompanied by deep-drawn sighs from the one, and a shower of pearly tears plentifully distilled from the closed eyes of the other. Mr. Deacon again stood astonished, and again addressing himself to the parties, he asked them whether there was not some mistake, hinting the probability of there being a misconception of what they had to perform, as it was the solemnity of a funeral, and not the ceremony of a marriage, that usually excited the feelings which they had manifested. He obtained, however, no other answer than sighs and tears; when the Clerk, craning out his neck over the altar-rails to a prodigious extent, like the opening of a telescope, whispered to him, that "all was right." He proceeded, therefore, in the duty, and then accompanied the several parties into the Vestry to sign the register.

The decent-looking man now put on a pair of spectacles, which, by griping the extremity of his nose, assumed an erect position; turning his tongue a long way out at the extremity of his mouth, and curling it in the direction of his left ear, he grasped the pen in a huge unbending hand, and after some toil and turmoil subscribed his name. His bride now taking the same implement, as if it had been the handle of a toasting-fork, into her left hand, that she might the better place it between the thumb and forefinger of the other, and having in the operation squirted all the ink upon the book, commenced the labour of graving her maiden address; when laying the vacant hand upon the undried signature of her consort, after an interval of some minutes, accomplished, in the palsied perturbation of her nervous system, the point of having drawn, in a sort of Chaldee character, her Christian name; then returning the pen into the hand of the Curate, she declared her inability to do more, for that she was " all over in a twitter." It was, therefore, completed by proxy; and being attested by their witnesses, the couple, instead of quitting the Church together, now separated, the men issuing from one door, and the women from another, to avoid the observations of the multitude without. The second party, who had commenced the ceremony with so much gaiety, seemed likely to end it in a very different manner. Their companions and attendants, some of whom were not the youngest, had conceived the circumstances of the ring to be of an ominous and unpropitious nature. They bad understood that a vein, pro-ceeding directly from the heart, terminated in the fourth finger of the left hand, on which account that member had been chosen as that to which the pledge of matrimony was to be affixed, and consequently that none other could be substituted in its place; and what was not of a less alarming import, the ring, in this instance, had been distorted from its circular form, so emblematic of constancy, into another as inconvenient as it was ill-omened and unseemly.

"My friends," said the Curate, witnessing their dismay, " I commonly find ill-timed levity accompanied by a corresponding portion of serious discomfiture; and I must say, that the giddiness you have so recently and unseasonably manifested deserves a check. However, as I trust your hilarity has proceeded more from thoughtlessness than intentional misbehaviour, let me assure you, for your satisfaction, that the opinion to which you have alluded respecting a vein issuing from the heart, and extending to this finger, is altogether erroneous, being none other than a vulgar mistake, the truth of which, any person at all versed in the science of anatomy will corroborate: no, the choice of this member, in particular, has been made from the consideration, that of all the fingers, this, while it is the most conspicuous, is the least used, and, therefore, the better adapted to the preservation of this token of such a sacred union; and with respect to the ring itself, I have no doubt, if you make the request, the Clerk here will change it for another of a less size, and a more perfect form."

This was no sooner mentioned, than the Clerk, taking a small drawer out of his writing-desk, produced a variety of the articles in request, and immediately suited the bride, having enter-ed into an assurance, that the ring exchanged was of the purest metal, and therefore a fit symbol of the generous, sincere, and durable affection that ought to subsist between those now joined together in holy matrimony. Happiness was again restored, and a smile brightened the countenances of the party, which spread to the face of the Curate himself, when he saw the bridegroom, now thrusting his hand into a pocket extending from his hip to his knee, buried his arm in the profundity of it, in search of his money, asking, at the same time, the Clerk, who held out his hand to receive the fees, — " Pray, Sir, what may be the *damage* ?"

No sooner had this pair and their attendants disappeared together, than the remaining couple came forward to sign the book.

" My friends," said Mr. Deacon, " I have felt much uneasiness on your account; but I trust, as you commenced with so much apparent uuhappiness, you will now complete the contract with real emotions of joy. What is it that can have occasioned you these sorrowful feelings?"

" Sir," replied the man, " we do not enter into vulgar and worldly feelings in the performance of this ceremony; we marry not for this world's comfort, but for that which will be hereafter; we are here united, not from terrestrial, but heavenly considerations;"— and as he uttered these words, his eyes were fixed upon , the ceiling, and his hands clasped, more like a lover making protestations to the un-complying object of his affections, than one who had actually obtained the hand of a fair maiden in marriage.

During the time thus passed by Mr. Dear con in his duties, Oswald and his bride, accompanied by the Doctor, had reached Mr. Lorraine's house, and received those usual compliments of their assembled friends, which, in this case at least, deserve a better name: it might be said, the dictates of the heart, glowing with grati-fication, and winged with wishes untaught, were interchanged. The Doctor, now seated on an easy chair, with his eyes lighted up with more than usual brightness, thus addressed the happy couple :—

" My dear young friends! hear the words of one whose sand is nearly run, and who has experienced both joy and sorrow, happiness and affliction. I began life with ardent expectations:' my heart beat in unison with one . whose many virtues excited hopes that were soon blasted by the dullness of death; but the memory of them still lives, in dear and honoured characters. I lost my wife, I gained a child,— one, in whom was imaged the dear picture of my lost Emily, and one, who, alas! too, like her, in early life followed her mother to the house appointed for all liv-ing. To-morrow completes the five-and-twentieth year since my Emily was called hence. God only knows, whether, on that day, ' my soul may be required of me.' But why do I mention these things? Why throw over this day of brightness, the cloud of darkness ? Why infuse into the cup of pleasure the ingredient of woe? Why self-ishly talk of my sufferings, when your hopes are burning with fondest anticipations

? It is, my young friends, to teach you, that life, however its morning rises with sunshine, is liable to continual glooms, and obnoxious to encroaching clouds. It is to warn you against indulging, what, indeed, is natural, in the hope of uninterrupted happiness. How kindly affectionate soever you may be, however well disposed to promote mutual comfort, you must not expect to pass your days without being the cause of some pang to one another, or dimming, though transiently, the mirror of one another's joy. Besides this, which will sometimes happen, (and well for us that it does,) there are and will be rougher and more unyielding monitors, that will convince you of the futility of allowing earthly joys to engross all your attention, or make you believe that this world is your home. We need all the trials and afflictions which we have to encounter, to wean us from unsubstantial pursuits, and engage , us more heartily in the service of that Sovereign who claims our duty from the cradle to the grave, and of this you are put in mind when you repeat till " death us do part." There is no true happiness but in Religion. Where it is the directing star, all other en* joyments are incalculably enhanced. Never, then, forget who and what you are, and for what purpose you were born. Let not the comforts of your happy condition sensualize your hearts: rather, whilst they burn with affection, ripened and mellowed by a con-tinued reciprocation of- domestic duties, let them also burn, as the disciples' at Emmaus, with that flame which derives its influence and effect from your Saviour, and which, under God's grace, depends for its continuance on your own exertions. Oswald, your hand; cherish, as you have sworn, this lovely plant — shield her from rougher cares, but exclude her not from your inmost self:—support, direct, love her!" — Maria, your hand; secure your husband's affections by gentleness, by confidence, by deference, by affection. Heaven bless you, my children! Be good, be religious, be happy!" — His voice faltered; nature was too powerful for his strength—the image of his dear child floated before him — his eyes were upraised to Heaven; they seemed to be calling down blessings — his lips faintly whispered, " God bless you both." ---- He stretched forth his hand, — he beckoned farewell, — and he left the apartment as Mr. Deacon entered it; who, having attended him to the Rectory, re-turned, at the Doctor's solicitation, to join the party. His words sank deep into the hearts of Arthur and Maria Oswald. In the hour generally devoted to the luxuriant ebullitions of youthful enthusiasm, they felt, that the ' web of life is of a mingled yarn, good and ill together,' —and they mutually acknowledged, that however dear to each other, they placed their hopes of happiness in their union, only as it might tend to stir up within them lively feelings of Religion; without which, in vain had their faith been plighted, their hands joined, blessings imprecated, and admonitions given.

THE RECTOR'S DEATH.

CHANGE of air and scenery, the excitement of travelling, of society and new objects, and re-laxation from ordinary pursuits, though, in their several ways, they tended to give a temporary stimulus to the mind, and thence dissipated thoughts of the debility of the body, failed to produce that alteration and amendment which could alone yield a permanent stay to the life of the venerable Rector. Outwardly he seemed to combat with the weakness of his body, and with those infirmities which, though not apparent to other eyes, he felt were gradually getting advantage of him. He knew the nature of the struggle in which he was engaged, and the power of the enemy that assailed him; he had, therefore, long secretly armed himself to meet the foe in the only way that man can engage him, — by submitting to his power for a season, in the assurance of gaining, by an all-conquering arm, final conquest — by making preparation for a change — by intercession through the Redeemer of mankind to the Throne of Grace — by " setting his house in order," knowing that he must " die, and not live." The Doctor had some time passed what is called " the grand climacteric," when he was seized by a second attack of paralysis, which had now deprived him of the use of his limbs, and the utterance of speech. This befel him on the evening of a day that had been particularly devoted to retirement and reflection. It was a day that never passed without being dedicated to religious contemplation; — it was that on which a beloved wife had been suddenly removed by the inscrutable decrees of Providence, leaving the void, which her loss had made, to be filled by another to whom life had been given at the ex-pence of her own ; and yet that second object of endearment, that representative and possessor of all his earthly affections, had been untimely snatched away, leaving the afflicted survivor, as it were, alone upon the earth.

His excellent Curate had for some time perceived a serious change in the health of his friend and Rector. He had, with deep sensibility, observed his memory impaired, and his faculties clouded; and though he had watched him with unceasing attention, he did so without betraying suspicion of his fears. He had made repeated visits, daily, to the Rectory on some pretence or other of consulting upon matters connected with the duties of the parish, and under further pretence for prolonging his visits, continually consulted works in the library, from which he read and made extracts; and by such means he contrived to become the constant guardian of his sinking friend, without giving him cause to suspect his object. But upon this day, knowing the good Doctor's habit of abstaining from any participation of his usual avocations, and of denying himself to every visitor, he refrained from trespassing upon his retirement; so that with the malady upon him, without the physical power to bear up his mind, either by deriving consolation from it, or by diverting the current of his thoughts, the latent disease seized upon its victim, and left him a wreck, the shell of a vessel once so majestic and so well manned; one, that had sailed so long upon the ocean of life, superior to the storms it had encountered; one, that had been triumphantly buoyed upon the troubled surface of existence, despite the perils of the deep, and having now answered the highest purposes of its destination, lay on the sand dismasted, the surf pertinaciously endeavouring to snatch it from the beach to submerge it in the profundity of its element

The hand of Providence had been laid by this affliction on the Doctor, as he sat in his library late on the evening of the day we have mentioned. His old servant, much beyond the usual time, had been waiting for his master's summons to attend him to his chamber, when at length hie determined, under some trifling pretence, to hint his own impatience to retire to rest With his candlestick in one hand, and the slippers in the other, honest John, (for so the Doctor called him,) having previously thrown down the snuffers in the passage as a preliminary announcement of his coming, gently opened the library door, when, to his infinite amazement, he saw his master extended helpless on the floor. The poor fellow, horrified, made the most violent discovery of his alarm, which speedily brought the assistance of all who were within hearing; and no time was lost in carrying the sufferer to his bed, in summoning the attendance of Mr. Deacon, and in calling in the aid of the faculty.

The first who obeyed this sudden call was the good Curate, who took upon himself the direction of every thing connected with the interest, welfare, and comfort of his venerable friend. He ordered ah adjoining apartment to be prepared for himself, and resolved not to quit the house until the Rector were either relieved by some material alteration for the better, or, if it were the will of Heaven, until he were reprieved by death.

Several days elapsed before the worthy Pastor regained sufficient power of utterance to make himself understood; at length, though he gra-dually spoke with more ease, his conversation was laboured and disjointed, and kept up with every apparent difficulty. After a few weeks had passed over, he remained nearly in the same situation; his utterance, indeed, more distinct and free, but with his faculties impaired, and his limbs benumbed. During all this time Mr. Deacon had never left him, but at a few short intervals to discharge those various little duties which the kindness and assiduity of friends could not execute. Nothing could exceed the strength of that feeling for the infirmities of his friend; nothing, the fervour of that disinterested concern—that deep-rooted sympathy—that melancholy regret for the decay of a mind lately so strong and active, a body so firm and vigorous,—as was manifested in the outward demeanor, and the many proofs of internal suffering, of this excellent young man. He saw that the physician's aid was vain that disease walking in darkness had entered, without noise, the mansion of mortality; that, in silence, the hand of pain had struck a staggering blow, from the effect of which experience could give no consolation, philosophy was confounded, and art was baffled. All this had been seen by the sufferer himself, who had already considered his end approaching, and had therefore brought his mind to regard the gathering storm of disease as the summons issued by his God to call him to a better state ; and long had he leaned upon an Almighty arm to support a mind vigorous with trust, and warm with devotion, though now encompassed with bodily infirmity. " Seven times a day," it might be said in the language, and after the pattern, of the pious son of Jesse, did the worthy Rector join in fervent prayer with his sympathizing companion; and, at other times, how seasonably did this ministering friend throw in those just and holy reflections, which, while they inspired hopes of a future acceptance, created consolation and composure of mind, the result of a well-disposed heart throbbing with aspirations after that state, " whither Christ himself is gone before."

Human frailty is never so well understood as in the contemplation of the sufferings of man* kind; the instability of our nature never so forcibly felt as when we visit the bed of sickness. Go to the couch of the sick and dying man, whose heart is fixed upon his God, and offer him all the idols which worldly men worship: talk to him of fame, and he heeds it not; show him beauty, and he disregards it; wealth, and he despises it; pleasure, and he loathes it! Bring before him instruments which invest him with unlimited powers, lay the crown and sceptre at his feet, and see if you can beguile him of a minute's agony; or, now the hand of death is upon him, whether you can check his anxiety to go on in his search of that better country, where there await him joys permanent, and unchangeable as the God he adores.

The truth of this was never more strongly exemplified that) in the instance before us. This " Man of God" had now accomplished the pilgrimage of life: he had in his journey seen every variety of woe; much he had himself felt; more, by the ministration of his sacred functions, he had relieved; yet he had kept the even tenor of his way, turning neither to the right hand, from any motive to avoid the inconveniences that met him, nor to the left, from a desire to reach his destination by an unfrequented, though shorter, path. Religion was ever his invisible guide; and to whatever object she pointed it was his aim to aspire, and his determination, under all hazards, to obtain. The joys of life, though no one relished them more, never raised him into transport; and the evils that befel him, never plunged him into gloom arid despondency: he knew by whose appointment these things came, for experience had taught him how transitory are sublunary ills and pleasures; and though he possessed a heart peculiarly susceptible, and endowed with the most refined sensibility, and consequently indifferent to nothing; yet his mind took into its comprehensive view only such objects as led him to prosecute his way to something more substantial and durable. In early life he was full of vigour and expectation, traversing the fields of literature, and culling from every flower that flourished in them the latent sweets with which it was stored; He formed acquaintances and connections with the good and virtuous, and was the theme of common praise: ever cheerful, ever gay, but, at the same time, ever mindful of the end for which he was destined, he passed the morn of life untouched in virtue, unblemished in reputation. In middle life, the cares of the world had accumulated upon him, and his connection with mortality was strengthened by additional ties of domestic and public affection; but in every department of life, he exhibited the same fortitude, the same regard for futurity, the same love of religion, and the same natural cheerfulness. His domestic sorrows and afflictions struck a blow which staggered the outward, while it invigorated the inner, man. His feelings were acute, his grief was poignant; but his confidence and hope in the Divine aid were never shaken. These calamities had cut the cord that, had bound him to the world, and he lived from the time of their occurrence for the benefit of others more than for the comfort of himself. Divested of domestic ties, he had made his parish his family, and had connected himself to it by every possible affection; and it was only the reflection of a final separation from it that now threw over him a shade of regret. No one was ever more beloved, for none could be more deserving of it: he was, indeed, the father of the orphan; the guardian of the oppressed; she supporter of the afflicted; and the lover of religion.

> " To them his heart, his love, his griefs were given,
> But all his serious thoughts had rest in Heaven.
> As some tall cliff that lifts its awful form,
> Swells from the vale, and midway leaves the storm ;
> Though round its breast the rolling clouds are spread,
> Eternal sunshine settles on its head."

The report of his sudden and alarming state had been widely spread: it had raised an universal commiseration among every class; and it was the sole occupation of honest John, his servant, to return answers to the never-ceasing enquiries of those who thronged the Rectory House door with the desire of receiving intelligence of a favourable change.

It was on the afternoon of a day when the good man had partaken of the sacrament, administered by that hand from which alone he had received every thing in this illness calculated to benefit his body and soul, that he thus bespoke the attention of his companion: —

" Deacon," said he, " how thankful am I to a gracious Providence that I have been permitted to enjoy a partial return of my speech; and I think, also, a perfect restoration of my mind, at a time, when death has possessed himself of the outworks of this brittle tenement. I am the more thankful, as it enables me to enjoy the only pleasure of which I am now capable; for after what I have now to communicate, my soul aspires for a release from its captivity here, that it may 'return unto the God that gave it.' Deacon, tell our friends, in whose society and converse we have taken so much delight, that I have recalled each and all of them to my remembrance, and have implored a blessing upon them. In my will, I have constituted you my sole executor; and you will find that I have left some trifle as a memento of my unfeigned regard to each of them. It is my desire to be interred between my wife and my daughter, beneath that altar where I have so often officiated, and where, in perfect love and charity with the world, I have administered the holy elements of the Eucharist. Let me be carried thither by the several officers of the Church, followed only by yourself and my servants; and as I wish to show how much I have ever deprecated the vain pageantry of funeral processions, let nothing be done more than is actually necessary; and let that be attended with the least possible expence: by these means something more can be added to my charitable bequests. I request that no funeral sermon may be preached; for I know, by experience, how apt we are to give way to our feelings upon such occasions, and to make them vehicles, more for commendation of the dead, than as warnings to the living: besides, I hold that no man is to be praised while living, nor his memory afterwards to be held in peculiar reverence for the mere performance of his duty, however just it may be properly to censure others for a wilful neglect of it. I believe you have heard me not unfrequently say, that I have no very near relations who survive me: but even those distantly connected, will find that I have not forgotten them. And now, my dear friend, I come to the consideration of yourself; and it is the provision which I have been enabled to make for you that gives me much of the fortitude I now possess; for with it is connected the vital interests of our sacred charge. As this object has ever been that nearest my heart, as soon as I had been able fully to estimate your worth, I took an opportunity of seeing my patron, and he, very readily, consented to grant me a request, which my long acquaintance with him, and his knowledge of my attachment to this situation, gave me the confidence to solicit; and he has since repeated the promise, in the event of my death, of making you my successor here.—Deacon, why should you be so much moved by what I have done ? It is due to your merit and to your character; I owe it to your strong attachment to me; but above all, I owe it to that high consideration of duty I bear my charge, and the love I entertain for our tender-hearted friend, check your emotion and hear me, for my time and strength will not admit of my saying much more. The house as it stands, with my books and furniture, and all my personal property, I have bequeathed to you, together with a suf-ficient sum to put it into complete repair. I need hardly add, as my last injunction to you, to maintain with all the ability with which God has blessed you, with all your zeal and devotion, that ' form of sound words' which it becomes a son of our National Church to support by word and deed. I die as I have lived, in the conviction that the doctrines and principles of our Establishment are those which are the most scriptural and true. I have endeavoured by every exertion, and by the fullest exercise of my intellects, to implant this belief in those committed to my care, and while I have studied to do the same myself, I have enforced the mani-festation of it in those with whom I have been connected, by every act of faith and practice. This charge (and great it is) I deliver over to you; and I entrust it with con-fidence, knowing that you will keep guard over it with the same watchfulness and assiduity, and the same tenderness of conscience that I have felt,; and while I have prayed, and still implore Heaven to accept of the very imperfect manner in which I have discharged this great duty, I have breathed a fervent prayer, that your per-formance may be less defective, and more beneficial.—-Deacon, your countenance bespeaks all the assurance I require; I am satisfied, perfectly satisfied,—so much so that I feel I have little more left me than to die; but I would fain accomplish another wish which concerns me nearly,—it is the desire to see around me the servants of my household, that they may receive the benediction of their dying master."

As soon as Mr. Deacon had made the Rector's wishes known to John, the old footman, he immediately communicated the matter to his fellow-servants; and pre-viously closing the lower shutters of the windows of the house, as a precaution against interruption, he accompanied them to the chamber. The curtains of the bed were now drawn aside, and the patient so raised as to be able to take the group into his view; when this was accomplished, an awful silence ensued, which for some time nothing but the sobs of those around disturbed. The dying man seemed gathering up all his strength, to make one expiring effort More than once he essayed to speak, but he could not; and it was only upon the falling of the drops which trickled down his venerable face, that his utterance was finally unlocked. Honest John wiped these tears from his master's face with the same homely handkerchief that absorbed his own.

" My good and faithful creatures," said the dying Christian, " I have sent for you to witness the departure of one whose only hope is in his Maker: of one who knows that the merits of his Redeemer alone can make atonement for his manifold deficiencies, and finally reconcile him to God. To you I owe much for the assiduity and care which you have ever shown in my service; it is my wish to impress you with the notion of that dignity which, however apparently lessened by the lowliness of your birth and stations, you, in common, enjoy with the highest of mankind. Look now at me, and see that man, unaided by his fellow man, is the most weak and powerless of created beings. Placed beyond the reach of the kind, watchful, sympathetic aid of others, his first sufferings would be his last: believe me, therefore, that those placed by Providence in your situation can never, while they are faithful and virtuous, become the objects of a good man's contempt. The proudest of mankind will find that those whom they despise as the meanest of their fellow-creatures, can lay them under obligations which they can never discharge; and with respect to myself, I declare that I have looked upon your many patient, condescending, and untired offices of fidelity with the most grateful admiration; and these acts have ennobled you in my esteem. After my death, you will find that your services have not been forgotten by me; and as I trust you have long looked upon me as your friend as well as master, let my last injunctions sink deep into your hearts. I am now hastening to that blessed and eternal country, where all who have loved and obeyed God are already gone before me; and to this state all my hopes lead, from the conviction that I have made sincere and earnest endeavours to make myself, by the death and merits of my Redeemer, in some respect fit to receive the blessings and promises which the Gospel holds out both to you and to myself. If it be your future desire to become inheritors of the same kingdom, and partakers of the same promises, you must live ' virtuously, soberly, and godly in this present life ; — but here is your advantage over us: God has been pleased to entrust to your care, perhaps, a single talent; to us he has given many more: our responsibility is, therefore, much greater than yours; and if, with all our exertions, our zeal, and ability, we have not converted these many talents to a proper use, take care that the solitary one in your possession is not neglected; — in other words, do your duties honestly and conscientiously, and labour for the acquisition of the knowledge of Religion. If you attain to any degree of it, you will find when you come, like me, to lie upon your last beds, that it will administer consolation when all other sources fail; that it will inspire you with heavenly hope; that it will disarm death of his sting, and make you welcome the ' coming of your God.' Take, therefore, back to the world with you this my last admonition: the day and hour will assuredly come, when he will be the happiest who best follows this advice. To the care of my true friend here I now commit you; and as long as you deserve, I am assured you will experience, his favour and regard. I give you my hearty thanks for all your kindness, for all your offices of love towards me; and I pray Heaven eternally to bless you!"

The good man seemed wholly exhausted by his efforts; but yet there played upon his countenance a holy serenity and composure, which seemed the result of an inward satisfaction, — a glow it was of the heart flushed from the first chill of death: his eyes were lifted upwards, as if in prayer, and Mr. Deacon, seizing the opportunity, knelt down with all the servants around the bed, and read with a fervent and impassioned devotion, the Litany of Bishop Andrews, so admirably suited to the time and occasion; at the close of which this holy man of God, turning his glazing eyes first upon his friend in acknowledgment of all his kindness, and then gradually upon those surrounding him, and finally casting them upwards, as if to draw down his last blessing upon them all, with one gentle sigh yielded his soul to those angelic spirits that awaited to bear it to eternity!

The news of the Rector's death was received by all classes of the parishioners with unequivocal symptoms of regret; while the families of his particular friends were thrown into such a state of unfeigned sorrow, that time alone could dissipate it. Social intercourse was stopped; mirth and cheerfulness gave way to feelings of a more solemn cast The eye was no longer arrested by outward objects; the mind dwelt upon nothing earthly; There was a void created in society, without the prospect of its being sup-plied. While the departure of the friend was mourned, there arose a desire with many to follow him: in short, the various feelings of regret, which the dissolution of a human being who has been universally beloved, when it is too late to recall him, took possession of the neighbourhood ; and in silence they awaited for the time when all that remained of their pastor would be consigned to the earth. The day determined upon for that of the funeral was notified by the awful tolling of the deep-toned ' passing bell,' which inspired with its protracted sound that melancholy feeling, which awakens in the human breast such according sentiments. Soon after three o'clock in the afternoon of a day which had been remarkable for the violence of a storm with which it had been ushered in, the door of the Rectory House was thrown open, to close again for ever upon its late possessor. The street and avenue to the Church, and the Church-yard were thronged by multitudes of people, among whom the body was borne, through a passage which opened to receive it. So unusual with large assemblies of this kind, not a voice raised to its natural pitch was heard; nothing assailed the ear but the whispers and footsteps of the throng, whilst on every countenance was depicted the expression of respect and sorrow. When the great folding-doors of the Church were extended to receive the mortal remains of the pastor saint, the organ was heard louldly and solemnly pealing through the aisles, in tones that overwhelmed the din created by the movement of those passing on-ward to obtain a situation where they might witness the spectacle, or participate in the mournful solemnity. The coffin was carried forward into the body of the Church, and laid upon tressels, placed in front of the reading-desk. Here might be estimated the degree of respect to which the deceased had risen in the hearts and minds of all around him. Scarcely a friend that had cherished the acquaintance of this great, good man but might now be seen to bear the last testimony of regard and love for one so dear. Crowded in every part, the Church was occupied by an indiscriminate mass of parishioners, who, however differing in other respects, upon this occasion united to pay their last tribute to the memory of a Christian minister so generally venerated. Those late daughters of affliction, Matilda and Ellen Montagu, were in possession of their seats; and behind them all their household. The families of the Lorraines, Trustwells, and Eustaces, with all their branches, and all their dependents, were there also; the whole clad in the deepest habiliments of woe. Other friends of the deceased were present, as well as the many constant attendants upon his ministry; and one large pew was filled with the preachers of the various dissenting congregations, drawn together from respect to a man, who, though firm in his attachments to the principles of his Church, never curtailed the boundaries of charity to exclude a brother man from the pale of social communion, much less, from the same hopes of happiness with himself, or even from his own prayers for their salvation. The two psalms which commence the service were sung by the Choir; and then followed the beautiful chapter from St Paul, read by a brother clergyman of the neighbourhood, with such dignity and pathos, that whilst it was rendered intel-ligible, and carried all its consolation into the breasts of the hearers, evinced the reader's feeling of the profound sublimity of the Apostle's reasoning. Again the organ played a solemn plaintive dirge, and the coffin was once more raised to be carried to its final resting-place. It was then that Mr. Lorraine and Arthur Oswald, Mr. Trustwell and his son, approached it, two on either side, to hold the pall; Matilda and Ellen Montagu, Mrs. Draymore and Mrs. Oswald followed next as mourners, succeeded by the companion and fellow-labourer of the departed, whose demeanour, throughout the whole of this trying scene, though supported by the servants, now, of his own household, evinced the deep regret of the man, softened and supported by the fortitude of the Christian.

Who that has been present at the interment of a relative or friend has failed to experience a thrill striking through the frame, when the coffin, lowered to its place, has returned a hollow sound when the mould was cast upon it, responding to the emphatic words, ' Earth to earth, ashes to ashes, dust to dust ?' Who, even among strangers to the deceased, if possessed of the true feelings of nature, can fail to have their minds impressed by the solemnities of a service calculated in all its parts to awaken in them a sense of their own frail nature, or to inspire the highest, the most exalted hopes of futurity? Perhaps there was nothing that exhibited so strongly the innate feeling of a benevolent heart, which the good man, whose loss was now so deeply deplored, possessed, as his manner of performing that service, which was the last now done for him. We know how apt repetition is to cloy, and what exertion of sense and duty it requires to keep the mind alive to that which so often recurs; yet, though for so many successive years this pastor had himself officiated in the consignment of hundreds of his fellow-creatures to the grave, he never failed, upon every instance of it, to give the full force and efficacy to every portion of the service, and to assimilate his feelings with those of every series of mourners that presented themselves. Repetition never wearied; habit and custom never beguiled him into a per-formance of the duty, undivested of a sympathy which made him 'weep with those that weep.' Who then can wonder, if the spot which was now doubly con-secrated as the repository of the ashes of one so beloved, was this day moistened with tears that fell ' like the dew of heaven' upon, it? Who can wonder, that every friend returned to his home, with at least another band loosened which tied him to mortality, better than when he left it? The imagination is more powerfully seized upon at such times as these. It is when we witness the departure of one eminent for virtue,—one who has shone as a star in the expanse of intellect; who, by his. exer-tions, has dignified the character of his species, and, by his exemplary deeds, has elevated the lowly, humbled the proud, or raised the oppressed,—that we not only become sensible of our loss, but learn to reflect, that such endowments, great as they are, cannot ward off the fatal shafts of death; that they are no security against the corruption of the grave; and are then led to infer that all acquisitions are use-less and unavailing, unless as they tend to prepare ourselves and others for another and a higher state. It is when we perceive mankind hastening onwards towards something greater and better, that the evil passions of our nature die away; that we see the futility, the impiety of harbouring in our breasts feelings of hatred towards any of our fellow-mortals, and that it is beneath the wisdom and the dignity of man to contend for trifles, when there are consequences so much more important which claim all his time and attention. Did we reflect, as we ought, upon that state to which the dead are gone, as often as we see their mortal remains passing before our eyes, or when, upon such occasions as the present, they are consigned to their kindred dust, we should be more forcibly reminded of the precariousness of our state; and should see the greater necessity of acquiescing at all times in the will of God. By observing the sufferings and frailty of our nature, we should practise more generally our love for each other; and by contemplating the striking instances of his power, we should better learn our duty to God. In short, we should estimate the value of life with more accuracy, seeing that it is ' a shadow which passeth away; a ' vanity that has nothing real or solid;' 'a flower which fadeth;' ' grass which withereth and is cut down;' a vapour ' which dissolves in air;' a ' dream' it is which leaves no trace after the sleep is gone; a thought which presents itself to the mind, but ' abideth not;' an apparition, a nothing before God!

Happy is he who lays these things to his heart; and, convinced ' that few and evil are his days,' resolves to dedicate the reflections of his mind and the actions of his life to the great purposes for which they are designed! Happy is he, who, whether called at the first or last watch of the night, is found ready at his post! Happy, thrice happy, is he, who, like this good and holy man, being full of hope and immortality, can receive the summons with calmnness, and obey it with alacrity; and having united the services of the mortal, with the best duties of the immortal, part of his nature, can render back his BODY to its kindred earth, in the joyful expectation that the SOUL will ascend to the God who gave it!

The Codes Of Hammurabi And Moses
W. W. Davies

QTY

The discovery of the Hammurabi Code is one of the greatest achievements of archaeology, and is of paramount interest, not only to the student of the Bible, but also to all those interested in ancient history...

Religion   **ISBN:** *1-59462-338-4*   **Pages:132**
MSRP $12.95

The Theory of Moral Sentiments
Adam Smith

QTY

This work from 1749. contains original theories of conscience amd moral judgment and it is the foundation for systemof morals.

Philosophy   ISBN: *1-59462-777-0*   **Pages:536**
MSRP $19.95

Jessica's First Prayer
Hesba Stretton

QTY

In a screened and secluded corner of one of the many railway-bridges which span the streets of London there could be seen a few years ago, from five o'clock every morning until half past eight, a tidily set-out coffee-stall, consisting of a trestle and board, upon which stood two large tin cans, with a small fire of charcoal burning under each so as to keep the coffee boiling during the early hours of the morning when the work-people were thronging into the city on their way to their daily toil...

Pages:84

Childrens   ISBN: *1-59462-373-2*   *MSRP $9.95*

My Life and Work
Henry Ford

QTY

Henry Ford revolutionized the world with his implementation of mass production for the Model T automobile. Gain valuable business insight into his life and work with his own auto-biography... "We have only started on our development of our country we have not as yet, with all our talk of wonderful progress, done more than scratch the surface. The progress has been wonderful enough but..."

Pages:300

Biographies/   **ISBN:** *1-59462-198-5*   *MSRP $21.95*

The Art of Cross-Examination
Francis Wellman

QTY

I presume it is the experience of every author, after his first book is published upon an important subject, to be almost overwhelmed with a wealth of ideas and illustrations which could readily have been included in his book, and which to his own mind, at least, seem to make a second edition inevitable. Such certainly was the case with me; and when the first edition had reached its sixth impression in five months, I rejoiced to learn that it seemed to my publishers that the book had met with a sufficiently favorable reception to justify a second and considerably enlarged edition. ..

Pages:412

Reference   ISBN: *1-59462-647-2*   *MSRP $19.95*

On the Duty of Civil Disobedience
Henry David Thoreau

QTY

Thoreau wrote his famous essay, On the Duty of Civil Disobedience, as a protest against an unjust but popular war and the immoral but popular institution of slave-owning. He did more than write—he declined to pay his taxes, and was hauled off to gaol in consequence. Who can say how much this refusal of his hastened the end of the war and of slavery ?

Law   ISBN: *1-59462-747-9*   **Pages:48**

MSRP $7.45

Dream Psychology Psychoanalysis for Beginners
Sigmund Freud

QTY

Sigmund Freud, born Sigismund Schlomo Freud (May 6, 1856 - September 23, 1939), was a Jewish-Austrian neurologist and psychiatrist who co-founded the psychoanalytic school of psychology. Freud is best known for his theories of the unconscious mind, especially involving the mechanism of repression; his redefinition of sexual desire as mobile and directed towards a wide variety of objects; and his therapeutic techniques, especially his understanding of transference in the therapeutic relationship and the presumed value of dreams as sources of insight into unconscious desires.

Pages:196

Psychology   ISBN: *1-59462-905-6*   *MSRP $15.45*

The Miracle of Right Thought
Orison Swett Marden

QTY

Believe with all of your heart that you will do what you were made to do. When the mind has once formed the habit of holding cheerful, happy, prosperous pictures, it will not be easy to form the opposite habit. It does not matter how improbable or how far away this realization may see, or how dark the prospects may be, if we visualize them as best we can, as vividly as possible, hold tenaciously to them and vigorously struggle to attain them, they will gradually become actualized, realized in the life. But a desire, a longing without endeavor, a yearning abandoned or held indifferently will vanish without realization.

Pages:360

Self Help   ISBN: *1-59462-644-8*   *MSRP $25.45*

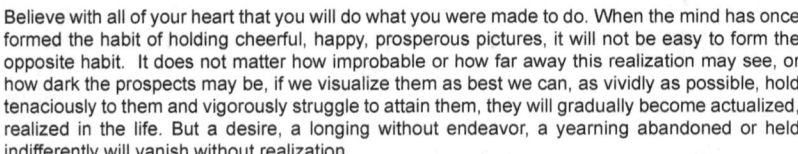

www.bookjungle.com *email: sales@bookjungle.com fax: 630-214-0564 mail: Book Jungle PO Box 2226 Champaign, IL 61825*

QTY

The Rosicrucian Cosmo-Conception Mystic Christianity *by Max Heindel* ISBN: *1-59462-188-8* **$38.95**
The Rosicrucian Cosmo-conception is not dogmatic, neither does it appeal to any other authority than the reason of the student. It is: not controversial, but is: sent forth in the, hope that it may help to clear... New Age/Religion Pages 646

Abandonment To Divine Providence *by Jean-Pierre de Caussade* ISBN: *1-59462-228-0* **$25.95**
"The Rev. Jean Pierre de Caussade was one of the most remarkable spiritual writers of the Society of Jesus in France in the 18th Century. His death took place at Toulouse in 1751. His works have gone through many editions and have been republished... Inspirational/Religion Pages 400

Mental Chemistry *by Charles Haanel* ISBN: *1-59462-192-6* **$23.95**
Mental Chemistry allows the change of material conditions by combining and appropriately utilizing the power of the mind. Much like applied chemistry creates something new and unique out of careful combinations of chemicals the mastery of mental chemistry... New Age Pages 354

The Letters of Robert Browning and Elizabeth Barret Barrett 1845-1846 vol II ISBN: *1-59462-193-4* **$35.95**
by Robert Browning and Elizabeth Barrett Biographies Pages 596

Gleanings In Genesis (volume I) *by Arthur W. Pink* ISBN: *1-59462-130-6* **$27.45**
Appropriately has Genesis been termed "the seed plot of the Bible" for in it we have, in germ form, almost all of the great doctrines which are afterwards fully developed in the books of Scripture which follow... Religion/Inspirational Pages 420

The Master Key *by L. W. de Laurence* ISBN: *1-59462-001-6* **$30.95**
In no branch of human knowledge has there been a more lively increase of the spirit of research during the past few years than in the study of Psychology, Concentration and Mental Discipline. The requests for authentic lessons in Thought Control, Mental Discipline and... New Age/Business Pages 422

The Lesser Key Of Solomon Goetia *by L. W. de Laurence* ISBN: *1-59462-092-X* **$9.95**
This translation of the first book of the "Lernegton" which is now for the first time made accessible to students of Talismanic Magic was done, after careful collation and edition, from numerous Ancient Manuscripts in Hebrew, Latin, and French... New Age/Occult Pages 92

Rubaiyat Of Omar Khayyam *by Edward Fitzgerald* ISBN:*1-59462-332-5* **$13.95**
Edward Fitzgerald, whom the world has already learned, in spite of his own efforts to remain within the shadow of anonymity, to look upon as one of the rarest poets of the century, was born at Bredfield, in Suffolk, on the 31st of March, 1809. He was the third son of John Purcell... Music Pages 172

Ancient Law *by Henry Maine* ISBN: *1-59462-128-4* **$29.95**
The chief object of the following pages is to indicate some of the earliest ideas of mankind, as they are reflected in Ancient Law, and to point out the relation of those ideas to modern thought. Religiom/History Pages 452

Far-Away Stories *by William J. Locke* ISBN: *1-59462-129-2* **$19.45**
"Good wine needs no bush, but a collection of mixed vintages does. And this book is just such a collection. Some of the stories I do not want to remain buried for ever in the museum files of dead magazine-numbers an author's unpardonable vanity..." Fiction Pages 272

Life of David Crockett *by David Crockett* ISBN: *1-59462-250-7* **$27.45**
"Colonel David Crockett was one of the most remarkable men of the times in which he lived. Born in humble life, but gifted with a strong will, an indomitable courage, and unremitting perseverance... Biographies/New Age Pages 424

Lip-Reading *by Edward Nitchie* ISBN: *1-59462-206-X* **$25.95**
Edward B. Nitchie, founder of the New York School for the Hard of Hearing, now the Nitchie School of Lip-Reading, Inc, wrote "LIP-READING Principles and Practice". The development and perfecting of this meritorious work on lip-reading was an undertaking... How-to Pages 400

A Handbook of Suggestive Therapeutics, Applied Hypnotism, Psychic Science ISBN: *1-59462-214-0* **$24.95**
by Henry Munro Health/New Age/Health/Self-help Pages 376

A Doll's House: and Two Other Plays *by Henrik Ibsen* ISBN: *1-59462-112-8* **$19.95**
Henrik Ibsen created this classic when in revolutionary 1848 Rome. Introducing some striking concepts in playwriting for the realist genre, this play has been studied the world over. Fiction/Classics/Plays 308

The Light of Asia *by sir Edwin Arnold* ISBN: *1-59462-204-3* **$13.95**
In this poetic masterpiece, Edwin Arnold describes the life and teachings of Buddha. The man who was to become known as Buddha to the world was born as Prince Gautama of India but he rejected the worldly riches and abandoned the reigns of power when... Religion/History/Biographies Pages 170

The Complete Works of Guy de Maupassant *by Guy de Maupassant* ISBN: *1-59462-157-8* **$16.95**
"For days and days, nights and nights, I had dreamed of that first kiss which was to consecrate our engagement, and I knew not on what spot I should put my lips..." Fiction/Classics Pages 240

The Art of Cross-Examination *by Francis L. Wellman* ISBN: *1-59462-309-0* **$26.95**
Written by a renowned trial lawyer, Wellman imparts his experience and uses case studies to explain how to use psychology to extract desired information through questioning. How-to/Science/Reference Pages 408

Answered or Unanswered? *by Louisa Vaughan* ISBN: *1-59462-248-5* **$10.95**
Miracles of Faith in China Religion Pages 112

The Edinburgh Lectures on Mental Science (1909) *by Thomas* ISBN: *1-59462-008-3* **$11.95**
This book contains the substance of a course of lectures recently given by the writer in the Queen Street Hail, Edinburgh. Its purpose is to indicate the Natural Principles governing the relation between Mental Action and Material Conditions... New Age/Psychology Pages 148

Ayesha *by H. Rider Haggard* ISBN: *1-59462-301-5* **$24.95**
Verily and indeed it is the unexpected that happens! Probably if there was one person upon the earth from whom the Editor of this, and of a certain previous history, did not expect to hear again... Classics Pages 380

Ayala's Angel *by Anthony Trollope* ISBN: *1-59462-352-X* **$29.95**
The two girls were both pretty, but Lucy who was twenty-one who supposed to be simple and comparatively unattractive, whereas Ayala was credited, as her Bombwhat romantic name might show, with poetic charm and a taste for romance. Ayala when her father died was nineteen... Fiction Pages 484

The American Commonwealth *by James Bryce* ISBN: *1-59462-286-8* **$34.45**
An interpretation of American democratic political theory. It examines political mechanics and society from the perspective of Scotsman James Bryce Politics Pages 572

Stories of the Pilgrims *by Margaret P. Pumphrey* ISBN: *1-59462-116-0* **$17.95**
This book explores pilgrims religious oppression in England as well as their escape to Holland and eventual crossing to America on the Mayflower, and their early days in New England... History Pages 268

QTY

The Fasting Cure *by Sinclair Upton*   ISBN: *1-59462-222-1*   **$13.95**
In the Cosmopolitan Magazine for May, 1910, and in the Contemporary Review (London) for April, 1910, I published an article dealing with my experiences in fasting. I have written a great many magazine articles, but never one which attracted so much attention... New Age/Self Help/Health Pages 164

Hebrew Astrology *by Sepharial*   ISBN: *1-59462-308-2*   **$13.45**
In these days of advanced thinking it is a matter of common observation that we have left many of the old landmarks behind and that we are now pressing forward to greater heights and to a wider horizon than that which represented the mind-content of our progenitors... Astrology Pages 144

Thought Vibration or The Law of Attraction in the Thought World   ISBN: *1-59462-127-6*   **$12.95**

by William Walker Atkinson   *Psychology/Religion Pages 144*

Optimism *by Helen Keller*   ISBN: *1-59462-108-X*   **$15.95**
Helen Keller was blind, deaf, and mute since 19 months old, yet famously learned how to overcome these handicaps, communicate with the world, and spread her lectures promoting optimism. An inspiring read for everyone... Biographies/Inspirational Pages 84

Sara Crewe *by Frances Burnett*   ISBN: *1-59462-360-0*   **$9.45**
In the first place, Miss Minchin lived in London. Her home was a large, dull, tall one, in a large, dull square, where all the houses were alike, and all the sparrows were alike, and where all the door-knockers made the same heavy sound... Childrens/Classic Pages 88

The Autobiography of Benjamin Franklin *by Benjamin Franklin*   ISBN: *1-59462-135-7*   **$24.95**
The Autobiography of Benjamin Franklin has probably been more extensively read than any other American historical work, and no other book of its kind has had such ups and downs of fortune. Franklin lived for many years in England, where he was agent... Biographies/History Pages 332

Name	
Email	
Telephone	
Address	
City, State ZIP	

☐ **Credit Card**   ☐ **Check / Money Order**

Credit Card Number	
Expiration Date	
Signature	

Please Mail to: Book Jungle
PO Box 2226
Champaign, IL 61825
or Fax to: 630-214-0564

ORDERING INFORMATION

web*: www.bookjungle.com*
email*: sales@bookjungle.com*
fax*: 630-214-0564*
mail*: Book Jungle PO Box 2226 Champaign, IL 61825*
or PayPal *to sales@bookjungle.com*

Please contact us for bulk discounts

DIRECT-ORDER TERMS

**20% Discount if You Order
Two or More Books**
Free Domestic Shipping!
Accepted: Master Card, Visa,
Discover, American Express